LAST SCORE

LAST SCORE

OR

The Private Life of Sir Richard Ormston

BY

STORM JAMESON

THE REPRINT SOCIETY LONDON

FIRST PUBLISHED 1961
THIS EDITION PUBLISHED BY THE REPRINT SOCIETY LTD
BY ARRANGEMENT WITH MACMILLAN AND CO LTD 1962

PRINTED IN ENGLAND BY HAZELL WATSON AND VINEY LTD
AYLESBURY AND SLOUGH

TO

A. D. PETERS

in friendship, and without asking leave

The colony in which the action of this book takes place is an imaginary one: the characters are imagined. If the reader discovers accidental similarities with events which have taken place anywhere in the world, in Africa, Europe, Asia, that will only be because all revolts against what can be represented as an occupying force follow the same unhappy pattern and take the same disconcerting shapes. The situation in the book is an invented one, but might, at some time, in some place, among people of one nation or another, occur. The events related are a vehicle for an account of the workings of that strange organ, the human heart.

CHAPTER ONE

GOURAUD caught them as they crossed the hall of the hotel, between the dining-room and the courtyard. He laid his nervous bony hand on the young man's arm.

'Where are you going? How? You are walking? Then let me send you in my car.'

'That's kind of you,' Andrew said, 'but we'd rather walk.'

'You are very foolish, I think.' He spoke English as an educated Frenchman does, with an extreme precision and purity of the vowels, nothing slurred, nothing flat, too rounded, too pure. 'At least you will persuade Miss Leng to get into the car.'

'Why, yes, if she'd like to,' Andrew said, with a glance at her.

The girl smiled at Gouraud. 'Thank you, but I'd sooner walk.'

Gouraud jerked a shoulder and an eyebrow in a gesture of polite indifference, or defeat. A distinguished old man in his way, rich, an amateur archaeologist, he looked, with his sallow sunken cheeks and tight mouth, like a shopkeeper, a small failing shop at that.

'Did you drink coffee after your lunch? Come upstairs and let me give you some more. I will show you something.'

Bored, but not knowing how to get out of it, they walked with him to the lift and were carried to the third floor of the hotel, where he had his three very large rooms, furnished by himself with the greatest luxury and the greatest number of valuable objects, almost all of the First Empire and earlier—the tapestries were much earlier—that he could fit into them. It must, Andrew thought idly, be like living in a museum or a place shown to tourists: as a home, a place to eat and sleep in, it was ludicrous, impossible. Sarah, he knew, felt the same about it.

Gouraud sent for coffee, then went away into his bedroom; he came back with a tiny figure in dark reddish clay, and laid it in the girl's hand.

'We turned it up yesterday.' His smile was a twitch of lipless mouth and a gleam in black boot-button eyes. He had been given permission to dig in a village north of the city, the site of a Roman temple, of which only the stump of a column remained above ground: all else was buried or had been carried away piecemeal over the centuries to build a house or a barn. 'It's interesting only because it's less crude than most. Look at the navel. And the line round the neck and wrists.' He touched it with a finger-nail. 'And the hint of shoulder bones.'

'What is it?' asked Sarah.

'A pregnant woman—an offering. The woman who offered it may only have hoped to be pregnant, or she was so already and wanted a safe childbirth, or had had one.'

Sarah handed it back. 'It's lovely.'

'No. But—appealing.' The boot-buttons rolled very rapidly across the girl's thin sunburned throat and shoulders . . . How old is she? Twenty? Older? Intact? Probably not . . . 'And not even the dust of the woman herself is left. Let me give you some more coffee—these cups are too small.'

'No, thank you.'

She was glad to be rid of the cup, which she knew must be as old and valuable as it was thin, nearly transparent. She glanced briefly at Andrew. He got up at once, setting his own cup on a papier mâché table, from which Gouraud discreetly moved it.

'Must go,' he said. 'Thank you, sir. We don't get coffee like this very often.'

'Change your mind and let me send you away in the car,'

Gouraud said warmly. 'It irritates me to see people run unnecessary risks.'

'It's not much of a risk.'

'That's nonsense.'

'Well, I'm sorry,' Andrew said, smiling, 'but the fact is
you either live, within reason, as if things were normal, or
you couldn't live here at all.'

'I'm fond of your father, and I believe he has no other
child?'

'My father is used to risks.'

'I respect him passionately,' Gouraud said. 'You know,
I am in love with England and the English—unlike most
of my countrymen, I am sorry to say. At the same time, I
think you are acting foolishly here, because you are doing
precisely what we should do ourselves in a similar situation.
As we do act ourselves. I am sorry you are not better than
we are.'

'Why do you stay here, sir?'

'Ah. I'm safe—no one will cut my throat or shoot me in
the back in the street. The question is why do Englishmen,
and Englishwomen, even when they have no business to
keep them here, stay? I will tell you why. Because of the
innocence. The happiness, exquisite, of living in a country
which is not cancered with fat living, suffocated by the
pressure on it of too much of everything it can be induced
to want, too many cars—thank God you haven't made roads
here—too many refrigerators, television sets, newspapers,
officials, too many children, far too many children. Here
there are hours during the day when nothing in the country
is real except the mask of heat on it, on the arid rocky hills,
the stunted trees, the all but colourless sky, except the dust,
the stony goat-tracks, the strong poor houses, except the
obstinate will of men to survive and make their living in
hard ways. Often when I wake up—I wake early, old people
do, you know—I don't recall at once whether I'm in Greece,

Cyprus, North Africa. It could be any country where the
dust is less mineral than human, dust of the uncounted
generations of the dead, from the naked savage staring down
from his hillside at the most radiant sea in the world to the
last English spinster who looks at the same sea and thinks—
but how do I know what an old Englishwoman thinks about
when she is near death? I only know why she stays here.
You English are merely the latest invaders, the latest carriers
of ideas which the sun and the poverty will rot. You won't
be the last. Even the violence here is innocent, because it
is so old, and never changes. The victims and their murderers change—and change sides. Only the violence remains the same, and the grief and the cries ... I hope I shall
be allowed to go on living here. I feel reasonably certain
that the freedom—I mean the moral freedom: no one is
bored, no one is stupid—and the poverty, the simplicity,
the freshness—freshness of the green seed in the dry husk—
the innocence, the myths, will outlast me. And the warmth
—ah, the warmth. My God, if I had to go back to Paris!'
He looked with a friendly malice at the young man. 'You
don't know what I'm talking about. You will.'

He insisted on going down with them in the lift, but stopped it at the first floor and led them along a service passage
to a flight of stairs, and at the bottom of them into a small
yard, with one dusty palm: at the far side a cracked grey
door.

'My very own private entrance,' he said. 'I should dislike
having to cross the lobby of the Astoria every time I go out
or come in. It will save you all but fifty yards of Urraca
Street. Goodbye, Miss Leng. Goodbye, Andrew—my
devotion to your father.'

He watched them out of sight. The girl, he said to himself, is any thin unformed attractive young female, all greeds
and ignorance. But the boy—ah, the boy is something else
. . . Andrew reminded him of a young Catalan he had

known for a few weeks: the long body, very thin and grace-ful, long nose, long narrow face, thick eyebrows, as straight as if ruled, wide mouth: in old age it might be a grim face, now it had the beauty of its lean ugliness, and the charm.

Gouraud sighed. Provided he doesn't get himself killed, he thought: or marry.

The heat of early September struck them a light searing blow. Most of the inner town's shops were in Urraca Street, dark burrows on the ground floor of neglected old houses, their open doorways the only refuge from the cars and lorries inching their way along a street that two loaded hand-barrows could choke. The sun shut down on it. In spite of the heat and the noise, and the fumes of petrol, dust, sweat, Urraca Street kept some of the charm of a provincial town, perhaps in southern France, where nothing has been planned, nothing repaired for generations except to prop up a collapsed wall, and where nothing marks off the four-teenth century from a newer building unless it be a more settled air of indifference and ease.

'He's very intelligent, old Gouraud.'

'Too eloquent,' Andrew said.

'Oh, I don't think it's bogus, do you?'

'No. Not quite. But too frequent. Too much of a good thing. But my father admires him.'

Sarah did not answer. He gave her a swift glance, and was silent himself. They stood, pressed against the window of a shop, to let a dray pass them, its wheels mounting the strip of pavement on both sides.

'Only three years ago,' Sarah said, 'when I first came here, you could dawdle down this street without its entering your head that you might be shot at or knifed. Who'd have be-lieved it could be spoiled so quickly?'

'It's not altogether spoiled. Some of what Gouraud said is true. You have time to breathe here and do nothing.'

Yes, and the sun, he thought—the diseases of the sun, and its benefits.

'Ah, but you didn't know it when it was any shabby easy-going little foreign city, the people in the shops and cafés smiling at you, and the country itself friendly, full of sun and silence.' They were passing the end of one of the several tortuous side-streets, narrower even than Urraca, which formed the web of the inner town. 'Eighteen months ago I should have dodged along there to get shade, but now . . .' She moved her thin shoulders.

At the corner of Urraca Street, where it opened into Government Square, was the best provision shop in the whole country, its window glorious with imported tinned food and cereals. It was shut. Under the vexed frowns of two young soldiers, an Englishwoman had paused to look in the barred window: her child, a little girl, drifting away from her, stood exactly where, forty-eight hours earlier, the body of an English civilian had lain, shot in the back by just such a slender supple fellow as loitered past her, drawing after him the narrowed glances of both soldiers.

Andrew recognised one of them as having been on sentry duty at Government House during the past week, and smiled at him. The other boy saluted, managing to convey by a slight twitch of his mouth that the salute was meant for the Governor's son, and the quarter-smile for a young man of his own age and class. He had missed the girl's face but, turning his head very slightly, he could appraise the line of her back, as straight as a bolt, bare-shouldered, and smoothly sunburned.

A few steps into Government Square gave them back the immense sky, blue, with a spidery veil of white cloud: the light for a moment held down their eyelids. This was the only part of the inner town on which English business and administration had made a noticeable mark: on one corner, the post-office, a squat ugly building encircled now by barbed wire and soldiers who had barely had time to learn mistrust: on the opposite side of the square, the file of anonymous yellow offices was defaced by the wrecked window of an English tourist agency—behind the steel screen a few scorched dusty leaflets and a photograph of York Minster. The square was only just inside the old city: the mediaeval ramparts, pierced by openings into thin twisted streets and lanes, formed two sides of it; houses had been thrust against them, and a café or two. At the side farthest from Urraca Street, a wide boulevard, beginning one of the few good roads in the colony, ran out towards Government House and the barracks and, two miles farther out, the airfield, running past streets, unmade, pitted crazily with stones and ruts, of bungalows and small white puny villas. They were not the only part of the city outside the walls. There was another and richer suburb, known as the English quarter, a number of large comfortable houses built on a north-facing slope, where every well-off foreigner, not only the English—and except Gouraud—had come together. None of these houses was in any sense splendid. And in the inner town itself, sophistication was limited to a couple of nightclubs too amiably shabby and simple to deserve the name, one moderately expensive restaurant run by an Italian, and a single large hotel, the Astoria, built less than twenty years ago: the other three hotels were all small, and had not given themselves the trouble to be even modestly comfortable. The country was, after all, primitive, lacking anything it could have turned into wealth, and unimportant except for the accident of its situation as—at one time—a coaling station and naval base, and now an air base, a dot on a line of defence.

Except for the young soldiers and an English civilian, the vast square was empty. Sarah stood still, shading her eyes with her hand to be able to look across it against the sun. The ramparts cut off the view except where the boulevard exposed a frieze of hills, their lean flanks given a Chinese delicacy by the blinding light; it reduced them to a washed-in line, effacing the vineyards at the foot and the rocks and dry scented shrubs and knotted trees of the upper slopes, and masking the crests of higher livid hills in the distance.

'We used to picnic in those nearest hills,' Sarah said. 'There's one ruin more fantastic than the others, storey piled on storey on the side of the hill, like a stone labyrinth built vertically, where I spent hours watching the lizards.'

'It all looks pretty bare.'

'That's almost the joy of it—the dry warm soil under your hands, the dry light, the scent, the sun on old walls. Up there you feel free. And if you saw it in spring, with water running over the white stones, so clear you can see to the bottom of the deepest pools, and flowers—flowers everywhere, on every hillside . . .'

'Perhaps I can get out then for a week,' Andrew said.

'Try.'

Was the gleam in her wide-set grey eyes mocking? Uncertain, he touched her hand, and felt the familiar light shock pass through him from his finger-tips. With an effort to speak easily, he said,

'By then you may be back in London.'

She turned on him with an exaggerated energy. 'I hate London, and I don't want to go back at all. I hate the end-less cold winters and the damp in my bones.'

'You can't stay out here for ever.'

She did not answer this. She asked impatiently, carelessly,

'How much longer have we got?'

'Another two and a half weeks.'

'And you start at the hospital—your clinical—as soon as you get back?'

'Yes.'

'You wouldn't have time for me then,' she said lightly.

'Don't be silly.' His voice made a caress of the sharp words.

The girl's face took on a look of obstinacy, even sullenness. 'I ought to go to the office now.'

She was on the staff of the only English daily newspaper in the colony, the *Compatriot*, owned and edited by her stepfather, Charles Cumberland. Born in the country, the son of a settler, Cumberland drew as much nourishment for his vanity out of his unpopularity as out of his decent liberal principles. Only his Maker knew which he cherished the more, but there was, in his devotion to his principles, more piety than his enemies gave him credit for, and less than he believed. He kept up a nagging and exasperated opposition to the policy of the Colonial Office and the government, spiced with sharp and sometimes witty attacks on Sir Richard Ormston, the colony's Governor. During the past two years—since the discontents in the country caught fire and became a revolt—he had hedged a little. But he still excused the rebels (they called themselves indifferently rebels, resisters, Partisans, Freedom Fighters) their murders and lesser crimes on the ground that they had a right to what they were seeking through murder—independence. (Gouraud, talking about him at a dinner-party in Government House, said, 'Oh, a dreadful fellow, as conceited as a bad actor, for all his brains, and a born politician, that meanest of animals, but—you'll forgive me the blasphemy, since I'm a foreigner and can't be expected to know better— in a sense he is right. There are long periods or moments when it's possible to coax, discipline, or thrash the lesser breeds into subservience or submission. Centuries of poverty, of forced simplicity, of trust in God or His priests, are not shaken off quickly. Then one day, at another moment, a wild gust blows through the world, or over a single country, and men fight like cornered rats for what they call their freedom. What a thrashing does *then* is to drive them to fight with any weapons—the filthiest become clean in their eyes; they can only be defeated by being choked in their own blood. Ironically, the only modern governments capable of doing this are those stiffened, like Soviet Russia, by an unshakeable conviction of their own righteousness. All the others have lost this saintly Calvinistic energy, and their efforts to be brutal earn them nothing but contempt, execration—and finally, too late, they give in, not out of virtue, out of a weakness. This is what you, alas, will do. Charles Cumberland is the reckless angel of your apocalypse . . . He is also engagingly immodest—I have seen him behave with his wife as if he had just brought her in from the street.')

'Oh, nonsense,' Andrew said, 'it's Sunday, you don't need to be in the office until after five—it's only just three.'

As if she had been protesting for form's sake, the girl let him turn her away from the *Compatriot*, housed in a ramshackle building behind the post-office, and towards the boulevard and Government House. Before they reached the gate of the courtyard a sentry recognised Andrew and swung it open. Instinctively, instead of crossing the scorched iron-hard earth of the centre, Andrew turned left into the feeble shade thrown by yellowing acacias and pepper trees planted along the wall. Frowning, eyebrows drawn into a single angry line, Sarah followed him. There were soldiers before the open doorway of the house, in the great marble-floored hall, and at the foot of the enormously wide ceremonial staircase. Andrew hurried her up it, past the closed doors of the official rooms, turned to the right into a narrower landing, round another corner, and up a less imposing flight of stairs to the second floor and the private wing. His room was at the end of the very long wide corridor.

They had crossed no one except the soldiers. Shutting the door of his room, Andrew smiled at her.

'Safe.'

A grey flash from her eyes answered him. 'Aren't you ashamed to make me creep into a house where I'm not welcome? I was a fool to come. I won't do it again.'

My love, he thought. 'You're talking nonsense again.'

'You know your father loathes me.'

'He loathes your stepfather and his foul paper—that's all.'

He would have taken her in his arms but she pulled herself away. 'I shouldn't have come. Why did you keep under the walls as we came in? Hoping that no one would see us?'

For a guilty moment he was not sure himself whether he had been thinking only of avoiding the murderous heat. He forced himself to a reasonableness he knew would be no use, might even irritate her further. 'Need we quarrel about it?'

'Don't treat me as if I were in the wrong,' she said, raising her young rough voice to its loudest.

Looking at her thin arms, at the childishly small bones of her wrists and shoulders, at her thin and seemingly—it was only appearance—frail body, he felt as much anguish as love. Her quick temper exasperated him and melted his bowels. He was too young himself to be able to deal with her anger except by hitting back.

'What the devil does it matter to us if they loathe each other?' he said.

'Yes, but you agree with your father'

He knew—both of them half-consciously knew—that they were going to quarrel again about politics and the revolt only to delay the far more difficult and dangerous quarrel waiting to be fought out between them. The flashes of hate and rage in their arguments came from a depth that had nothing to do with politics.

'I agree, of course I agree with him that you can't surrender to a gang of murdering brutes—knifing people in the back, sneaking into hospitals to cut some poor devil's throat

in his bed, shooting a pregnant woman and letting her bleed
to death——'

'She got in the way,' the girl blurted.

'You shock me, Sarah.'

She blushed deeply. 'I didn't mean that . . . It's horrible,
I know it's horrible, but it's the government's beastly fault
—the only remedy they can think of is arrests and hangings
—and your father approves.'

'He has to keep order.'

'But he approves! So do you. It's frightful.'

Andrew clenched his hands to keep them from reaching
out to touch her. Speaking in an exasperatingly smooth
voice he said,

'Would *you* hand this country over to squalid killers? Or
even talk to them?'

'People should be free,' she retorted. 'It's their country,
they didn't ask us to come here and cherish them, we came
because we had a use for it. It's unjust.'

He gave way to his impulse to punish her for his own
cowardice—at this moment he believed that nothing but
cowardice kept him from dealing frankly and brutally with
his father's disapproval of her and her resentment of his
father: it never occurred to him that a compromise might
be possible.

'You're being sentimental,' he said, smiling, 'your stepfather's muddled sentiments. It's a civil war, too, don't
forget. Have you ever seen any of their victims? The other
day they got hold of one of their own people, a schoolmaster, battered him to death, then dragged what was left
back to his house and dropped it in front of his wife and
child. That proves their fitness to govern themselves,
doesn't it?'

'Don't tell me any more,' Sarah said. She shivered.

His anger turned over in him and became a crazed tenderness. 'I'm sorry, my darling, forgive me.'

The girl was not ready to forgive him, nor adroit enough. 'I don't like your father. I disliked him even before I knew he had a son he has brought up to be as hard and self-centred as himself.'

'You don't know my father.'

She moved away from him, then turned back impulsively. 'Andrew, I'm sorry, I'm sorry. I shouldn't curse your father, it's disgusting bad manners.'

'He did bring me up,' Andrew said. He smiled at her with extreme sweetness. 'Pity you don't like the result.'

She said fiercely, 'I love you. You are a hard selfish beast and I do love you.'

'He was a pretty good father to have. He gave me a fine life and the most exciting holidays any child ever had.'

'Didn't your mother have anything to do with it?'

'My mother?' He made a light gesture with his fingers, as though trying to free them of dust. 'Poor darling, she was always kind, I don't think I ever knew her lose her temper, and—if you want me to tell you the truth—she was, compared with my father, rather dull.'

'But you're fond of her!'

'Of course.'

The pupils of Sarah's eyes narrowed, giving her the look of a spitting cat. 'I'd rather my son hated me than spoke about me with that sort of kindness. No, I shall never like your father. And since he thoroughly dislikes and disapproves of me, such an adoring and obedient son ought not to have anything to do with me.'

Deafened by a rage which set the blood ringing in his ears and left no room in him for anything but his violent need of her, Andrew looked at her without answering.

Trembling a little, she mocked, 'What will you do when your father refuses to have me in his family?'

'He won't.'

'What will you do? Which of us will you drop?'

He found the calmness to say, 'Don't go on with this, my darling.'

An acute pleasure filled her. 'Me—would you choose me? Or would you say: So sorry, my dear girl, but my father—who gave me a wonderful time when I was a child —says nothing doing with that gutter cat, Sarah Leng, so away you go, take yourself off.'

'Shut up, Sarah.'

Is there a happiness in the world sharper than that of inflicting a wound only one person, yourself, can cure? Her eyes wide-open and gleaming, she stared at Andrew's face, its lines for a moment what they would become in twenty years' time.

'I'll talk as I like,' she said, smiling with pleasure.

Andrew took a step forward; she ran into his arms, with a cry he stifled against a blind mouth, pressing herself against him with surprising force. She drew back to be able to say,

'I'm ashamed. I wish I was different.'

'I don't,' he said. 'Even if I could I wouldn't change a thing in you, not one—not one of your appalling faults.'

'If you knew more about me you would.' She astonished him by contorting her face to keep back tears. 'I must really go now.'

'Not now,' he said. 'You can't go.'

In his arms she was very thin, hard and unbearably yielding: for a few moments he was conscious of her eyes looking at him through thick straight lashes, of a line of bright hair, of the fine bones of her shoulders in his hands, then, in the feverish impatience of his body, only of himself.

CHAPTER TWO

SHUTTING the door on his visitor, an English politician, Colonel Frent went back to the window at which, a minute or two before, the easy fellow had paused to say,

'A magnificent view. I suppose you no longer notice it.'

'Oh, I look at it,' Frent answered.

'With pleasure?'

'With interest, rather. Splendid guerrilla country, all these hills.'

Calling on what he believed to be his tact, the visitor said, 'Ah, yes. Each of us sees what he has been bred to see. You as a professional soldier see men in uniform, where I see them as, ah, individuals.'

What does he imagine a soldier is? Frent asked himself. An animal, a sawdust-stuffed doll? He contented himself with a faint smile. 'This wall'—he laid a hand on it—'was part—the only fragment that remained—of a mediaeval fort built into the ramparts. There was no window, of course. That was opened up when this place was built. You can see the thickness of the old wall—nearly three feet. Nothing else in the building above ground is as solid.'

'Was it built for the—ah—security police?'

'Yes. Except that, fifty years ago, they were called police.' He smiled again, as briefly. 'You said *security* as though it were an indecent word. Why?'

He knew why, but it amused him to needle the fellow—who was, he saw, disappointed by his visit to police headquarters: he must have expected the squat ugly building to be deliciously sinister. He had been shown over both floors: the upper floor, composed of this large handsome room (with a view) which was Frent's private office, and beyond it, his much less splendid living quarters: downstairs, on

the ground, other administrative offices, and the cells. The
place was not a prison, but a half-dozen barred and shuttered rooms, cut off from the rest by a steel door, were used
as temporary cells for suspects waiting to be examined.
They were empty—as were the basement storerooms he was
not shown. The visitor's nostrils, dilated to pick up whatever smell he had expected, were no use to him. A pity,
Frent thought. We should have laid on at least one rascal,
something for his television pap.

Alone, he allowed himself a rare minute's idleness. This
view nourished and delighted him in a way he could have
explained to no one except his dead brother—who would
not have needed the explanation. The barren hills with their
darkened rock and grey calcined soil reminded him sharply
of the country behind Manosque, where in 1943 he had spent
some months on one of his missions to Resistance groups in
the area. This country was as old and hard-boned, and the
men hiding in it were surely as like his French partisans as
one rifle is like another of the same bore. Somewhere up
there, in a pocket of shadow and silence, a man was thinking
the thoughts of a Frenchman lying out in the maquis. '*My*
thoughts during those months,' he said under his breath.

For a moment he had an extraordinary sense of intimacy
with the unknown guerrilla leader: he felt the parched earth
and dry brittle herbs under the skin of the other's hand, and
saw the shape of the ground through a pair of sun-reddened
eyes. It was an intimacy without a trace of kindness.

Turning away from the window, he looked at his watch.
Half-past two. Ormston should be here now, he reflected.
He walked briskly to his desk, and began to look through
papers already docketed and arranged. The telephone rang
at his elbow. He listened, holding the receiver a little way
from his ear because the voice at the other end jarred
him.

'Yes, a damnable business . . . Yes . . . Yes, I agree . . .

No . . . You know my opinion . . . Certainly. Can you be
here at eight this evening? . . . No, I'm afraid not. Eight is
the earliest . . . Right. Eight o'clock . . .'

He glanced at his watch again, frowning. Damn Ormston,
he thought, irritated, no idea of punctuality, we should have
had a soldier in charge here. No, I'm unjust . . . Ormston
had been anything but weak in his handling of the crisis.
He was also brave. Until it was pointed out to him that his
chauffeur was in as much danger as he was, he refused an
armed escort in the city, and had behaved with the greatest
coolness on the occasion, a year ago, when his car was
ambushed on a country road and himself wounded, slightly,
in the arm: one of the soldiers was very badly hurt, and
Ormston had insisted on staying with the boy until the
ambulance came, and ridden in it with him to the hospital
. . . Yes, yes, courage enough—courage or vanity; one
takes over from the other at these times—but why the hell
can't he be punctual? . . .

The door was too thick for footsteps to be heard on
the stairs. It opened at this moment, and the Governor
came in.

At fifty-three Richard Ormston was still almost insuffer-
ably good-looking: a smoothly feminine line of cheek and
chin, grey half-sleepy eyes, straight nose, mouth of classic
length and beauty. His body had become a little heavy.
Eats and drinks too well, Frent reflected—not for the first
time. He stood up, with a cool affable smile.

'Ah, here you are, sir.'

With a sigh of relief, Ormston sat down in the armchair
placed for him. 'Yes, here I am. My God, it's a scorcher
outside.'

'I like it,' Frent said.

He nodded at the young man who had followed Ormston
into the room. His private secretary was one of Frent's
lesser black marks against the Governor: a young man of

no family, the son of a schoolmaster or some fellow of that
sort, commended to Ormston by his old tutor (also the
young man's tutor) at New College, to Frent no commenda-
tion at all. There must, somewhere in the Governor's acute
mind, be a streak of sentimentality, most unlike him and
unexpected. Robin Hind looked more ingenuous and
younger than his years. It would be a lie to say that he was
inefficient or lazy, yet Frent could not help feeling that a
degree in classics, and very good manners, did not qualify
him for so responsible a job. Nor did even his so obvious
admiration for Ormston.

It was only lately, within the last week or two, that
Frent had begun to wonder whether young Hind were not
ambitious—even capable of calculation. The fragments
of shell still clinging to him were perhaps being carefully
preserved?

'You like this heat, do you?' the Governor said. 'Well,
you're eight years younger than I am. I must say you look
infernally cool.'

'I don't eat lunch, sir. That helps.'

The Governor's sleepy glance passed over Frent's slight
body and round neat head. The mind of a middle-aged
clerk in the body of a monk and a soldier, he thought: a good
soldier and a damned bore. He respected, valued, and disliked Frent.

'Too austere for me,' he said lightly. 'Well—anything
new?'

Frent lifted a sheet of paper and turned it over before
answering. 'This morning, an elderly man called Durham
—he had a market garden two miles out—had had it for
thirty years—came home and found his wife lying with her
throat cut, head all but off. He was kneeling over her, poor
old chap, when he was shot in the back—the killer had waited
for him to come in.'

Robin Hind's face had turned the colour of slate. 'Good

God, I knew them—the Durhams. He was a nice old
boy.'

A grimace of pity distorted the Governor's mouth, and
for an instant Frent—whose moment of anger and disgust
had come five hours ago, when the news was brought to
him—hoped he was going to see a breakdown of what he
thought of as Ormston's arrogant aloofness. He was disappointed. The Governor said coolly,

'You haven't got the murderer, of course.'

'No . . . This doesn't make it any easier to keep the C.P.S.
chaps in line. I had Puckeridge on the telephone five
minutes before you came.'

Four months earlier, a Committee of Public Safety had
been formed, headed by a well-to-do business man, James
Puckeridge. Ever since, he had been asking that it should
be armed and its members taught to shoot.

'Asking for arms?' the Governor said.

'Yes.'

An image of Puckeridge—a big heavily-fleshed man,
efficient, intelligent, a bully—crossed Ormston's mind.
With distaste, he said,

'It's not the way to deal with terrorism.'

Frent's reasons for agreeing with him were a little different. 'I have no use for armed civilians, sir. Undisciplined
amateurs . . . Have you had time to read the report I sent
to Government House yesterday?'

'Yes,' the Governor said. 'Yes, very carefully.'

'Well, sir?'

The Governor's voice was the one he used, casual, very
pleasant, when—Frent believed—he meant, for the satisfaction of his self-importance, to take his listener down a peg.
'I'm never quite sure, Frent, how far you are crediting these
fellows with your own ability to organise and direct. Your
report speaks of a General Staff, with brigades and depart-
ments, training sections, intelligence, a courier service,

execution squads, sabotage squads, transport, and so on
and so forth. You're describing—picturing a—a military
organisation, aren't you?'

'Para-military,' Frent said. Much you know about fighting, he thought.

'Oh, if you like. At any rate an organised force.'

'I drew the picture, as you put it,' Frent said coldly, 'from
the information got out of prisoners. It's not over-drawn.'

Does he know how to judge evidence? the Governor
wondered. 'My dear fellow, aren't you, possibly, giving too
much coherence to a number of scattered groups, some
more murderous than others, but all essentially *dis*organised
—which in time and with patience can be mopped up one
after another?'

'Mopping up—one of those easy words—means as little
as most such terms, sir.'

Irritated, the Governor said calmly, 'What term do you
prefer?'

His hands folded, more monk than police chief, Frent said,
'When a force—call it what you like—guerrilla, resistance,
rebellion—when a force is already breaking down, it is
possible to isolate and destroy the separate bits. Mop them
up, if you like the phrase. All the evidence I have collected
since I came here five months ago points to one answer—
the force being used against us is *not* breaking down. On
the contrary. It is being skilfully, technically, built up. Very
well built up. And by a man who knows his job.'

'By one man?'

Frent shrugged. 'You can't run a war—or a revolt—in
committee. You need a man—a leader.'

Elbow on the desk, chin propped lazily on his hand, the
Governor seemed to listen attentively and coldly. 'You
don't in your report put your finger on any one man among
the so-called officers leading these gangs.'

'No, sir,' Frent said drily. 'For a good reason. If I could

put my finger on him he would be here in this building, now.'

'But you are sure he exists.'

The inflection of irony in the Governor's voice did not move Frent. 'I should be sure even if I had no other evidence than the fact that what started, as you say, with scattered groups, has grown into a decently organised force—which is becoming daily more efficient, co-ordinated, better armed.' He paused—and went on with startling energy. 'My God, if I had this country, these hills, to operate in, *I* could make a monkey of our thirty thousand troops and police, with a tenth of their number.' His face worked. 'I could do it with three thousand young men. Young fanatics.'

'Fortunately for us, you are not leading the rebellion,' the Governor said. The beginning of a smile softened his mouth.

'Someone is,' Frent said quietly. 'Let's call him X—' he had a laugh like a short bark—'Trouble is we know what X equals—and it doesn't solve the problem.'

Robin Hind had flushed crimson. He blurted, 'Excuse me, sir, I don't see how you can use the words *decently organised* about brutes capable of hacking off an old lady's head—and the other things that have happened——'

Frent did not snub him. Mildly, with only a trace of contempt, he said, 'These murders, y'know, are quite rational. I mean, they have an intelligible reason. If you have fewer men than your opponent, a much smaller and weaker force, one of the ways you build up your side is by spreading terror.'

'No, no, it's shameful, inhuman,' Hind stammered.

Frent folded his hands. 'Any resistance movement—that is, any small body trying to out-wit and out-fight a stronger enemy—is driven to do inhuman things.' He added slowly, 'I know what I'm talking about.'

'That's enough, Robin,' the Governor said. 'Colonel Frent is not excusing the murders—there's no point in our sitting here arguing the relative brutality of wars and rebellions . . .' He looked at Frent. 'You have no direct proof that your professional leader exists? Your X.'

Frent said coolly, 'Yes. I have.'

The Governor raised his eyebrows very slightly. 'Really? What is it?'

'Not all his subordinates are efficient—and they're not all brave. In the last week I've had two matching accounts from prisoners of a man they call—they don't seem to have a name for him—the English colonel——'

'*English?*'

'Why not English?' Frent said, with the same coolness. 'You have a disloyal ass like this fellow Cumberland running a seditious newspaper. Why should he be the only one? An ex-officer with a grievance. A politician—one of your ambitious left-wingers. Like the fellow I had here this morning —not that he looked like a rascal, except that he stank of the cigar he'd been smoking . . . These days you can be any sort of traitor and get yourself absolved as a lover of peace or humanity or what not.'

The Governor did not answer. Half turning his chair round, he stared through the window at the hills. Some change in the light had brought them nearer and sharpened the dark folds between the crests: he had a momentary sense of menace, of being hemmed in. Something old and subtle detached itself from the naked hills and moved towards him. This country had a long memory, reaching far behind any records except those in the soil, into the darkness before history, of invasions, massacres, treacheries, a fate too heavy and tragic for a pliant undemanding people, never exterminated by any conquest, and never, until now, in open revolt. It was as if the arid bony hills themselves had revolted. The thought of the 'English colonel', if he existed, shocked him.

Some perverted idealist, he thought: murder and the highest ideals have always been first cousins, if not blood brothers . . . He turned sharply.

'You think I'm too lenient with Cumberland and his unpleasant rag,' he said. It was not a question.

Frent said, 'Your responsibility, sir,' in an expressionless and matter-of-fact tone.

The Governor moved his hands—he had ugly blunt hands, plebeian hands, in surprising contrast with the rest of his body and the beauty of his features. 'The fellow attacks me personally.' He might have been talking to himself. 'If I shut him down, it will look as if I had felt it.'

'That may not be a good enough reason for allowing him to go on poisoning the wells,' Frent said with slow care.

'I have—I daresay you know—been under some pressure to silence him.'

'Mr. James Puckeridge is peculiarly bitter.'

'Oh, those fellows,' the Governor said contemptuously, 'I don't mean them.'

He had a feeling of uncertainty, and suppressed it violently. The line of support behind him was a thin one—he was not even sure how thin. It was composed only of the friends he had made in the course of his climb out of an all but friendless youth: without anything that could be called influence, the climb had not been easy, and he had never asked for help that he was not certain, beforehand, of getting because he was useful to the man he approached. Nor were any of his later friendships really intimate—he had only one intimate friend in his life, and . . . his mind served sharply . . . I can rely on no one, he thought. No doubt my own fault—I haven't the gift of friendship.

Frent had not answered him. Glancing at the police chief's sharp ascetic face, which hid all griefs, or his lack of them, he thought: Is he an enemy? He knows, he must know that in certain quarters in London I'm blamed for letting the situation get out of hand . . . Every new atrocity —the wretched Durhams—every young serviceman ambushed and killed, sharpened tongues against him. He said slowly,

'You are probably right. There has been an increase of brutality——'

'Of efficiency.'

'That, too.' He had been going to add: You came here with a reputation for efficiency, and you don't want to blot it . . . Rejecting the impulse, he said, 'Just now you reproved me for speaking of mopping up——'

'Mopping up will come later, sir,' Frent said with a tightly-drawn smile.

'In the meantime——' To his annoyance he forgot what he had been going to say. He went on rapidly, 'The rebels are getting more bombs and guns than they were. None of your prisoners has been able to tell you how, or where from?'

'No,' Frent said, 'no. My guess is the same as yours. But I have no proof.'

The question forming itself in Ormston's mind remained unspoken. It had to do with the relations between the police chief and the G.O.C., General Smith. Should he let Frent know what he had discovered: that his report had been in Smith's hands for a full forty-eight hours before it was sent to Government House? No. Keep that in reserve.

'Let me tell you now what you'll hear at Thursday's conference—I'm going to London next week, taking with me a plan the G.O.C. is preparing now'—and which you probably know everything about, he thought ironically— 'based partly on your report—a plan of operations on a more ruthless scale. It will be put into effect as soon as it's been approved—as it will be.'

'I see,' Frent said.

You see a long way before your sharp nose, my friend . . .
'I don't believe—I never did—in what our *Compatriot* calls
methods of persuasion. You can't persuade a rattlesnake.
You can only crush its head.' He laughed shortly. 'Pity
we haven't found its head.'

He stood up. Robin Hind jumped to his feet. Rising
more slowly, Frent said,

'If you can spare a few more minutes, sir, I'd like you to
listen to one of my agents——'

The Governor cut him short. 'Oh, I don't think so.'

Frent persisted. 'A disreputable enough type, but more
intelligent than the run of the mill.'

'What's his name? If he has one.'

'Oh, yes, he has a name. You possibly know it. He's
called Ward. Maurice Ward.'

'Is that how he earns his living? Good God!'

His look of fastidious distaste became loathing. He knew
more about Maurice Ward than his name. Before he came
out here, when his appointment as Governor had been
announced, an old lady who had once, when he was a young
man, done him a considerable kindness, came to see him
and asked him to find out for her about her nephew who
was living in the colony. 'I have never heard from him,'
she said unhappily, 'since he went back. His father sent him
to England to school, he spent all his holidays with me then,
and I loved him very much. When he went home, he never
wrote to me, and I'm told'—her voice faltered—'I'm told
sad things. I do beg you to see him.' He promised—and
meant to keep his promise. Soon after his arrival in the
colony he made enquiries, and learned at once what Maurice
Ward was—a man on his way down, nearing bottom. He
did not even try to see him.

'He doesn't advertise the fact, sir,' Frent said. 'Nor do
we. I inherited him with my job.' He smiled. 'At least he

knows the meaning of words. They don't all. Will you see him? I have him waiting.'

The Governor seated himself again, with a nearly peevish reluctance. 'If you think it necessary.'

'I'm very much obliged,' Frent said quickly. He lifted the telephone. 'Send Ward in to me, will you?'

CHAPTER THREE

THE man who came in crossed the room towards them with a slouching assurance. His big face and full loose mouth had an air of amiable cunning and self-indulgence, with a hint of something less soft, as though his adroitness and his vices had swollen his features round a thinner harder face: he looked older than his forty-five years, and unhealthy, but not in any way dissatisfied with himself. The Governor had never seen him; he had the absurd thought that if he had he would have known him: the fellow looked, down to his long dirty fingernails and narrow feet in worn-out rope sandals, what he was. The son of a rich well-born settler, he had inherited his estate at the age of twenty-two; he sold out at once to his father's Scotch manager, and in less than eleven years had drunk and lazed away the whole of his capital. An Englishman who owned a small dubious hotel took him in—perhaps in memory of the hundreds of pounds of Ward's money he had taken over the bar—and employed him, when he was sober enough, as a clerk, paid him nothing, and when he was too drunk let him sleep all day. No one else did anything for him—no one could. For his father's sake, one or two men had tried and been defeated by his insolent determination to ruin himself. During the last five years he had drifted, more or less by accident, into the habit of bringing scraps of information, some of them useful, to Frent's predecessor, a man who had been his father's close friend. No doubt he was listened to at first out of pity. But he had relations with the native inhabitants of the colony which were not without value—now especially. He still spent much of his time with the woman he had seduced—or she seduced him—when he first came back to the colony from his English school: her three children were his. When no one else had a word for him, or food, she had. Possibly he was fond of the garrulous emotional object she had become, all cries and ready tears and animal warmth.

He had to cross almost the length of the room to reach the desk, and took his time. A smile, half leery, half affable, slackened his mouth as he looked from one to the other of the three faces turned to him. A short distance from the table, he halted, pulled a chair out, and sat down. His drawling voice had traces of a stutter.

'Good afternoon, gentlemen.'

Frent spoke with a detached cool civility. 'Good afternoon, Ward. I kept you waiting for a good reason. I wanted His Excellency to hear anything you can tell us. I gathered that you have something.'

The glance Ward turned on the Governor was curiously insolent, an amused insolence. He said lazily, 'I don't know that I have anything to say that Sir Richard will want to hear.'

The Governor's cold annoyance included Frent. 'I can give you five minutes,' he said to Frent.

Surprisingly, Ward sniggered. He pulled himself up at once, and said, 'Sorry, sorry. I happened to see a copy of *The Times* this week, and the editorial began: If Sir Richard Ormston has given five minutes' thought to . . . Damned if I remember what you were asked to think about, and I don't suppose it was of the faintest importance. People in London know all about what's happening here except the truth.'

The complete lack of respect in his manner struck even the Governor as involuntary. The man's quite obviously cracked, he said to himself. His instinctive repugnance for a drink-sodden wastrel was not without a tinge of guilt. I ought to have written to old Mrs. Ward, he thought very briefly.

'And what in your view,' he asked, 'is the truth?'

'The truth? Oh that, short of a miracle, we're going to

lose the place.' He sniggered again. 'We, I said. Did you
notice? I keep on forgetting who the devil I am.'

Something like a flicker of warmth moved in the Governor's mind, at a great depth, the obscure attraction that
failure, shamelessness, disgrace, have for the successful and
upright. He said abruptly,

'I knew your aunt, old Mrs. Charles Ward. If I can do
anything for you . . .'

And now Ward did a very surprising thing. Edging his
chair close to the desk, he leaned forward and scrutinised the
Governor's face with intense curiosity, before saying in a
malicious voice,

'What d'you expect me to do? Fall on your neck? Don't
worry, I shan't remember your generous offer. I know you
better than that.'

Frent had half risen. Before he could speak, the Governor
said coolly, 'If the fellow can say anything in three minutes,
tell him to go ahead.'

'Thank you, sir,' Frent said. He turned on Ward the
glance his subordinates tried to avoid. 'Go on.'

Ward did not seem intimidated. He leaned back, crossing
one leg over the other with the ankle resting on his knee.
'I suppose you know that our Mr. Puckeridge is running
about the place asking'—he smiled and stressed the words
—'for *His Excellency's* head on a charger. I don't know
whether he's prepared to dance for it. He's anyhow dancing
with nerves. They all are.'

'I don't think we need to know anything about Mr.
Puckeridge's nerves,' Frent interrupted him.

'Oh, quite,' Ward said easily.

He was sprawling clumsily in his chair now, jacket opened
to display a filthy old sweater, shirt unbuttoned on a sagging
neck, wide and fleshy like an old bull's. The Governor felt
a spasm of rage that he had been asked to give as much as a
minute's attention to this worthless nonsense. Frent must

be out of his mind, he thought drily. In the same moment he realised that he was less angry with the police chief than with himself, with his lapse of weak sympathy for the unspeakable Ward. He was pushing his chair back to go away when Ward began speaking in an altered harder voice.

'Excuse me, I'm not trying to play the fool, and I'm not drunk. It's only—to be exact, yesterday I got a—no, I can't call it a hint, since it wasn't meant for me—' he paused, and some change of expression took place, strangely under the sallow skin of his face—'I was supposed to be too far gone to take in anything that was said. And I damn near was—and damned little was said. A couple of sentences. Enough, when you laid them alongside two others I heard dropped a week ago, to make five.' He looked, insolent again, round their faces, and jerked his head at Robin Hind. 'Is this child to be trusted?'

The young man had been eyeing him with a half pitying, half naïve curiosity. His face sharpened angrily.

'Don't be an ass,' he said.

Ward smiled, sucking in his lower lip. 'All right, sonny boy, I'm a suspicious old man . . . In any case, I haven't anything startling to say.' He lowered his head slightly to look under his lashless eyelids at Frent, his chin disappearing into the folds of his throat. 'Tell me something—have you a brace of characters spry enough to keep behind me this evening without even my spotting them?'

'I think so,' Frent said. 'Yes.'

'Well, don't think—be sure,' Ward said pleasantly. 'And tell them . . . let me think . . . tell them that if I know where I'm taking them—maybe I don't, but if I know, they'd better be good. Better than good. Ready to put their man out—I don't mean kill him, that would be a horrid mistake —but cold—before he knows they're there. Some of yours were commandos, weren't they?'

Looking at him with merciless attention, Frent nodded.

'I thought so,' Ward said. He yawned. 'Well, they ought to do.'

The Governor's distaste for the fellow's thick drawling voice and slack body became too much for him. 'If Mr. Ward has nothing intelligible to say, can't we excuse him?'

Ward laughed, gently and spitefully. 'What d'you want me to tell you? That every little brat sitting on his bare bottom in the dust—and every whore in this city—believes you're done for—you can't win. James Puckeridge has a right to be jittery. I would be—if I cared.'

The Governor stood up and nodded at Frent. 'I'll see you tomorrow,' he said, with marked curtness.

Jumping to his feet, Frent walked with his light springy step to the door, reaching it ahead of Robin. Opening it, he said,

'Very good of you to stay, sir.'

'Very unnecessary,' Ormston said. 'Goodbye.'

Still smiling his sharp smile, Frent stepped back into the room.

CHAPTER FOUR

To reach Government House from police headquarters, the car made a long detour, avoiding Urraca Street. Ormston was silent, his head pressed against the comfortable back of the seat. Now and then Robin Hind glanced at him, cautiously and with a solicitude that his youth made a little touching. Not that he was as young as he seemed. He was twenty-five and looked twenty. He was pale, with a clear smooth skin, his face a pure oval: everything about him had the same deceptive air of freshness and delicacy, bluish eyes, slender neck and wrists, slender body. He had a modest way of speaking and holding himself, a little maidenly but not without assurance, and a trace, a pleasant trace, of youthful nervousness. He did not obtrude his enormous admiration for the Governor, yet in one way and another, by an ingenuous tone in his voice, or a slight gesture, he managed to convey it. He was doing it at this moment by sitting without a movement, at once effaced and alert, steadying himself with his hands on the seat against the jolts of the car, which was being driven at top speed over a poor road.

The Governor spoke with half-humorous energy. 'My God, what a brute. Inexcusable for Frent to bring him in.'

'Sir, I'm frightfully sorry,' Robin said in his low cool voice, 'I apologise for what I said—I mean, about the murders. I lost my head for a minute. I'm terribly sorry.'

'My dear boy, it didn't matter.'

'You're very kind, sir, but I had no right to speak.'

'Of course you hadn't,' the Governor said kindly. 'Don't do it again. But'—he smiled very slightly—'I'm never altogether drawn to Colonel Frent.'

A sudden boyish gaiety broke through the young man's discretion. 'He's not very engaging, sir, is he?'

Although not aware of it, or so little aware that he could ignore it easily, the Governor enjoyed the moments when, without moving a toe outside the limits of respect, his secretary contrived to suggest that the gap separating twenty-five and fifty-three is less wide than it seems. Imperceptibly he became less irritable and tense. He sat up and glanced indulgently at the young man. It crossed his mind briefly that having Hind about, as it were in the family, was a little like having a son always there, without any of the anxiety, the feeling of responsibility and diffidence bound up with a real son—all the more inescapable when like Andrew he was a son to be proud of, responsive and highly intelligent.

He smiled at Hind. 'Ah, you don't like him?'

Robin hesitated and said quietly, 'He's a splendid man, sir, and must be a very good soldier. But it's not easy to like anyone who is so—so eternally unshakeably certain of his own righteousness.'

The Governor did not answer. I asked for it, he thought: I have no right to snub him . . . What was more, he did not want to. He was amused by these flashes when something cool and ambitious and very shrewd broke through the surface of the young man's modesty and simplicity. After a moment he said in an indifferent voice,

'He wasted ten minutes of my time on that unpleasant scoundrel.'

Robin spoke with a touch of anxiety. 'I hope you're going to rest this afternoon, sir. You were working at four o'clock this morning.'

'It's cool then. I like it . . . And, damn it, how d'you know I was working at that time?'

The secretary blushed. 'In my bedroom I can hear when you open the shutters in yours. I—well, in fact, sir, this morning I got up and got as far as your door. I thought you might need me. And then I lost my nerve about disturbing you, and went away without knocking.'

'I'd have sent you back with a flea in your ear,' the Governor said. He laughed, with a feeling of ease, and liking for the slender quietly self-contained young man. 'Four o'clock is too early for the young.'

The car with its escort of four motor-cyclists turned into the courtyard of Government House, and Robin was out of it and opening the door before the nearest soldier reached it. The Governor took the steps two at a time and hurried across the hall and up the staircase at a pace that had his secretary running to keep close to him. He went straight to the room on the first floor, originally the library and now also his working room—he had taken it for himself because it faced north. Glancing over his shoulder at Robin he said,

'I don't need you. I really am going to take a couple of hours. Off you go.'

'Right, sir. I'll be upstairs,' Hind said.

He had turned and was going away when the Governor's voice, pleasant and casual, halted him. 'Just a minute. There *was* something I wanted to ask you. Come in.'

The huge room was cool. Its uncarpeted floor, a mosaic of different woods, highly polished, the table with its island of letters and newspapers and the vacuum jug filled with cold water, the bookcases lining three walls, all added to the impression of coolness and peace—a country gentleman's library where he talked to his agent, saw tenants, and slept a little after lunch. At the end of the room, the window, uncurtained, had much the same view as the police chief's at the other end of the city, and changed as that did with every shift of light across the flanks of the hills, now pale, with crests like the spreading horns of bulls, and deep bluish-brown clefts.

The Governor settled himself into one of the leather armchairs in the window. 'Sit down, boy, sit down,' he said lightly. 'This isn't official.'

Robin turned round one of the chairs placed at the table,

and seated himself. He felt curiosity, and a little, not much, nervousness. He knew that he had given satisfaction, that he was liked, and he had never, even in the beginning, had with Ormston the difficulty many people had with him, with his polite arrogance, his way of evading personal relationships. One of the secrets of his success with the older man was, he almost knew, his feeling, instinctive, that Ormston was distant and evasive because he did not know how to be anything else. The same instinct usually told him how far he could go in a sort of respectful freedom. He waited to hear what was wanted of him now.

With the same lightness, the Governor said,

'You knew this young woman Sarah Leng—Cumberland's step-daughter—in England, didn't you?'

In spite of the careless tone, the implication—that he had no love for the young woman—was too clear to miss. What's Sarah been up to? Hind wondered coolly. Something to do with her beastly newspaper? . . . During the past six months—between working twelve or fourteen hours a day, and an affair, not serious but absorbing, that he was having with a young nurse at the Military Hospital—he had not so much as seen Sarah Leng. Feeling his way—what did the Governor want him to answer?—he said in a neutral voice,

'Yes.'

'Well—you knew her well?'

'Oh, very well indeed, sir.' He could be talkative about this, it was inoffensive and innocent, didn't involve him in any way. 'She and I are cousins, her mother is my mother's much younger sister: she was a widow, and when she married again, Charles Cumberland—heaven knows why she married him—and he brought her out here, they left Sarah in England with us. She was twelve then—three years younger than I was.'

'How long did she live with you?'

'Seven or eight years. Seven.'

The Governor's eyes were half closed, he had a little amused smile.

'Did you—do you like her? Is she—how shall I put it? —a clever young woman?'

Robin's mind jumped, in a familiar way. Talking to people was like a guessing game, in which you are given one end of a thread of thought and have to grasp the rest of it yourself: he felt quite certain now that the Governor would be disappointed if he spoke of Sarah with approval. He laughed gently.

'Oh, too clever by half, sir.'

A little genuine malice had crept into the game he was playing. He still remembered with resentment certain passages of their adolescence when the girl's sharp tongue had humiliated him, and before others.

'Clever—and not much worldly sense, eh?' Ormston said.

'What do you mean, sir—worldly sense?' He let his malice slip out of control, a rare happening with him. 'If you mean, is she as innocent as she looks, you can be certain she isn't.'

The Governor spoke in a sharp voice, no longer casual or amused. 'Not innocent? What do *you* mean, my boy?'

An acute discomfort seized Robin. He had not meant to say so much, and he had no wish at all to make mischief. For all their quarrels and her hot temper, he was fond of Sarah. He said quickly,

'Oh, I only meant that nowadays there isn't much girls don't know—even girls as young and well brought-up as Sarah.'

The crease at the ends of Ormston's mouth was one of ironical pleasure: it amused him mildly to use his power over the young man to twist his arm, morally and mentally twist it. He tapped him on the knee.

'My dear Robin, that isn't what you meant. I know you

too well. You were going to tell me something about Miss Sarah Leng—and you suddenly decided that I am too old —or too innocent myself—to hear it. Which of the two was it? Come now. Out with it.'

His voice was pleasant, almost gay, but Robin knew, he knew in his innermost mind, that if he dared hold his tongue now he would give real and unforgettable offence. He was caught in the trap of his own adroitness, his clever trick of guessing what would please the other person to hear. For all that, he still hesitated. He was uneasy and genuinely reluctant to harm Sarah. He caught a steely gleam in the Governor's eye and felt that he had no choice now. I must go on with it, he thought. He frowned, and said in a calm voice,

'It's not much of a story, sir.'

Leaning back in his chair, Ormston said, smiling,

'Never mind that. Tell it.'

CHAPTER FIVE

'THANKS, my dear boy. It's a very interesting little story. I can't say it surprises me.'

He caught sight of his secretary's hand, gripped on his knee, and realised that the young man was unhappy and very uneasy. Afraid that I shall give him away? he thought, amused. No—mortified because he has had to behave, as it must feel to him, shabbily: he doesn't mind who knows about the girl, but he would hate to be seen in the act of betraying her . . . Leaning forward, he said kindly,

'Don't feel sorry you told me. I'll be very discreet. And I'm immensely grateful. Now—off you go. And forget it.'

He sat for a minute, not so much thinking as turning the story he had just listened to over in his mind in a suspension of feeling, as though it were a stone he had picked up and could drop or use to throw at a bird. The feeling that seized him suddenly was one of savage resentment . . . It was intolerable that his son, *his* son, should be in danger of throwing himself away, spoiling his life, on anything so worthless as this wretched girl. He expected much from Andrew. To have brought him up with such passionate care not to spoil him, loving him as he did, with such justified pride, such delight in his intelligence, in the brilliance he had shown at school, and at Oxford in his medical work, and such pleasure in the boy's trust and affection, and now . . . No father ever had more thoroughly satisfying relations with a son. From the moment when, bending over the week-old child's cot, he had felt, ridiculously, with a pang of joy, that Andrew *knew* him, the boy had never disappointed him, never once: he had even skipped the awkward age his father expected and had prepared for, when he would be sullen and unmalleable. Always, he was always, with his

father, alert, clear, amused, easy. And now, if now, a girl
with less promise in her whole body than Andrew in his
little finger were to lay her deforming hand on him and on
his future, his career . . . Spoiling *my* plans, he thought
with anguish, spoiling my pleasure in him . . . No, it was
intolerable.

He stood up, and stood for a minute rigid, compelling
himself to put aside even the story itself. This needs tact
and a quiet mind, he warned himself. Looking at his watch,
he saw that it was still only four o'clock. Started up by his
anger, the restlessness in his body sent him to pick up the
telephone and ask for a number. He waited impatiently to be
put through. He had so little time. No time to live, he
thought, no time . . . Ah . . . 'Anne? How are you? . . .
Oh, not more than usual. Tell me, are you alone now? . . .
Good, that's splendid. May I come? . . . Now? . . . Not
long, I'm afraid. An hour. I'll come at once . . .'

He ran down the staircase like a young man. A sentry,
as he began to cross the hall, signalled to the car drawn up
in the shade at the side of the courtyard, waiting. One of
the motor-cyclists of the escort had taken off his helmet,
and another was lighting a cigarette. They moved, when
he appeared on the steps, like a machine. He told the driver
that he was going to see Mr. Gouraud. Visiting the Frenchman, once a week, rarely oftener now, was known to be the
only amusement he allowed himself, his only relief from the
crisis—a strange idea of amusement, his driver considered,
but it takes all sorts to make a world.

And indeed the old Frenchman was the only man in the
colony with whom the Governor was at all intimate, and
the only man he could trust—as he did trust him—with a
secret. He scarcely remembered now the circumstances, or
the accident, that had led him to put himself in Gouraud's
fine sensitive hands. When he did it, it had only been a very
slight sharpening of what was already a friendship, not a

so to speak blood friendship, and not a habit. What he liked in Gouraud was the alliance of an extreme delicacy and subtlety of mind with manners so good that they were like the colour of his eyes or the fineness of his skin, given him at birth; they came straight from his senses. A very highly-bred animal might be as naturally polite—it was as easy to be with him as with a friendly cat, if such a creature exists.

In the lobby of the Astoria, he made sure that Gouraud was in his apartment, then sent car and escort back to Government House. 'I'll telephone for you when I want you,' he told his driver. Two foreign journalists, sitting drinking in the lobby, stood up as he passed. He waved a hand at them: as soon as he was in the lift, they would inform themselves who it was he called on in the hotel. He spent two minutes in Gouraud's apartment, the time it took to bring the Frenchman's car round to his private door into the lane at the back of the Astoria. He had no need to tell the chauffeur where to take him: the man, an elderly Bordelais, with small black eyes corrupt with dead secrets, knew. The car, a battered Peugeot, was enormously roomy: leaning back in it, he was as far out of sight as if it had been shuttered, and safer than in his own escorted car, since everyone in the city knew the shabby black monster and that it belonged to the Frenchman.

They crossed the inner town and left it by the shockingly bad road that led to the English quarter. This was a much older suburb than the spatter of bungalows and little villas on the other side: a score or so of large houses, built up and round a slope, with terraced carefully-planted gardens and high walls: there were trees, acacias, pepper-trees, planes, breathlessly still in the heat, and a musky smell of dryness or dying sapless flowers: on one wall a long trailing white flower gave off an acrid tang, like a bitter herb. Behind its white walls, Anne Boyd's house was smaller than the others

in the suburb; the shutters at the windows, all closed, were
solid and had been painted grey, but the paint had long
since dried into streaks on the cracked wood; it was perhaps
they and their shabbiness which gave the house its blinded
look. The door, as Ormston expected, was open behind a
screen: he went in and straight to the drawing-room.

Even this room, the one most often used, its windows
opening on to a paved inner yard, had an air of dust and
neglect, as though the person living in it were wholly un-
interested in her surroundings: there was even a very slightly
foetid odour of dying plants, no one bothered to carry away
the dead flowers until they were rotten, or to sweep up the
parched leaves fallen in the yard.

All this was so familiar to him that he barely noticed the
shabbiness of rugs and silk chair coverings, or the half-dead
flowers in a large tarnished copper basin. There was nothing neglected or slatternly about the woman watching him,
from the sofa, as he crossed the room to her. Anne Boyd
was not beautiful, her features were too irregular, and she
looked her age, but she was almost overwhelmingly attractive: her skin had the waxen texture of a thick petal, startlingly white against the folds of dull black hair; her eyes
were very large, a brilliant brown, with deep lids. She was
wearing a sun dress—she who never exposed herself to a
ray of the sun—its top leaving bare generously rounded
white shoulders and arms and full throat. Stooping to kiss
her, Ormston had the familiar sense of burying his face in a
full-blown white flower, the same longing to draw in all at
once its scent, softness, coolness, to absorb it, feel it completely, possess it, and the same frustrated sense of failure.

'My darling, how cool you are,' he said.

'Is it hot out?' she asked.

Her voice was one of the things that had drawn him to
her and now held him: he amused himself sometimes trying
and failing to find the words to describe it: it was low, at

once warm and curiously flawed and metallic, like a deep-
toned bell with a crack in it that altered certain notes, giving
them a double sound, tormenting and seductive.

'Yes. Hot and dusty. Not a climate for hard work.'

'Where would you like to be?' she asked, smiling.

'If I weren't in this room? I think—in Scotland—a house
I know in Glen More. With you.'

Her smile pulled down the ends of her mouth. 'We shall
never be there.'

Lifting her hand, he pressed it over his eyes for a minute.
'Yes. One day before we're too old,' he said indistinctly.

'We're too old now, my dear,' she said, drawling the
words. 'You're over fifty and I'm forty-five. Too old
for anything except amusing each other for a few more
years.'

'Do I amuse you?' he said, with difficulty.

She shook her head. 'Not in the least. I'm much too fond
of you.'

He kissed the palm of the hand he was still holding, and
laid it back on her knee. Getting up, he went over to the
window and stared out at the courtyard without seeing the
shabby cane chair under a faded awning, or the bed of dingy
sun-baked earth and tangled bushes of jasmine. Everything
in him and outside him seemed at this moment to be de-
voured by the same aridity and emptiness, the same absence
—no other word for it. He felt an impatient, almost irritable
need to make love to her, a greed of his whole body. The
tension in his nerves and veins suffocated him. Turning to
look at her, he said,

'Would you, do you think, be as fond of me if we were
living obscurely somewhere, on not a great deal of money?
I could get some sort of job. Fairly easily.'

She looked at him with a half-indulgent mockery. 'My
dear Richard, you would never do it. I can as easily imagine
you a retired nobody, an *ex*, as I can imagine my dear

husband without his ridiculous international congresses and his quarrels and jealousies and the rest of his habits. Absurd. You are both egoists, you know, my darling.'

'You know me too well,' he said with a shock of bitterness.

'I'm right, though, aren't I? It's true?'

He came back and stood looking down at her, without speaking. It was true—yes. His success in the world, his career, came before even his hard greedy lust for her. 'Anthony,' he said, 'you've heard from him?'

'Yes. This morning. After more than ten months.'

'Well?'

Even now, when it had grown thinner and harsh with resentment, her voice kept its metallic resonance, coming from deep in her throat. 'He has found—somewhere close to the frontier, he says—a totally new species of orchis—orchis? orchid?—which do I mean? Growing on the edge of a crater.' She pulled a face of amused contempt. 'And he's coming home.'

'When?'

'Did you expect him to tell me when? That would be too thoughtful. Tomorrow—next week—next month——' A light glancing bitterness made her seem older and tired. 'After all, he's not coming home to me, but to his study, his books, and to read the letters waiting for him from colleagues he despises—and will insult by the first post he can catch after he gets back.'

'Why are you still so angry with him?' Ormston asked her uneasily. 'Why do you mind so much?'

'Mind? I don't mind,' she said swiftly. 'I don't exist for him.'

'Nonsense, my darling.'

She laughed. 'My dear, if I were dying, and Tony heard that some expedition or other was setting out for Tibet to collect . . . whatever grows in Tibet, he'd pack his things and go. It's always been like that—ever since I married him—long, long before we, as they say, grew apart. Indeed, should we have grown apart'—she mocked the phrase by her tone—'if he hadn't, from the first, made it quite clear that a botanical congress was infinitely more important to him than I am? I don't know.'

Ormston was silent. His jealousy of her husband was an offence to him, to the raw edges of his self-love: for months he could ignore it, then a moment came, as now, when it wrenched him with the pain of a torn nerve.

'You still think about him.'

'With hatred,' she said calmly. 'No, no, that's far too— too interested. With an utter weary indifference.' Her voice rose. 'Oh, if only he would never come home again. If one of his ridiculous expeditions would go on for ever and ever —to the moon—to his grave. I should be delighted to hear that he had died on the next one. The coward!'

Ormston felt something like shame. He had loved Boyd in the past, the not, after all, so distant past. To be joining in abuse of him was somehow meaner than to have become the lover of his neglected wife. Yet he felt—only now and then, when she had managed to disturb him brutally—a curious guilt about that, too: curious because, apart from everything else, it gave him a deep, the deepest satisfaction to injure the other man, to punish him. Boyd had always been reck-lessly careless and self-indulgent, always obeyed every im-pulse, even when it would destroy him. Born rich and well-placed, he had kicked away every chance, every advantage. To be so sure of yourself, so free, that you can lash out all round . . . Boyd deserved to be punished for it . . . Almost without intending to, he said,

'He's not a coward. Anything but.'

Anne had recovered her calm. 'You're fond of him, aren't you?' she said, smiling. 'Still.'

The pressure round Ormston's heart lightened suddenly.

'After all, I've known him for nearly forty years,' he said lightly. 'That's a long time.'

'Was he always'—she hesitated—'always self-centred, moody, always quarrelsome?'

'He was always difficult—liable to fly off the handle for no very good reason—even as a boy.'

She laughed, a short laugh. 'Difficult? You mean impossibly touchy, completely unspeakably selfish.'

'No, not selfish,' Ormston said, with sudden energy, 'you're wrong. Except as a dedicated man is selfish. The thing he cares for—whatever it is—when he was at school it used to be snakes, now it's rare plants—obsesses him to such a point that——' He stopped, abruptly conscious of her again, her nearness, her cool indolent body. 'I can see that it might be hard for you, for any woman to take.' He touched her shoulder lightly, running his hand upwards over the side of her throat to her temple. 'A very beautiful woman.'

'D'you think I feel he should have dedicated himself to me?' she said derisively. 'I'm not a complete fool. But between dedication and the—the indifference he shows, there is a desert. No, no, my dear, I married a man who feels that the world doesn't appreciate him and his genius—and he takes his disappointment out on the person who happens to be nearest him.' She added in a harsh voice, 'If I'd been more submissive, stupider, I might not have objected so violently—and he might have been kinder. As it is . . .'

With something like grief, a jealous grief, Ormston thought: Why is it that neither of us can forget him when he's not here? 'It's true he hasn't had as much success as he ought to have had,' he said slowly.

'Why should he?' she cried. 'He has always quarrelled with people who could have been useful to him. Gone out of his way to quarrel with them. If his career is ruined it is his own fault.'

'He'd have been happier as a soldier. I mean if he had stayed in the army—as he meant to, surely?'

'My dear Richard, in the war he made an enemy of the G.O.C., and bitterly offended my brother in the War Office. You'd have thought he hated both of them more, far more than he disliked the Germans he was fighting.'

'Perhaps he did ... But he was a good soldier—as brave as you like.'

A gleam of malice came into Anne's eyes, making them for a moment bright and cold, like peaty water in sunlight. 'Yes ... He had some very sharp things to say about you at the time.'

Ormston refused to let this reach him. 'I spent my war in the Foreign Office,' he said calmly.

'I know.' She dropped her voice to its deepest and most deliberately caressing. 'Tony said it was wise of you.'

A jet of bitterness sprang in him. 'Need we go on talking about him?'

'No,' she said. 'No, it's not very important.'

She stood up and began to move about the room, idly, not as if noticing things: even when she ran her finger down a worn place on the arm of a chair, she did not see it. One wall of this room, the longest, was covered from ceiling to floor by bookshelves: she had two interests, the care of her body, and—surprising anyone who did not know that she had been one of the more intelligent young females of her year at Oxford—modern philosophy. She was too lazy, bone lazy, to want a career. But on the day a new book reached her from London, she did not take the trouble to dress: she sat all day, in dressing-gown and slippers, reading it, and brushing her hair, or turning pages with a finger kept for the purpose out of the jar of face cream. What if she had not married would have become of her? Ormston wondered.

'Tell me,' she said with her back to him, 'things are getting worse here, aren't they?'

'In what way?' he asked, momently vexed. 'No.'

'Oh, they are, they are,' she exclaimed, turning on him. 'Why do you pretend—to *me*? One has only to go out. I can feel it—the way they look at me in the streets, in shops. And our own people are much more nervous now, you know. There's a—a tension.'

'Nothing is really any worse.'

'The murders are worse . . . the Durhams . . . that poor woman, Richard!' She shuddered. 'I find myself eyeing Agathe, my dear Agathe that I've had all these years—with her dramatic ways and her devotion—and wondering if she's about to round on me and cut my throat.'

'If you feel like that, get rid of her,' he said, with energy.

'And get what or whom in her place? No, it's frightening, Richard, I'm frightened. I feel that anything—some horrible thing—can happen now. And I'm not abnormally nervous, you know. Everyone I talk to—not that I see many people—feels just the same. It's getting, yes, unbearable.'

He watched her, frowning. Why now? he thought, exasperated, why in God's name now? He had meant, when he came here, to soothe himself by making love to her; the talk about Anthony, that fool, had distracted him, and now when he ought to be leaving, his need became acute, so acute that she had ceased to be anything but a body he wanted to violate.

'You shouldn't live here alone——'

With one of her swift changes of mood, she interrupted him. Coming to him, she put her hands on his shoulders, pulling him to her, and kissed his cheeks, his mouth. 'Never mind, never mind,' she murmured. 'If I'm going to die in some unpleasant way, I don't want to think about it. I'll think about you instead. You still love me, don't you?'

The last rags of his self-control vanished. Again, bending over her, he tried to lose himself in her, to take her in

his mother seventy-two, Rose Bain two years younger: they had been at the same finishing school—what a phrase!—in Paris, and he imagined that the relationship between them had remained essentially unchanged since then, one of superior to adoring submissive emotional inferior. Caroline Ormston was tall, elegant in mind and body, and dress, with fine aquiline features and a fine skin, very clear and curiously lightless, as though made of some delicate unliving material which had been crumpled and then smoothed out: she used no make-up except on her lips; these were a pale pink, faintly and skilfully rouged. She had always been a delicate woman, but she took care of herself and had never had a serious illness—nothing worse than a headache. Her headaches were a threat that waited on her, and were responsible for the only marks of strain on her handsome face, two deep, very deep vertical lines between her arched eyebrows . . . As for Rose: there was no elegance in her, no self-assurance either, only generosity, devotion, irrational antipathies and loves, clumsiness—traits visible in her long bony face, sunken eyes, even in the hair she neglected so that it stood out like strands of white horse-hair above her small ears and the thin nape of her neck. She was continually in awe of her friend, whose companion she had been since he could remember, certainly since he was a child at his first school. Nowadays she spoke of herself as Caroline's secretary, but her devotion was greater than her efficiency or her commonsense, and her duties were carried out in an anguish that would have been a better comedy if it had not been so obviously real. It was still comic. Ormston listened, smiling, while his mother, speaking in her loudest, most authoritative voice, but slowly, as to a child, repeated her instructions about the letter to be written to the Board of one of her many charities. She was active, even at this distance from England, in several works: clothes for the reputable poor, the Conservative League, a hospital for old women.

There were others he had forgotten. Rose, nodding her head wildly, scribbling notes with pen quivering between her gaunt fingers, repeated emphatically,

'Yes . . . yes, Caroline . . . yes, I do understand . . . yes, yes.'

Does she? Ormston wondered. Poor old girl . . . Only a woman so good and generous as his mother would put up with this grotesque.

The large room was filled with light the colour of honey; this same light had soaked into the hills visible through the window, so that the sculptured rocks now had the translucence of pale wine, and in the deep folds the violet shadows opened and shut like the sticks of a fan. These rooms were the best of the living-rooms, the largest and coolest. They were meant to be used by the Governor himself, but he had insisted on her taking them: she protested, but agreed as soon as she saw how anxious he was for her to be as comfortable as possible in a situation that was uneasy even before the revolt soured and turned murderous. She had brought out with her a few of her possessions, just those which would create round her the setting she needed: a pair of ivory figurines of saints, a small very fine Corot, books in her own bindings, a George I silver kettle on its slender mahogany stand, grey French silk curtains, rugs. To visitors who marvelled that she would risk her 'lovely things' in the colony now, she said in her cool way, 'I couldn't live, even for a short time, in a place I hadn't done something to civilise.' Rose, if she were there, would cry, 'Oh, Caroline's a genius. D'you know, she once redecorated the whole of a flat she had only rented for six months, because it had been done so badly by a woman without any style.'

One other object in the room went with her everywhere, even on short visits—the cast, in bronze, of her hands, made when she was thirty, while they were still without a flaw. They had been of the most startling beauty, long, narrow, each nail the half of a peeled almond. They were drawn in various poses by a famous artist, photographed, and finally—the suggestion of a sculptor—cast as a death mask is cast, and worked over by him in the bronze. They were separate, and she liked to alter their pose. Today, for instance, they lay with the fine finger-tips touching: another day, they might lie, one palm upwards, the other lying across it. Her son had always found something disturbing in these hands cut off at the wrist; in some strange way it was a mutilation. But that might have been due to his life-long awareness of his mother's hands as in some obsessive way different from the hands of other women; for one thing, she disliked having them caressed or even touched; when, as a child does, he had seized one and begun to play with the fingers, she drew it sharply back and told him, in a voice he never forgot, and never risked hearing again, to keep his hands off hers. The ritual of caring for them lasted a long time, morning and evening.

They were still, for an old woman, remarkable hands, but they were covered with lines, some of them as deep as wrinkles. Watching them, as she turned over the pages of a letter she was reading through before giving it to Rose, her son wondered briefly why, now, they roused in him a slight, the very slightest repugnance. Was it only because he could remember them when they were as smooth as the smooth metal, or because they made him think of two long lean animals moving across her knees? The thought vanished almost before he had noticed it.

She had, he now saw, one of her headaches. He knew it because she was sitting with half-closed eyes: the deep heavily-veined lids, a little discoloured, were like the remains of a double bruise on her face, and the impression she gave when her eyes disappeared behind them was curiously one of disdain.

Many years ago, when her son was a child, these headaches

had been much more severe, killing her, as Rose put it, for two or three days. She lay in her bedroom, with blinds drawn, eating nothing. Each time it happened, he fell into the same agonised fear that she was going to die. It was a terrible fear, completely out of his control, like a madness. It woke him at night, and he lay trembling, sweating, praying. Once, unable to endure his terror a moment longer, he got out of bed in the early morning and went downstairs to the door of her room; for a long time, hours, he sat outside it listening, straining his ears to catch the faintest sound. Nothing—not a breath. In the end, when he thought that the servant would soon be up and find him here and laugh at him, he turned the handle, slowly, with infinite pains, and went in. His mother was awake. As his head came round the door she raised herself on her pillows, looking, with the compress across the upper half of her face, terrifying, a stone woman. 'What do you want?' she said, in the voice she used to keep him from touching her hands. 'Go away at once.' He asked her, shivering with the cold of his vigil, if she were all right. 'Go away,' she said again. He went.

Later, a great many years later, he knew that it was not her headaches, or not only the headaches, that gave him his feeling of fearful anxiety and responsibility for her—as though it had been born with him. As though he were the parent and she the child. And as though he were, in some way, guilty towards her. Yet the guilt was not, wholly not his. Was there ever a time when he had not known and been wrung by the knowledge of her disappointment and unhappiness? His father was to blame—only his father . . . Even now, when George Ormston had been dead forty years, his son could not remember him without a throb of the resentment he had felt, the anguish of the child helpless to prevent his mother being treated brutally. They were allies, he and his mother, against the husband and father—

an unspoken alliance: she would never have allowed him to put his hatred and disrespect into words. And she herself was severe with him, no spoiling, no weakness to make up for his father's rough violence. He understood that, too, now. She was hard, merciless on his small sins, because of her fear that he might grow up like his father, a beast who drank and had women.

He had forgotten much of his childhood—most. But one incident remained, a living worm in his mind. It happened when he was about nine: he had been lying in his bed, listening to the argument that went on, louder and more insistent, until his father left the house: then, after a time, not able to go to sleep, he crept downstairs and stood in the darkness and cold at the door of his mother's bed-room, and heard her crying. He had never known it to happen before, never imagined her in tears. She cried, with a misery, a quietness, he found terrifying. He could not go back to bed, leaving her in this wretchedness, nor dare he go in to her: in the end, it seemed to him calmly, as if nothing could be simpler and more ordinary, he decided to wait up until his father came home, and kill him. Searching in the kitchen for a knife, he chose the ham knife because it was thin, long, and dangerously sharp, and went with it into the sitting-room: the door of this room opened into the passage leading from the front door to the stairs, immediately opposite a table and the coat-stand; if he stood here in the darkness he could jump out and drive the knife into the brute's left side as he stood in the light, his back to the sitting-room door, hanging his coat up. How long did he wait there? Four, five hours, going over in his mind, over and over, the instant of killing, raising his arm, lowering it, touching the point of the blade gingerly, body and mind so concentrated on their purpose that, cold as it was in the doorway of the room, he did not shiver. His father came in about two, and stood there, head thrown back, smiling at his handsome image in the glass above the table, a perfect target. And the child could not move, paralysed by fear—and by some other unrecognised emotion which filled him from head to foot and kept him rigid until his father went away upstairs, humming under his breath gaily, then threw him on his knees on the floor, then flat on his face: he lay there, shaking with hate, cold, and bitter shame that he had turned out to be a coward . . .

Looking round the room, with its white-painted walls and the window with its frieze of ancient dark-veined hills, and at her still handsome face, its fine bone structure visible under the skin, he thought: I have done as much as anyone could to make things up to her . . . The thought gave him a sensual satisfaction.

Rose had stopped scribbling. Rolling her eyes nervously in their deep sockets, she said,

'Oh, Caroline, do you think you ought to say that? Won't it make things awkward for, what's his name, you know, the secretary?'

Her agitation was ridiculous and funny, but Mrs. Ormston did not smile. She very rarely smiled—though she could laugh, a half-tittering laugh, like a girl's—and she had a way, when one of her certainties had been questioned, of speaking as though from a great height, with all the energy of an unconscious arrogance.

'What on earth have Mr. Core's personal feelings to do with it?'

'Only that he does the work.'

'This is a principle,' Mrs. Ormston said.

'Yes, yes, of course,' Rose murmured, 'I just thought——'

Unexpectedly, Mrs. Ormston tittered. 'Oh, Rose, you know it's no use your trying to think.'

This was an old joke, and Rose smiled in relief and love. 'Yes, Caroline.'

'Well, now run off,' Mrs. Ormston said very pleasantly.

'And try not to make too many mistakes.' She watched in a detached way Rose blunder across the room, then turned to her son. 'Well, my dearest?'

'How are you feeling now?' he asked. 'Is the heat too much for you?'

She closed her eyes as she spoke. 'I'm very well.'

'Your head aches.'

'It's nothing,' she said, eyes widely open, 'it will pass.'

'Is there anything you need? Shall I ask Fielding to have a look at you?'

'No, no, certainly not,' Mrs. Ormston exclaimed. 'I dislike him. And I know far more about myself than any doctor. But you might draw the curtains across the window again. Quite enough light comes through them for anyone but Rose. And besides, she likes the barbaric view.'

The curtains were almost always drawn, or half-drawn, to protect her eyes, the Corot, the leather bindings of her books. And it was true: the light in this country could press through the eyeballs to the skull, like a tooth.

'That better?'

'Yes. And that's enough about me, my dear. Talk to me about yourself. Is there anything new? Why don't you sit down?'

If he sat down, facing her, on the chair she was pointing to, he would also face the cut-off hands. He said quickly,

'If you're not too tired, I wanted to talk to you about the great man's visit next month.'

Her face came alive with pleasure. 'Ah, yes.'

'I've been told privately that he hates being bored on an official tour, and that the ambassador or Governor who bores him too wretchedly gets a lasting black mark.' He smiled. 'That's no doubt an exaggeration, but still . . . I wondered whether we could manage to alleviate in some way the dullness of official dinners and so on.'

'Why not?' Mrs. Ormston said calmly. 'He'll be here for three days, won't he? It's the easiest thing in the world to fit in one or two informal luncheons. There are three or four very pretty women we can ask—who would be out of place, or badly placed, out of his sight, at the official things. Let me think it out.'

'Good.' He bent down to kiss her: she moved slightly and his kiss landed on the tip of her ear. 'What on earth should I do without you? Sophie, poor girl, is hopeless at these things.'

Mrs. Ormston spoke with emphatic kindness. 'Sophie is the best woman in the world, and it's not of the least importance that she has no social graces. They don't matter, you know.'

'Only because you supply them,' he said coolly, 'and have done ever since I married.'

'Sophie,' his mother said, 'is a *good* woman.'

'Yes, yes.' He added quietly, 'Fortunately I don't have to depend on her goodness too much—or not officially.'

Mrs. Ormston laughed a little behind her hand. 'Do sit down,' she said again. When he obeyed, placing a chair sideways so that he need not have his eyes on the hands, she leaned forward and stroked his face lightly with a living one. 'Tell me, what's the latest news?'

He kept nothing from her; it pleased her to be trusted, and did no harm: she was as secret as the grave. Shall I speak about the Durhams? he thought, and said, 'I wonder whether I'm being selfish to let you stay here? If—when —we put our plans into operation, things will be more unpleasant. At least for a time.'

'My dear boy, I'm not nervous. I shouldn't dream of leaving.'

'You're very brave, but——'

She interrupted him to say, with immense assurance and energy, 'You can't be too ruthless. These people are savages

... I haven't seen you since Rose and I went out to do a little shopping yesterday. It was very disagreeable.'

He frowned. 'I wish you wouldn't shop. Send for anything you want.'

'No, no, I can't live like that.' She made an impatient movement. 'We came out of the shop where I'd been trying on shoes, and there was a child, squatting at the edge of the road. She jumped up as we came out, lifting her face'— she lifted her own, its lines deeper in the filtered light— 'and deliberately spat at me. That wasn't very much, but it was her *eyes* ... I have never seen such hate. And in a child! My dear Richard, that child was evil. She should have been thrashed, or shut up somewhere. A creature like that, so vicious, would be better dead than allowed to grow up. Those black evil eyes! I'll never forget them.'

His anxiety made him rough. 'Do as I ask—and keep out of the streets. I can't stand your running into danger— even the danger of being spat at by a child.'

'I shouldn't have told you ... Richard, you look tired.'

'I shall be all right after dinner. A bottle of claret ...'

He saw her frown. She disapproved, sharply, of his liking for good wine and food. He knew why she did, but he had always to stifle a moment's irritation when she showed it. This time she did not comment. 'I want to talk to you about something else,' she said, and stopped.

'Yes?'

She was either reluctant or, for once, doubtful. 'It's horribly disturbing, my dearest. I wonder if I ought to tell you.'

He smiled. 'You must,' he said, 'now.'

She looked at him with a curious blank steadiness, like the stare of an intelligent animal in the moment before it springs. 'You know how dearly I love Andrew. He comes only second to you in my—my heart.'

He said sharply, 'Andrew?'

'My darling, I'm sorry . . . forgive me . . . He had that girl—Sarah Leng—in his bedroom this afternoon. She was there an hour or more. I happened to see them when they came upstairs—my door wasn't quite closed.' Her look of distress changed to one of intense loathing, as though she had a filthy rag pushed into her hands. 'It may be perfectly all right. But nowadays, I know, young people—even supposedly well-bred young people—think that there's no need to wait until they're married. I find it quite horribly distasteful.'

'Marriage?' Ormston said harshly. 'He's not thinking of marrying Sarah Leng.'

'I'm afraid he does think of it, my dear.'

Unable to sit still, he got up and walked about. He was coldly angry. 'In the first place, he's much too young to think of marriage. A young man who has hardly begun his career, and has ambitions . . . He has years of hard badly-paid work in front of him. I don't expect him to live like a monk, but—marriage——'

'He might be better married than living a sinful life,' his mother said, in the same tone of overwhelming distaste.

For what seemed the first time it had happened, a flash of his rage turned against her. What does she know about it? he thought. He controlled himself at once. 'And this girl —of all the young women he might have chosen. It's not fit. She's not fit.'

'Really? What do you know about her?'

'Enough to dislike intensely the idea of my son marrying her.' A bewildered grief had begun to weaken his anger. 'I don't understand him—he knows perfectly well what I think about her stepfather and his foul rag—for which she works. And yet he brings her into this house behind my back.'

'Yes, they crept along the corridor like a couple of thieves,' his mother said softly. 'Her fault, of course. She must have suggested it.'

Ormston's face twitched. 'Andrew is old enough to know what he's doing.'

'Oh, my dear,' she exclaimed, 'I wish I hadn't told you. And we're making too much of it, I feel sure. He's a *good* child.'

'I must talk to him,' Ormston said. With an effort he added warmly, 'Thank you for telling me.'

'Promise me you won't worry,' she said tenderly.

He smiled. 'I promise.'

When he had gone, Mrs Ormston leaned back on the sofa, closing her eyes. After a minute or two, the door opened cautiously: Rose Bain came in, moving her gaunt body with infinite care not to make a sound. It betrayed her, as it usually did, knocking itself against a chair. Mrs. Ormston raised her eyelids a little, and sighed.

'You're in pain,' Rose said.

'It's nothing. My head aches.'

'Oh, what can I do? Yes, eau de cologne. On your poor forehead. I know you won't take aspirin. I'll get the eau de cologne from your bedroom.'

She was hurrying off. Mrs. Ormston sat up, and said with languid amusement, 'Rose, you remind me of no one except the White Rabbit in *Alice*. I don't want the eau de cologne. But I shan't dine this evening, I'll have a tray here. You might go along to Lady Ormston's room—' she laughed, with a trace of malice, a frank malice—'I don't know why, but it always makes me smile to think of Sophie as Lady Ormston.'

'It should be the other way round,' Rose said energetically. 'She should be Mrs. Ormston and you should have the title.'

'Tell her I shan't be dining—no, wait. You can run and tell her just before eight o'clock. I don't want her in here condoling with me in that disconcerting way of hers, poor annoying creature. Such a pity.'

She lay back again. Her eyes closed. For a minute Rose stood, looking down at her with an expression of the purest devotion on her long equine face, then tip-toed away.

CHAPTER SEVEN

ABOVE all, thought Ormston, no sign of annoyance, and no criticism of the young woman. That would be stupid . . . He felt calm now, and lifted the telephone. 'Find my son—he's probably in his room—and ask him to come to the library, will you?'

A cupboard in the angle between two bookcases held decanters of sherry and whisky: he filled two glasses with sherry and carried them to the end of the table nearest the window. When Andrew came in he looked at him with something like astonishment, realising, for the first time, that his son was partly a stranger, not any longer the charming malleable intelligent boy, but a young male, to be handled carefully. He even thought he detected, in the young man's long thin face, a resemblance to his own detested father: the two were not alike—his father's good looks had been heavier, a little gross—but there was something, a hint of recklessness in the lines of the mouth, that recalled the older man. They were both born to please, he thought briefly: it's the only thing the boy has inherited from him . . . With a smile, he pushed one of the glasses towards Andrew.

'Sherry?'

'Thanks, dad,' Andrew said. Seating himself in an armchair, he waited without a great deal of interest to know why he had been sent for. 'Anything happening?'

'Nothing fresh . . . Are you dining at home this evening?'

'No. D'you mind?'

'Not in the least. You're not going to a restaurant in the town, of course.' He was careful not to give this the form of a question.

With a scarcely perceptible hesitation, Andrew said, 'I'm going to the Astoria.'

'With Robin?'

'No . . . I'm taking Sarah Leng there.'

Ormston said gently, 'I'm not very anxious for you to show yourself in public with a reporter for the *Compatriot*.'

A look of discomfort, even a touch of remorse, came into his son's face. 'I know, dad, but—well, I shan't be here much longer.'

'Long enough to do damage.'

'It can't damage you, sir.'

'For you to be seen on friendly, very friendly terms with someone from the staff of a newspaper which spends its time undermining authority in the colony . . . encouraging disorder, even treachery——' He stopped, and went on in the same unemotional voice, 'I won't say anything about its abuse of me.'

'Don't think I don't worry about that,' Andrew said. He looked suddenly defenceless and haggard. 'I do, but——' He moved his thin hands in a confused way.

'But this girl is important,' Ormston said gently, 'more important——' He hesitated. How—without a clumsy appeal to it—to make the boy feel that he was betraying their affection? . . . With the same light gentleness, he said, 'More important than anything to do with me.'

'The two things don't conflict.'

Ormston smiled slightly. 'They do, my dear.'

'I don't see that they need.'

'Yes, you see it. But'—against his will, his voice hardened—'you're trying not to see it. Andrew, if I ask you . . . the situation here now—my responsibility, my job, could hardly be more difficult——'

'I know that,' Andrew interrupted.

'Of course you know it.' He allowed himself a hint of irony. 'Any young serviceman who arrived yesterday knows

it. Very well—if I ask you to drop Miss Leng—completely?'
He saw Andrew's body stiffen, but he answered in a calm
voice,

'Don't ask me.'

Harshly, Ormston said, 'I must.'

'There's nothing I wouldn't do to please you,' Andrew
began, 'but this really is—' his control broke abruptly—'I
beg you not to ask me. You never have asked me to do
anything for you that I didn't want to do. This is the first
time and I——'

Ormston waited. 'Well, Andrew?'

'If you knew her better . . . After all, Cumberland is only
her stepfather, she's not even remotely like him . . .'

Ormston was silent. He was surprised by the intensity of
the bitterness he felt against the young woman. *My* son,
he thought. How dare she lay her hands on him . . . He
got up, and refilled their glasses, then went to the window
and stared without seeing them at the tormented hills.
'You had her here this afternoon, didn't you? In your room.'

'How did you know?' Andrew said after a moment.

He sounded very cold and very young. Turning to look
at him, his father said,

'Your grandmother saw you come in.'

'None? None saw us?' His tone made the use of his
childish name for her—she had taught him to use it—
sound like mockery. 'Was she on the look out?'

'You passed her door,' Ormston said drily, 'it was open.'

Half taken aback, half irritably, his son said, 'Whosever
business it is, it's not dear old None's.'

Ormston felt, almost to despair, the distance that separated him from this stranger whose first words had been
spoken to him. 'Anyone who loves you,' he said in a low
voice, 'would want to stop you from making a bad mistake.'

Andrew looked at him with his charming smile. 'I'm not
making a mistake, dad. I know what I'm doing.'

This smile, so familiar, so much part of the simpler past, gave his father back his confidence, his adroitness in handling people far more difficult to cajole or impress than a clever but inexperienced young man. He said quietly,

'Oh, I didn't for a moment suppose that Miss Leng hadn't told you everything about her life before you knew her. And yet—no, no, I must confess, Andrew, I wouldn't like you to marry her. Anything short of marriage——'

He had spoken exactly as he meant to, in a friendly, almost teasing voice. The hostility in Andrew's glance chilled him, but he waited.

'I shall marry her as soon as I can.'

'Even . . .' his hesitation was genuine. 'No, no, she's not the right wife for you, Andrew. A young woman who was Julian Hind's mistress for as long as three years . . . no, no, no.'

His son looked at him without a change of expression, without any expression at all. Ormston had a moment of acute anxiety . . . Is he going to pretend that he knew all about it? Have I lost him?

'What are you talking about? Who is Julian Hind?'

Ormston's relief was almost physical. A pressure at the back of his skull seemed to have been lifted. He's still mine, he thought joyfully. He still, thank God, trusts me . . . He was doubly careful to keep any hint of triumph or satisfaction out of his voice.

'She didn't tell you? But you said——' He stopped—as though he had realised that he was showing his astonishment much too frankly. Above all, he reminded himself, don't provoke him to defend her. He said in a warm moved voice, 'I don't, I can't blame her, Andrew, for holding her tongue. She couldn't know how you would take it—and she's young and she naturally wants to be admired. You can forgive her.'

'Who is Julian Hind?'

'Robin's older brother—several years older than Robin.'
He caught sight of his son's hand, the only thing that gave
him away. The boy is suffering, he thought with anger.
'If I hadn't thought you knew,' he said. 'But you certainly
ought to know.'

'Yes. Yes, of course.'

There was a silence. He watched this man who was his
son closing his mind over the wound dealt—to what? His
pride? Vanity? Love? What is love at that age? he
thought. An agony that doesn't last long . . . A muscle in
Andrew's cheek twitched like a pulse: he was otherwise
unmoved, but he looked older; his youth had had its first
shock. His father felt a mingled pride and grief. He's taken
it extraordinarily well, he thought. No fuss at all. He's a
good boy . . . He felt at this moment that the way he had
brought Andrew up had been tested and proved. He had
been absolutely justified. Not only that the boy could take
a hard knock without showing that he was hurt—something
a merely vain person can do—but he could look at an
unpleasant truth without any impulse to dodge or soften it.
He was not only hard-grained, he was cool, lucid, unsenti-
mental.

Involuntarily, he made a gesture of tenderness, laying his
hand on Andrew's arm. He felt the arm become rigid, but
it was not drawn away. With an apologetic half-smile, he
dropped his hand. Andrew said calmly,

'Yes, I ought to have known. Thanks.'

'Perhaps these things don't matter much in themselves
. . .' He left unspoken the implication that what mattered
was the young woman's lack of frankness.

'I don't know,' Andrew said in an indifferent voice.

His father smiled slightly. 'A question of taste,' he said,
'or feeling.'

Andrew stood up. He got up easily, as a reed straightens
itself. 'May I use your telephone?'

'Yes, of course,' Ormston said.

He walked over to the window again, as if to keep out of the way, but, by turning his head a fraction, he could watch Andrew give his number, then stand holding the receiver without fidgeting. He got through quickly. 'This is Andrew Ormston speaking. Is Miss Leng in the office? . . . No, I don't want to speak to her, I want to give her a message, if you will. Tell her: I'm very sorry I can't see her this evening, I'll ring her up tomorrow . . . Yes . . . Yes, thank you.'

He put the receiver back very slowly and carefully, as though it were alive.

'I'm sorry, Andrew,' his father said impulsively—a real impulse.

Andrew smiled at him—the smile that gave his lean face its momentary sweetness and beauty. 'Don't bother. I'll have to think about it a little. That's all.'

'You'll have dinner here?'

'Yes.'

He turned, and went out of the room.

CHAPTER EIGHT

ORMSTON felt tired but satisfied. The game had been played and—perhaps—won; in either event there was nothing more he could do now: and on the whole he believed he had won. To Sarah Leng as an amusement for Andrew he had no objection—or only a moderate one. Abruptly, he thought: I'd better warn Sophie . . . He felt a weary reluctance to talk to her about anything at all, even to see her, but at last, shrugging his shoulders, he got up and went upstairs to her room.

It was at one end of the long immensely wide corridor of the private wing, the opposite end from his own bedroom and his mother's three rooms: a large very bare room which his predecessor had used as a schoolroom for his younger children. Sophie had chosen it for herself; he had left its decoration and furnishing entirely to her, to make exactly what she pleased of it, and what she had made vexed him afresh every time he set foot in the place—not often. The walls had been painted white, a white without any nuance of colour, and the chairs, the sofa, the bed, the rest of its sparse anonymous furniture, were placed about the room carelessly, with no attempt to give it a personal or any other style. Her indifference not merely to comfort but to the way a room looked irritated him unreasonably. Why, since he did not care anything for his wife, should he care what she chose to live with or sleep in? But it was all part of her negligence, her unpardonable social clumsiness and inadequacy. The strange thing was that she had had a luxurious upbringing: her father had been a merchant banker and she his only child, on whom everything, every comfort, every costly and beautiful object, had been heaped. Why then, in the name of sanity, did she want to live in a cell? If she had chosen, deliberately, to make of herself and her surroundings something in as harsh contrast as possible with his mother's exquisite taste, she could not have done it better. Perhaps, he reflected, she was always irresponsible, and what at the time had seemed the rawness and silences of a narrowly brought-up girl was really moral and mental vacuity. There was nothing malicious in her, there was merely nothing.

She turned her head as he came in. She was writing letters, sitting sideways at the table of bare ink-stained wood, a schoolroom table, which had been left behind in the room and she had kept.

At forty-five, Sophie Ormston had the look of a child who has passed through youth and womanhood without ever, as it were, opening: her face, with its few lines, on the flat eyelids, at the sides of the mouth, between strongly arched eyebrows, was young and not young, old and not old, its fine bones stretching the skin between wide temples and narrow jaw. Something in it—impossible to her husband to say what—had remained childlike while its surface aged slowly. Her dark eyes had little movement in them. She might have been the weathered Madonna, dark-grained and ageless, in some obscure dusty church in a Basque village. There were incongruous echoes of her son in her—both faces were of the same lean hard sort—but she had little of his ugly good looks: as a girl, when her eyebrows were a fine black line, her straight hair dark and thick, and her face as smooth as an egg (it had the same shape), she had been what older women looking over the marriage market called *very presentable*. Not that she knew how to present herself.

No more now than then did she make any attempt at elegance. The clothes she preferred were all country clothes, as if she expected at any moment to have to tramp across moors: her feet, long and very narrow, were made clumsy

by the strong shoes she put on them. She never used make-
up. Her hands—she had remarkably small hands—were
ringless except for her wedding ring. A plait of grey hair,
looking like an archaic diadem, circled her small head
without giving it dignity. Poor Sophie, what could do that?

She had a small monkey she had bought in her first week
in the country. Her husband had never taken the trouble
to ask her what kind of monkey it was: a reddish-brown
running to bronze, it was very small, not so long as many a
new-born infant, slender, with a long tail, and in the black
mask of its face dark brilliant eyes: its head was tiny, no
larger than a baby's fist. Indifferent to animals, Ormston
hated the human habit of bringing them into the house:
there is something unclean, he felt, about sharing your room
with an animal, any animal. Though he had never spoken
unkindly to Sophie's monkey—nor spoken to it in any other
way—it was either afraid of or disliked him, and whenever
he came into her room, it hid. It ran away now, making a
wild leap from the chair it was squatting on, and vanished
behind a small sofa.

Glancing round him with the familiar annoyance, Ormston thought drily: My God, if I had to leave any side of my
life to her. He asked,

'May I sit down for a minute?'

His wife raised her eyebrows slightly. 'Why, Richard, is
something wrong?'

'No.' He took the one half-comfortable chair in the room.
'Why?'

'You don't come here often.'

There was a sly hint of a smile in her glance. This flicker
of humour was the most adult thing about her. When it
came it was nearly imperceptible, like a tadpole flashing
across the bed of a tadpole-coloured stream: an instant afterwards, her husband could tell himself that it did not exist.

'I wanted to talk to you before dinner.'

'Not, I imagine, about the Secretary's visit?'

Surprised, he said, 'No, no—my mother is seeing to all that.'

'Yes, of course,' Sophie said.

During all the twenty-three years of their marriage, she had given no sign that she resented her subordinate position in the household. Why, at this moment, did the thought jump into his mind that possibly she did? Heaven knows, he thought drily, my poor mother did what she could to train her . . . Her efforts had broken against the wall of Sophie's mute obstinacy: the shy carefully-bred girl, who before her marriage had seemed malleable, a sane and serene young creature, became in less than three years a woman disconcerting in her silences, unable to grasp any of the lessons, in social strategy, that his mother insinuated, gently at first, then with natural exasperation: in the end, without protest from the young wife, she kept everything in her hands, making the arrangements, giving orders, spending, wisely, with a politic eye to his career, the money Sophie had brought into the family . . .

'You might ask her about the visit,' he said. 'She would be glad of your help.'

Sophie did not speak. Irritated, he said sharply,

'I came to talk about Andrew.' He hesitated. How far would she understand?

She said in an absently polite voice, 'What has Andrew done?'

'Did you know—no, of course you didn't—that he has involved himself with Cumberland's step-daughter, the Leng girl? He had her here only this afternoon, in his room.'

For the first time, his wife looked at him with attention. 'How do you know that?'

'None saw them come in.'

A silence. Then Sophie said calmly, 'And she told you.

How wise of her. Your mother *is* wise.' A tone of half-amused curiosity came into her voice. 'I suppose she was very upset. It's just the sort of thing that would upset her.'

She might be talking about people who are complete strangers to her, Ormston thought. He controlled his impatience.

'The girl isn't good enough for Andrew. Quite apart from all the other things—her stepfather—the fact that she's useless to him, no family, no money—she's had one affair already. With . . . oh, never mind who the man was.'

Sophie's glance became erratic again, shallow and deceptively clear. 'Does Andrew know?'

'He didn't know. I told him.'

'When, Richard?'

'A few minutes ago.'

'Poor Andrew,' she murmured. 'How did he take it?'

'He took it extremely well,' Ormston said. He added abruptly, 'What d'you expect? He's after all my son.'

'Oh, yes, quite,' his wife said. The faint gleam of amusement in her eyes came and went. 'Mine, too, of course—which just might have put a flaw in him . . . But do tell me—the once or twice I've seen Sarah Leng I liked her—why do you feel that she's so awful?'

He made an effort, smiled, and managed to reply with the gentleness and polite tolerance he rarely failed to use with her: it hid, decently, he thought, the cold purgatory of boredom his marriage had day by day become. 'That depends what you mean by awful. She's a loose young woman. That's surely enough.'

'I feel very sorry for her,' she said, with surprising warmth.

'But why?' It was when he was most exasperated with her that his voice became kind and charming.

She moved her hands. 'It's so easy—when you're very young—to make a mistake that costs you far more than you ought to have had to pay.'

Nothing irritated Ormston more, in her or anyone, than sentimental pity of this sort. He saw it as purely a question of sick nerves, a form, and a vulgar one, of egoism. He had taken the greatest pains, since Andrew was a tiny child, to see that no trace of it could root itself in him, and he had, thank God, succeeded. Whatever other faults Andrew had inherited, from either side of the family, sentimentality, a habit of cheap easy compassion, was not one of them.

'The girl has no morals, and—what's much the same thing—no manners either,' he said drily.

Her head on one side, Sophie looked away from him. 'Yes, I see. She's flawed, too. Not the kind of young woman you'd hand your dearest possession to. That wouldn't do, would it?'

She really is a goose, he reflected wearily. 'Well, don't talk about her in his hearing. That's all I came to warn you about.'

He stood up, catching sight as he moved of the monkey peering round the edge of the sofa, its eyes for a moment so like his wife's in their stillness and flatness, yet so filled with a simulacrum of irony, that he was startled.

'Oh, are you going?' she said. 'You don't stay long. Is there any news? I forgot to turn the wireless on this evening.'

'Nothing you need worry about,' he told her gently. 'The less you read the newspapers and listen to the wireless the better. I'd tell you if anything more serious happened.'

'Would you really?'

'Of course.'

She got up, with a clumsy gesture which knocked off the edge of the crazily littered table an untidy pile of books. Ormston stooped and began to pick them up. One book sprawled face downwards and open. When he lifted it, a photograph fell out. He looked at it with astonished disbelief. It was a photograph of his father in the uniform of a second-lieutenant, taken probably in 1914 when he enlisted.

'What the devil are you doing with this?' he asked sharply.

His wife smiled, a quick evasive smile. 'You threw it away. Years and years ago.'

'I daresay I did. But what's it doing here? Why have you kept it?'

'I don't know,' she murmured. 'Yes. Yes, I do. I felt sorry for it, being thrown away.'

He was too angry to master himself. 'What idiocy!'

He bent the photograph between his hands. The yellowing paper of the portrait itself tore easily, but the cardboard mount was too tough to be torn across more than twice. He gave up trying, threw the pieces into the wastepaper basket beside the table, and went out without another word.

His intense exasperation with her lasted until he reached his bedroom at the other end of the corridor. Then he repented. It was only at these moments—very few—when the surface of kindness and politeness cracked across, that something like a point of guilt moved in him at a great depth—guilt for what? For his indifference to her, his shocking boredom? For having married her at all? It vanished as soon as he was able to say to himself: It was her childishness that made her keep it, not any sort of malice. I must say something to her at dinner that will comfort her . . . His dinner jacket and the rest had been laid out on the side of the bed. He rang the bell for his servant. At the same instant, the telephone on his table rang.

He listened for a minute to Colonel Frent's precise colourless voice, said only, 'Yes,' and put the receiver down.

His servant came in.

'Give me a thin overcoat,' he said. 'Thanks. Let them know I'm not dining here, will you?'

CHAPTER NINE

ALONE, Sophie scrabbled in the wastepaper basket for the pieces of the photograph. Clearing a space on the table with a movement of her arm which sent more books and papers on to the floor, she put them together, to have one more look at the face before throwing it away for good. The monkey had come from behind the sofa: he sprang on to the table and began, as he did often, to join in what she was doing: he looked with an intent stare at the photograph, turning his head when she turned hers, and touching the fragments delicately.

'Don't move it,' Sophie said.

She was not sure whether she had begun to talk to herself before she had the monkey. Very likely I did, she thought ... The solitude in which she lived, in this room which was as like a cell as makes no matter—not that she had wanted to live in a cell: it had come to seem the easiest thing—had to be peopled somehow, since she was not, never had been, a contemplative. Talking to the monkey was pleasanter than talking to herself, and—if she were overheard—it was not a crazy thing to be caught doing. In a queer way, too, the monkey was her double, her youth and unused mischief and gaiety. When she looked in the glass to plait her hair, and he came to sit on the dressing-chest and look with her, she mocked herself by tracing the likeness between their two faces: the same fixed eyes with, she thought, as little in the way of logic behind them, the same air of sadness and wisdom, ridiculous in both. What have you and I to be sad about, she thought, and what do we know? Nothing ... Like the monkey, too, her very small hands were lighter in colour on the palms.

The face in the photograph had not been torn; it looked

up at her with a cold smile in the dark eyes, a face older and more formed than most of the photographs of that time, but recognisably of the same family as all those smooth young faces with something of the child still in the shape of the mouth and the unlined eyes, those bodies restless with life, in their second-lieutenant's uniform, so soon to be nothing, so soon gone. At twenty-nine George Ormston was handsome in a hard robust way, with a hint of coarseness in the jowl and neck, probably not there ten years or so earlier when a headstrong girl of eighteen ran off with one of her father's stable-boys, a year older than she was. The two of them managed to hide themselves for a month —by which time it was too late for her parents to put anything right. They were wretched about it, and angry, but not unforgiving. It was their daughter herself, it was Caroline who, in pride, in vanity, in rage because she was unhappy, cut herself off from them completely, and from her own class. Deliberately, she stepped down in the world and stayed down, with her husband she had taken from the stable-yard. All she allowed her father to do was to pay for her son's education at the best and most fashionable of preparatory schools and then at Winchester.

George Ormston was killed at Ypres, a day after he was thirty.

As she had done many times before, Sophie searched his face for any likeness to his son. There was none she could detect. Richard Ormston was the spit of his mother, his beauty a clearer and masculine version of hers. He was like her, too, in character. They are both, she thought idly, very elegant, both of them are always right, they both, in their different ways, like to be very comfortable, and they're both ambitious.

'Both of them,' she said aloud, 'are what my nurse used to call: All for number one . . . But don't take it into your head, monkey, that I'm incapable of appreciating Richard—

he's a fine man, very fine, he knows four languages and a
great deal about several countries, he can make people do
what he wants, he works hard. It was foolish of me to
marry him, I ought to have known better, even at that age
I ought to have known better . . .'

Smiling without knowing it, she thought: My God, how
ignorant I was—sillier and more ignorant than any girl
would be now. Sarah Leng would be wiser—ah, poor
Sarah, she hasn't a chance against him. I should like to tell
her not to be sorry for herself, that she won't die of grief,
no woman ever does . . .

'Some people, my dear monkey, will tell you that Richard
is cold and arrogant, not approachable, but let *me* tell you
something—he can't help himself, he keeps his distance and
makes other people keep theirs because he doesn't want to
be looked at closely. Or to look at himself. Now why?
I declare humbly that I don't know. If I did I'd tell you.'

She bent to look nearer at the smiling face on the table.
The monkey jumped on to her shoulder, and scratched the
nape of her neck, very gently, a caress. What a shame he's
been torn up, she thought lightly. So good-looking—a
little vulgar, perhaps, but so much energy. I'm sorry.

'What do you think? Could a man possibly breed a son
in whom there was nothing of himself, nothing at all, not
a single habit? And Caroline—even if she hated her husband how could she form her unborn child in her own image
entirely? But she can't have begun to hate him as soon as
that, you know . . . D'you want a fig? Is that what you're
scratching for? Here. Here you are.'

The box of dried figs was open on the table, under a book.
She prised a fig loose and held it out: the monkey took it,
jumped off her shoulder on to a chair, and began to eat,
delicately, with concentrated attention.

'I wish I knew more about this girl,' she said. 'You
haven't seen her, monkey—she's charming and I'd think

sensible and brave, but . . . Oh, get on with you, Sophie, you think a lot of nonsense . . . Heavens, it's a quarter to eight. I must change.'

She pulled off her jacket, skirt, blouse, and ran across the room to the wardrobe. There was a knock at the door. Frowning, she said,

'Come in whoever you are.'

Rose Bain came in gaily. 'Oh, you're dressing,' she exclaimed. 'I'm sorry, I thought you would be ready.'

'I ought to be,' Sophie answered.

Rose spoke in a peremptory tone to the monkey, wanting to know if it were enjoying its fig. The animal ignored her. 'Why is it so uppish?' she asked, with a noisy laugh.

'He's not much of a talker,' Sophie said. 'But you didn't come to talk to him, did you?'

'No. I came to say that Caroline, poor darling, has one of her terrible headaches, and she won't be dining.'

Thank God for a small mercy, Sophie thought with calm pleasure. For a great many years now she had been familiar with Mrs. Ormston's handling of her on public occasions. She had two gambits: the one in which she left her significantly out of the conversation: another, less often used, when she made brave and obvious efforts to include her in it. Either was easy—almost, she felt, disgracefully easy—to endure. But she disliked being alone with her superb mother-in-law. At these times Caroline did not open her mouth. It was a principle with her not to talk when she was bored, or in the company of her intellectual inferiors. Very trying for the inferiors.

'Oh, then I needn't take much trouble,' she said.

She took a dress from its hanger and began to pull it on over her head. When it was half-way over she heard Rose say loudly,

'That brute!'

'What? What did you say?' Freeing her head and arms,

she saw that Rose was looking down at the pieced-together photograph on the table. She came over to look at it again herself over the other woman's shoulder. For an instant she imagined an ironical complicity in the eyes looking into hers. She said coolly, 'A brute perhaps, but was he the cold brute Caroline and Richard say he was? He looks to me warm. Violent, but warm and reckless.'

'He was a devil.' Rose's powerful voice was the only thing about her that could remind anyone of her birth in a once ruling class. With age it had become over-emphatic, and she had added wild gestures to it, to mark her points, like a boisterous schoolboy. 'Yes, a devil. And he knew exactly what he was doing.'

'Then why, why did she marry him?'

'Poor darling, she was a child—eighteen. She didn't know what she was doing. Running away with him was the only wrong thing she ever did in her life, and how she paid for it in misery!' Her voice took on the depths and resonance of a tragic actress. 'And bore it nobly, yes, nobly.'

'Need she?' Sophie murmured.

'What on earth do you mean? Brought up as strictly as she was—two governesses and a maid of her own—how did she know what a brute, an ill-bred brute, he was? He was teaching her to jump.'

Sophie burst out laughing, her clear bubbling laugh. 'To jump? Oh, Rose!'

'I mean on horseback, of course ... You don't know what she went through with him. No one knew. *I* did, but what could I do? And she kept everything from her child, everything. It was only after the brute had been killed that it had to come out—the women he'd been keeping and the rest of it. Drink. Cruelty. Oh, noble, I tell you, noble.'

'It might,' Sophie said, 'have been better for everyone— her son especially—if she had been a little less noble.'

'I can't *imagine* what you mean, Sophie.'

'But I'm not sure myself! Except that very virtuous people are not—not always loving.'

'You know nothing about it,' Rose cried. 'Nothing. I'm the only person who knows that she could have left the brute for another man—of her own sort. He was a cousin. She was in love with him, too. And she refused. Think of it, she refused.'

'Why?'

'You may well ask! I begged her to take him. Begged her. But, no, she wouldn't, she said, she had sinned mortally once and she wouldn't add another and worse sin to it. Oh'—she gave a brief angry snort of laughter—'I'm on my knees to her. Day and night. On my *knees*.'

Your poor bony knees, Sophie thought. You are the best woman in the world, the warmest most wildly generous heart—and mad, an innocent mad old maid. It is because you are so loyal and so silly that Caroline is able to exploit you, shamelessly.

'Of course one wouldn't want her to sin,' she said gently. 'But to be so noble as that must have been a great strain.' She moved, almost, in her haste, sprang away. 'Very gratifying, too, I daresay.'

'And so kind as she is!' Rose exclaimed. 'Do you know how many charities she works for? Eight!'

'You do the work,' Sophie said.

'Nonsense, nonsense. I do what she tells me.'

Sophie laughed again. 'We all do.' Coming back to the table, she swept the torn photograph into the wastepaper basket. Now I shan't remember you again, she thought lightly. A pity—but not everyone is remembered. 'We'll go and dine,' she said to Rose. 'Come along.'

CHAPTER TEN

IN Sophie's eyes this room, never used except for family luncheons and dinners, was a looking-glass image of her life. It was very narrow, with traces of elegance in the gold and olive green panelling; it had only one window, at the narrow end; and, built on an outer wall of the house, it faced an immense waste lot of dry dusty earth patched with reeds. Here and there in this waste a dilapidated shed housed a family—tethered goats, and three or four infants all apparently the same age like a clutch of sparrows, scratching in the dust. Outside the window was an iron balcony: it had once been pleasant with flowering shrubs and sun blind; now, because it could be fired at from the waste lot, it was never used. The view was all the same splendid. At this side, a distant headland detached itself from the line of hills and threw out two long bony flanks like shadowy wings opened in the steep empty sky.

At this hour, darkness coming, the shacks and dusty reeds disappeared; only the hills remained, and the arched shadow of wings. Warmth and that insolently handsome view came into the room through the open window. Once the lights were switched on, it would have to be shut out. Better the half-dark than a room behind iron shutters.

Rose's voice, booming as she would not have dared if Mrs. Ormston had been there, flowed through the courses. Excited by a single glass of wine, she leaped from subject to subject like an elderly goat scrambling among rocks. Few of her remarks were directed to the two people facing her across the table. If one chanced to be, Sophie struggled to find an answer: Andrew sat silent, opening his mouth only to eat.

At these family meals, coffee was served at the table. The

servant placed the heavy silver tray at Sophie's elbow and went away. She did not notice it until her son broke the silence to ask,

'Aren't we to have any coffee, mother?'

Flustered, she said, 'I'm sorry. I'm so sorry. I'm not used to being in charge.'

Rose went off into a cackle of laughter. 'Poor Sophie!' She drank her coffee, gulping it. 'If you don't mind I'll leave you now. I must get Caroline to bed. Don't move, Andrew.'

Still talking, she stumped off on her strong bony legs, opening and shutting the door on herself before the young man had done more than begin to get up. He sat back, and said moodily,

'My God, what a fool she is. How do you stand her?'

'I don't know what your grandmother would do without her,' Sophie said. 'She's a gentle-hearted creature, kinder than anyone I know.'

Andrew did not answer. Getting up, he walked out on to the balcony and stood there, gripping the railing.

'Don't stand there,' Sophie said.

'Don't fuss, mother. It's safe enough.' He added, without turning his head, 'Only another three weeks. Less.'

Sophie left the table, and stood watching him, his long lean body profiled on the greyness; she felt a useless grief. 'Please do come in . . . Are you so bored with us?'

He turned quickly, and came back into the room. 'I didn't mean that. I'm sorry.' His face suddenly contorted. He did something he had not done since he was a very little boy. Taking her arm, he drew her with him to the sofa placed in a recess, made her sit down, and knelt beside her, his head against her knee. 'I don't know what's the matter with me,' he said in a young baffled voice, 'my head's all over the shop. I can't think straight.'

Sophie moved her hand over his hair, timidly. It was too

many years since her child became a stranger, not an unkind
stranger, but one who had nothing to say to her, whom she
daren't question about himself, at whose biting hopes and
ambitions she could only, awkwardly, guess. But would it,
now, have been in any way different if she had been able
to dispute their lively little son's heart and mind with his
jealously loving father? (And, perhaps, been defeated?)
The distance she was afraid to reach across was only an
aggravation, a widening, of the abyss between generations.
Sooner or later, she thought, tomorrow, next week, in a
year, it will open at Richard's feet and he'll discover that
the young are walled up behind their egoism, their
feverish greeds, absorbed in the life thrusting through
them. It's only later, when the thrust has grown weaker,
and the fever cooled, that they know they are not, but not,
different from their parents, not wiser, or bolder or more
vulnerable.

She was afraid, if she said anything, that it would be the
wrong thing, would bore instead of comforting him. How
they torment themselves at his age, she thought, and they
don't know that it's all nonsense . . . A fold of irony narrowed her eyelids.

'It's Sarah, isn't it?' she said.

Andrew straightened himself to glance at her. 'How did
you know that? What do you know?'

'Only that None watched you going to your room with
her this afternoon—and told your father.'

Her son frowned. 'Are you as shocked as None?'

Her expression became very slightly malicious. She shook
her head. 'No. But then I'm a less imposing character than
None.'

Andrew mumbled something she did not catch.

'What did you say?' she asked.

He stood up and moved away a few steps, turning his
shoulder on her. 'You don't understand things, mother.'

After a moment she said, 'And None does?'

Andrew turned to look at her. A little remorseful, he came back to the sofa and seated himself at her side. 'I ought not to worry you with this business,' he said gently. 'Or with anything else.'

Whatever I say won't make a hair of difference, Sophie thought. 'If you want my opinion, it's that None has always thought too much about—what shall I say?—physical things. I can't see that that's more virtuous than doing them. If you know what I mean.'

Her son stared at her with amusement. 'I don't believe I do.'

'Well, never mind.' Lifting her hand, she touched the centre of his chest with one finger, as delicately as an infant exploring the body of an adult. 'It gives you a pain here, doesn't it, to argue with your father?'

'I hate vexing him,' Andrew said, vehemently. 'He's so decent himself, so generous. I . . .' He made a gesture of despair and rage. 'And he may be right, I may be a complete fool—I may have been made a fool of . . .'

'By Sarah?'

'Yes, by Sarah,' he said roughly. After a moment, he repeated it in a lower voice. 'By Sarah.'

He must hear her name spoken, his mother thought. 'Do you love her very much?' she asked.

She spoke with more diffidence than she felt. These fearful tragedies of the very young, she thought slyly, so exaggerated, and sincere and pure—as ours aren't pure. Too many things creep into the tragedies of the old, too many fears—fear of loneliness, vanity, the fear of injuring our dignity, lies, the lies we tell ourselves to keep going. And the rest of it and the rest of it. But—but the young recover and we don't . . . Her thoughts hardened. If, she thought, the boy is not irrevocably in love, why, why should Richard have his one fully satisfying possession spoiled for him by

this young woman—my poor Richard? . . . A smile came
and went on her face. Mine? she thought briefly. Mine?

Andrew did not answer. He put his head in his hands, as
she had seen him do in moments of childish unhappiness.
She stroked it cautiously. 'You could be making a mistake,
my darling. If you are, if this is something you can get over,
it's not worth disappointing your father. He expects so
much of you, you know.'

He shook her hand off and sat up. 'If you think I enjoy
disappointing him! I'm not a brute.'

He brought you up, oh, with the best intentions, she
thought, to be hard, to know clearly what you want and to
push others aside to get it—and to want only sensible wordly
things. This is your first lapse. Could I, if I'd tried, have
made any mark on you? Too late to try now . . . She smiled
at him.

'You were a very little boy, not five, when you said:
Poor mummy, you're not clever, are you? But never mind,
I'll look after you.'

He laughed. 'You kicked my bottom, I hope.'

'No. Oh, no.'

He stood up, touched her forehead with his lips, and said,
'I must go.'

She knew that her anxiety irritated him. But before she
could stop herself she had said,

'You're not going into town, are you?'

'No, don't worry,' he said with impatience. 'I've nothing
to go for.'

He went away. I didn't manage that very well, she
thought wryly. My own fault—I thought about Richard
when I ought to have been thinking only about Andrew and
his unhappiness. Inside families, one is always guilty towards someone, it's impossible to be just . . . Without
thinking, she went out on to the balcony and stood where
Andrew had stood, looking into the darkness. The black

bubble of the sky was empty except for the blacker crumpled line of the hills, and a few, very few, points of light. It was easy to see this hard country under an earlier sky, before either gods or men had broken into it with their lusts, fears, cruelties, and their loves. Anyone must love it, she thought: the short bright springs, the long summers with their dry river-beds and burning suns, the friendly winters, soften all wounds . . . She caught the scent of jasmine. The silence laid a heavy hand on the darkness. During her first months here, when *the trouble* was only an affair of slogans scrawled on the white walls of houses, the night would have been alive with warm sounds, voices, a burst of laughter, boys singing, bicycle bells, a flute. Wiped out by the curfew. There was nothing now in the darkness except fear—an old fear. The young English soldiers brought here were not the first to stumble in the folds of dry savage hills over the broken walls of forts—only the latest, the kindest and most innocent.

She turned to go in. The light scent of jasmine came again for a moment, with the smell of dust and dry reeds and goats.

CHAPTER ELEVEN

THE streets, when the Governor drove through the inner town on his way to police headquarters, were almost empty. Curfew was less than five minutes away and . . . better be safe than sorry: here and there in the shadow of a doorway a man effaced himself before the sweeping ray of the head-lights. More sharply than the pairs of sentries behind their rolls of barbed wire these solitary crouching figures evoked the tension, the unsleeping anger and hate paralysing the colony, a sluggish poison in the veins.

Deliberately, leaning back in the car, he let his mind drift. Useless to waste energy on guesses. Frent had said only: Something that may be important has just happened. If you were able to come . . .

Something important enough for the police chief to ask him to come instead of bringing the news to Government House himself . . . He could not crush out entirely the prick of excitement, the sense of a coiled spring of energy in his body. Nothing had happened that he could not deal with, nothing.

When he came into Frent's room, the sight of James Puckeridge levering his heavy body out of a chair infuriated him. He detested the fellow. If Puckeridge had been less intelligent, less (as a figure in the colony) respected, he would have disliked him less. But he was more than a sound man of business, he was a man to whom his associates listened; he had political ambitions, and friends in London well placed to help him to them when he chose to come home. The power latent in him was the same kind of power Ormston enjoyed using and intended to keep. In a muffled way he felt that Puckeridge was, not a rival but a distorted copy, a caricature—the thing he might have been himself

if he had had no social prestige, no training in the human-
ities. He detested, too, the successful bully. Nothing, no
instinct of prudence, tempered Puckeridge's fits of bad
temper. With the Governor he kept every polite form, but
a subtle inflection of mockery came into his voice and
glance, as though he were doing it to amuse himself, not out
of respect. Strange that he had friends. But perhaps a
greed for power—if it is only overbearing enough—puts
people on their knees quicker than kindness.

Dropping his hat on the desk, the Governor settled himself in the chair Frent pulled out for him. He drew his
gloves off, slowly, yawning, and made an effort to be amiable.

'How d'you do, Puckeridge?'

'I'm glad of the chance to speak to your Excellency,'
Puckeridge said. 'I've been telling Colonel Frent that either
he authorises our people to carry guns, *and use them*, or
they'll do it without his orders. This last bestial outrage
. . . poor Durham . . .'

Surprised by a momentary feeling of agreement with him,
the Governor said in a friendly voice,

'I didn't expect civil disobedience from you, of all people.'

'Call it what you like, sir, you can't expect us to rely on
being protected by boys in uniform—who can't be everywhere—when we're a damn sight better able to protect ourselves. If one of the brutes attacks me you won't punish
me for defending myself. But that's not good enough.
What I want is the right to get him first—when I have
reasonable grounds for thinking he's going to attack me.
Or my property or my wife . . . Colonel Frent seems to
think I'm not to be trusted.'

His manner was more offensive than the implied threat,
and the Governor was unable and unwilling to keep out of
his voice the contempt it roused in him.

'Would reason come into it?' he asked.

'I don't think trust does,' Frent said, with his sharp smile.

'I'd trust Mr. Puckeridge to show every sort of courage and energy. But, at the moment, to have the admirable Committee of Public Safety taking pot shots at terrorists, or potential terrorists, won't help.'

The bald place on the top of Puckeridge's head started to pulsate, a sign that sent any of his subordinates scuttling for cover. 'I'd like to know what the devil will,' he began. He controlled himself. 'No doubt you know far more about it than I do—but I hear everywhere, from all sorts of people —and some of them are not English—that worse devilry is coming. I'm not panicky, I tell you, but I don't like it.'

Leaning back, the Governor played with his gloves, tapping one with the other. 'We can deal, in the short run, with anything that can happen—anything possible. In the long run, Mr. Puckeridge, the problem isn't soluble by individual violence.'

He had managed at least—easily—to wipe out any derision in the glance Puckeridge turned on him. 'If you'd tell me what will solve it . . . sir. That swine Cumberland babbles about educating people, easing their lives and so on and so forth. But these animals never had an easy life! Why the devil, because we happen to be here, should we give them what they're not used to? And suppose we did, how does the fool think we could exist and make reasonable profits? Does he want to ruin us—his own people? If they're up, we're down. It's as simple as that. A choice, simply a choice.' A queerly dull look, as though the blood had thickened behind his eyeballs, came over his face. 'I'd like to have Cumberland in my hands for a few hours. I'd twist his guts—and no metaphor intended.'

'I wonder,' the Governor said coldly. 'You might not enjoy it.'

'Just give me the chance.'

Frent had listened with his eyes on a sheet of paper on which he had been scrawling a pattern of criss-cross lines:

he drew a thick rectangle round them, laid the pencil down, and said,

'Mr. Puckeridge, I suggest that you give me a week—to look into your request again. I can't take the decision. But' —his tone became dry and sharp—'I may tell you that there are circumstances—I can conceive circumstances— when I should take your side. I hope they may be staved off.'

He stood up. After a second's hesitation, Puckeridge rose. His thick underlip protruded; the deep folds at the ends lengthened it grotesquely. 'I'll be on to you again in a week's time.' He turned his head slightly and said in a neutral voice, 'Good of your Excellency to listen to me.'

As the door closed on him, Frent said,

'I'm sorry, sir. I tried to get rid of him sooner, but he needed handling . . . I hope you'll forgive me for asking you to come here, but I couldn't leave to come to you— and I couldn't talk to you on the telephone.'

This was the first time the Governor had seen in him even a weak hint of excitement. It was disturbing.

'What have you to tell me?'

'I . . . we've got X.'

The shock the Governor felt came from deep in his own body. 'Are you sure?'

'Yes, quite sure,' Frent said. He gave a short dry laugh, the release of his stifled excitement.

'How did you do it? Where was he?'

Frent folded his hands neatly. 'When *we* found him—in bed with a woman. Less than fifteen miles from here—a village in the hills . . . call it a village . . . five houses.' He paused, coughed, and said drily, 'Ward was shot. Killed. There was no guard on the house—a house of two rooms, with a well outside the door—and my boys picked the fellow out of bed like kidnapping a baby, but when they were bringing him away someone fired at them from behind the well—one of these high stone jobs—and got Ward. I'd sent men to follow the two-ex-commandos, of course—they were keeping three or four hundred yards behind, and they went through the village without finding either a man or a gun. Their officer decided, quite rightly, to bring the prisoner in at once, and Ward along with him.' He shrugged. 'Ward is no loss, even to himself.'

The feeling of suspense and tension in the Governor had become almost suffocating. He made an effort, steadied his voice, and said calmly,

'I congratulate you. A pity about Ward. But the other fellow? Your X?'

Without moving his head, Frent stretched a hand to press a switch on his desk. He was keeping his sharp eyes, bright, with something inquisitive in their brightness, on the Governor's race. This irritated Ormston, as though the other man had been indiscreet enough to touch him. Dropping a glove on the floor at the side of his chair, he bent to pick it up. As he straightened himself, the door was opened by a lieutenant. His face struck the Governor as though he were looking at an image set in relief on a dark background: it was a strictly triangular face, running away from the temples to a minute rounded chin; very narrow half-smiling eyes, the pupil a dark streak; a small delicate mouth below a moustache like an eyebrow: the face of a girl and a pretty rat.

For an hallucinating moment, the Governor thought: But I know you . . . It was nonsense, one of those illusive recognitions welling up in half-sleep from a bottomless pit of the mind.

He had never seen the man before.

Coming into the room, the lieutenant saluted and stood back: he said briskly,

'The prisoner, sir.'

The prisoner, handcuffed, a soldier with a sten-gun on

his heels, stumbled as he came in. He was taller than the short young lieutenant, but not much taller, with a remarkably broad chest. He had a dark face, and bright arrogant eyes under a high forehead. A lock of his thick hair had fallen across it, and he made an ineffectual effort to rid himself of it by tossing his head back.

'Lieutenant Hadham, sir, is the officer who was in charge of the arrest,' Frent said.

The Governor had got to his feet. 'You?' he said. Not certain that his voice had been audible, he repeated it. 'You?'

Startled, the prisoner looked at him for the first time. The barely visible line of his eyebrows rose. He smiled, showing the edge of splendid teeth. 'Dear me,' he said lightly, almost merrily, 'I didn't expect to be given an official welcome. At the highest level, too.'

'Anthony,' Ormston said, and stopped. The effort to go on standing exacted all his energy; a drop of sweat trickled across his temple; to his horror he felt that he was smiling, but his smile was not a response to the other's. An immense feeling of satisfaction possessed him, a swelling wave of triumph, as though the other man's disgrace showed off his own merit, as though it made him safer, in some way exalted him. The pleasure he felt was sensual; it invaded his mind only as relief, excitement. Abruptly, as if he had caught his hand on a nail in the darkness, he felt wretchedly hurt.

A wholly foolish thought crossed his mind: I expected this . . . It was not true. Only in the last two minutes had a disturbance too indefinite to be called a warning started in him: in his nerves.

He turned to Frent. 'You know his name, of course.'

'Oh yes, I know him,' Frent said. 'That's to say, I know a great deal about him.' In the same off-hand way he added, 'He hasn't been questioned yet.'

The conviction that Frent knew about his relations with Anne Boyd seized the Governor. Of course. He was here to know things.

'That's your job,' he said. 'Get on with it. I don't want to talk to him now. Tomorrow—I'll see him tomorrow morning.'

CHAPTER TWELVE

In the early sun, the hills stood about absently, not so much enclosing the room as reducing it to a speck of dark grit embedded in amber.

'Will you want to see him alone?' Frent asked.

'Yes. Where is he?'

'I'll have him brought here.'

He seemed about to say more. Speaking curtly, the Governor said,

'I should be glad if you would.'

Frent went briskly off; the hind view of his shoulders conveyed efficiency, obedience, self-confidence. He left the door ajar. Turning his back on it, the Governor looked at the hills, at one in particular, which was beaked and fluted. Cooler up there, he thought. Really, I wish to God this hadn't happened to me . . . He heard footsteps climbing the stairs to the narrow landing, and turned to face the door.

Two guards edged Boyd into the room. 'Hullo, Ricky,' he said, drawling. 'They didn't tell me it was you. Nice of you to come.'

'Take his handcuffs off,' the Governor said. 'And go away.'

He watched Boyd's face as the soldiers undid the handcuffs. It was more than eighteen months since he had seen him. Why hasn't he changed? he thought absurdly. It was monstrous that, standing in this room, a prisoner, charged with the responsibility for who knew what bestial crimes, he should look exactly as he always looked: amused, slightly aggressive, slightly petulant. His eyes were as bright and quick as ever. His full flat lips, African in outline but nearly colourless, gave his face, when he was not speaking, a

curiously simple and youthful air: or, rather, they were what
remained of a very young man in the slightly tarnished ex-
officer of fifty-two. When he spoke this air of simplicity
vanished, and a hard and even supercilious look took its
place, a mask of stubbornness broken by a single peevish
line running from nose to chin.

He rubbed his wrists vigorously. 'Thanks. They're
abominably uncomfortable, let me tell you.'

'Sit down,' Ormston said.

He felt a sudden confidence. The warmth of the only easy
comfortable relationship he had ever had with another man
in his life hung in the air between them: they might have
been sitting in the room they shared at Winchester, beginning one of the wrangles which ended—almost always—in
Anthony, out-argued and completely unconvinced, throwing up his hands with a smile and an: All right, damn you,
I'm absolutely in the right, but have it your own way . . .
He'll give in, Ormston thought. And then what? Oh,
time enough after he had thrown his hands up to decide
what to do with him. I'll do my level best for him, he
thought. The instinct to protect his friend from his silli-
nesses, the familiar love—and the familiar twinge of contempt—stirred in him, at a depth where nothing, no
jealousy, no ambition, interfered with it.

'Sit down, man,' he said again.

Boyd dropped into the nearest chair. 'I'm tired. Your
bloodhounds kept at it the whole night.' He grinned. The
flash of white teeth was as familiar as the rest, as reassuring.
'D'you know, they surprised me. I was surprised how much
that foxy devil—Frent—knew about our—I should say *my*
organisation. He could be guessing, of course: he's a
soldier, he knows what he would have done in my place.
All the same, y'know, it's astonishing how much—and how
damned little—he knows. And, my God, is he naïve!'

Ormston had noticed the *my*. Still the same old Anthony,

he thought affectionately: the one efficient man in a mob of fools . . . He smiled.

'I know what you're thinking,' Boyd said sharply. 'But he's naïve, I tell you, as only a soldier can be. He seemed to think I'd be so shattered by his cocksure voice and his know-all that I'd be only too delighted to tell him the names of my officers, where I get my money and arms, and any poor little plans I might have had up my sleeve for the day after tomorrow. If I hadn't been so damned sleepy I'd have laughed in his face. His face! Is he a spinster, by the way, or does he only look it?'

'Your plans?' Ormston said. 'What did you flatter yourself you were doing? Running a war?'

Boyd ignored the irony. 'I told him: It's taken me less than a year to turn a crowd of easy-going coffee-swilling youngsters into first-class killers—what you're up against now, my friend, is an army, not a pathetic rabble.' His voice became harsh and boastful. 'It wasn't easy. Your precious staff and their over-fed troops, poor young devils, gave me less trouble, far less, than some of my subordinates, but I've pulled it off; in one year I've licked a score of unorganised gangs into something you can't laugh at—into a force.' He laughed. 'And Frent squinting round his thin nose at me—by God, I almost thought I was back in London being sent up by a bloody politician in uniform for knowing more about soldiering than he did.'

Ormston thought: If only he'd promoted instead of humiliating you, you wouldn't be in this room . . . He caught sight of Boyd's wrists, swollen and chafed, and felt a prick of grief. To get rid of it, he said drily,

'So it's the War Office you're fighting, is it? Aren't you carrying your little personal grievance a bit far?'

Sitting bolt upright, Anthony began speaking in a rough eager voice, words pouring from him, as they used to when he was an excited boy, his mind darting back and forth in a frenzy of impatience to get his arguments out, throwing them down in disorder, so that a cooler opponent had only to trap one in mid-air and demolish it, to bring him down, red and stuttering.

'You can't believe it, can you, beastly materialist that you are . . . you never put a foot wrong in your whole career, always the right word for the right man at exactly the right moment . . . you can't believe that anyone might care—my God, I don't care a s—— for anything or anyone else—about getting human beings their freedom and happiness . . . not just English human beings, or human beings who happen to be useful to you for the moment . . . simply any human beings . . . as Byron cared about the Greeks.'

Ormston raised his eyebrows. 'Byron? My dear boy! Though I suppose he had his share of vanity . . . Would you have taken to terrorism if your efforts during the war had been properly rewarded? I doubt it.'

'What the hell do you know about war?' Boyd said with anger. 'You spent yours bettering yourself.'

Ormston was silent. This was a queer moment to feel—what was it he felt? jealously? envy? sympathy? Sympathy for his friend's reckless and disorderly life, for all that had made him an outlaw, a breaker of the laws, a—the words rushed into his mind—a free man? A touch of fear brushed him, but it was fear of himself, of a self so deeply buried that it was unrecognisable, faceless, bodiless, not a body but an obsession in search of a body to inhabit. No, no, he thought, violently, with contempt, he's a fool, he could have been anything, and like a fool he has thrown everything away . . . The contrast between his own hard relentlessly careful youth and his friend's—son of a rich man, flanked by useful uncles and cousins on all sides—woke an old bitterness. Don't let him insult you into losing your temper, he thought. He said coolly,

'A point to you.'

Anthony went off into a jeering cackling laugh. 'You didn't miss your chances. You haven't missed them here, have you? With my whore of a wife.'

The anger Ormston felt was murderous, a pure impulse to kill. 'Hold your tongue.'

'Oh, come,' Boyd said, smiling, 'you've been sleeping with her. I knew about it from the start—my Intelligence is at least as good as yours or foxy Frent's. Don't think I mind—I'm not conceited enough to expect anything else. Why should she deny herself anything she wants? She's bed-worthy and I neglect her.' His eyes sparkled with triumph. 'I assure you I don't mind. A whore is good enough for a clever bum-sucker any day.'

Scarcely conscious of moving his arm, Ormston struck him across the face. He stared, his rage ebbing, at a thin trickle of blood running over Boyd's chin from his lower lip. Boyd passed the back of his hand across his mouth, looked at it—then looked up, with a mischievous smile.

'Well—now that you've broken the ice we're back on the old terms, aren't we?'

Despair, love, and a crazy desire to laugh seized Ormston. 'You devil,' he said.

'You're an idiot, Ricky, you knew I was baiting you.'

'Yes, I knew it, but'—he laughed—'I owed you that . . . you've blotted my copybook as well as your own.'

Affection and mockery softened Boyd's smile. 'Ricky, I love you and respect you—sometimes I respect you . . . and you know what you can do with your copybook, don't you?'

'What in God's name,' Ormston cried, 'made you—you —take sides with these squalid heroes against us? Your own people. It stupefies me. I don't—I can't understand it.'

After a moment, Boyd said,

'I'm atoning for us. Repaying your blood money.'

'Oh, talk sense,' Ormston said impatiently.

Boyd gave him a cool clear glance. 'This is sense. You—
we, so far as I can't help being English—come here, we take
possession, we put down airfields, barracks, base camps, we
make laws and fix wages, we behave as if we were a superior
race, and when the poor bloody inhabitants protest we say:
What's the matter with you, we're treating you nicely, aren't
we, better than some would—why complain? They complain that we're here at all!'

Bored, bored to the point of yawning in his face, Ormston
said,

'All these platitudes. *Aren't* we superior?'

He believed it as simply and coldly as he believed that
England has abdicated. It ought to have had the courage
to go on asserting its rights, as a superior race, to rule. Perhaps only—since the fatal blood-letting of 1914–18—its
right to go down fighting. Perhaps the only thing now
possible, in a world dominated by America and Russia—
and soon by China—is to keep up a show of dignity and
distance, not, at least not to spout nonsense about democracy
and equality from every slack weakened pore.

'You old romantic!' Boyd jeered.

'My dear chap, your friends may not know it, but you
know—as well as I do—that if we weren't here, someone
else would be—it's our mild hand against what might
be a very rough one. If a child came to you screaming to
be let run into a sea full of sharks, you wouldn't say: Right,
off you go . . . All these small nations are finished—helpless.'

In a light teasing voice, Boyd said,

'Their old gods are against you, you know.'

'Really? Which of their gods hacked off an old woman's
head yesterday, and shoots unarmed men in the back?
You talk about freedom and happiness like a—like a
politician. Don't tell *me* you believe they'll spring up out of

these sordid murders and betrayals, out of a filthy mess of vanity and ambitions and fears. Your first-class killers are as crazy with fear as their victims.' His contempt for a murderous romanticism got the better of him. 'You fool— the other day one of them let a woman bleed to death with her terrified child clinging to her. It seems a rather trivial bestiality for your famous army to brag about.'

Boyd's face changed as, without knowing it, he had known it would—had meant it to: its look of mulishness and fanaticism was the sign that he had stopped thinking.

'Wait. You'll see whether I'm only bragging.'

An irrational certainty seized Ormston. There was truth in the rumours running through the colony: something, something unpleasant, had been brewed. I must, my God, know, he thought. He felt a spasm of fury that he could not tear the facts out of the other's mind. Controlling himself, he said quietly,

'We know who is backing you—which country.'

'You do, do you?' Boyd mocked. 'Much good may it do you.'

'You weren't a communist. Have you been converted?'

'Don't be a goat,' Boyd said. He gave his cackling young laugh. 'I'm no more a communist than foxy Frent—I hate *all* policemen. Use your head—if you're fighting machineguns with your bare hands, and a man you don't like offers you a bomb, what do you do? Refuse it?'

'Anthony,' his friend said, with anguish, 'what you're doing is evil. Help me to stop it.'

Boyd smiled. 'Funny simple old boy you are, after all. Everything black and white—good one side, evil the other. Like a fairy-tale.'

'You're not doing even your own side any good. You can't win.'

'I'm backing the wrong horse, am I?' Boyd said lightly. 'Something you never did . . . No, no, wait a minute. I'm

not such a fool as you think. I boast, of course I boast.
Always did. But I know better than you, better than Frent,
that I can't make war on you. I'm not trying to. It would
be a waste of my men. I'm trying to run a terror—and by
God I'm succeeding. Aren't I? I'm not going to have *you*
assassinated, old boy. Not because I'm fond of you—I am,
but . . . But because I know where to draw the line. It costs
less and pays better to spread the terror thinner and wider
———'

'To murder defenceless men and old women,' Ormston
said savagely.

'Oh, as you like . . . But now—look at the score. There's
only one way you can deal with us—repression. Growing
more and more brutal as we resist. But the more brutal you
become, the more bitterly you shock people all over the
liberal world—including people at home, better men than
Charles Cumberland—and in the end, in the end, Ricky,
you'll negotiate with us. It's as simple as that. Simple
and nasty. Frent can't see it, but you see it. Don't you?'

Ormston stood up. 'It's no use going on talking. I'll
leave you to Frent.' His feeling of anguish returned, drowning his bitterness. 'If you come to your senses—send for
me. I'll come whenever it is, day or night. But, for God's
sake, remember that it's hopeless—hopeless.'

Boyd had not moved. For less than a moment, looking
down at him, his friend caught sight of an adolescent as
avid as a young dog for the taste, touch, smell of the life
offered to him, and as innocently direct. Boyd spoke in his
voice of that time, with simplicity.

'You're wrong, my dear Ricky. You have troops on your
side, arms, all the authority of power—and that's all you
have. We have the wishes, secret and open, of a whole
people. We shall win.' He stopped, and went on with
savage exasperation. 'Not so soon now—God curse me for
a randy fool—but sooner or later.'

'Give up now,' Ormston said harshly. 'I'll do everything I can for you, I'll make things as easy for you as I can.'

'Let me laugh,' Boyd said. He grinned. 'Ricky the saviour. What d'you want most? To be rid of the only person who knows you through and through and isn't impressed, or to score over me by saving me? Which?'

I can't reach him, Ormston thought. Despair and impatience filled him. Why must he ruin himself—and very likely ruin me? 'Don't you believe me that I want to help you?'

'Yes,' Boyd said. He yawned.

Turning, the Governor walked to the door. As he opened it, the guards jumped to attention.

'Take him back where you brought him from.'

He watched the movements of their fingers on Boyd's wrists. In an amused voice Boyd said,

'Can I have clean shirts sent in, or is stink part of my punishment?'

'Take him away,' the Governor said.

CHAPTER THIRTEEN

FRENT spoke behind him. 'Well, sir?'

He had gone back to the window. A day from his first weeks in the country returned to him. With Robin Hind and a visitor from London he had driven into these very hills and spent an hour climbing a rocky flank to the ruins of one of the eleventh-century castles, a shell for the wind: beyond it, milk-blue, the line of higher hills: he had promised himself other days of white scorching sun, thyme-blessed earth, and the silence. I shall never go there again, he thought. Reluctant—the moment he turned his back to them, the hills would close in and trap him—he turned.

'Nothing,' he told Frent curtly. 'I got nothing out of him at all. I made no impression.'

Frent's air of respectful attention did not change. 'It's just possible, sir, isn't it, that it was unwise for you to take the trouble to talk to him. It will inflate his self-importance. These fellows are incurably self-important.'

'What fellows?' the Governor asked. He sat down.

'Traitors. I've had some experience, a little, with the breed—we don't, thank God, breed many, treachery isn't one of our national quirks—and I never knew one who wasn't vain. Born vain.'

'You may be right. But all vain men are not traitors.'

'True,' Frent said. His tone sharpened. 'I've just had the report of another murder—a Red Cross nurse coming back from a farm in the hills where she'd been taking penicillin to a child. Two youths turned her out of her car, shot her, and drove off in the car. A filthy business, but less disturbing than something else—that happened between two and three this morning. Five men drove into a village—Torija —only five—dragged a couple of chaps out of bed, told

them they had been found guilty of helping the enemy—us
—and hanged them, in the square, as coolly as you please.
They'd fetched the rest of the village, even the children, out
to watch the hanging, and told them it was a rehearsal for
the show they would put on when they took over the country.' He drove his sharp narrow teeth into his upper lip for
a second. 'Very effective.'

'Infinitely less detestable than killing a nurse,' the Governor exclaimed.

Frent shrugged. 'Oh, of course. But—if you're a farmer,
or a shopkeeper or a village schoolmaster—it's the hanging
you remember.' His face lightened. 'Well, we have Boyd—
a God-given turn of luck. He can tell us who runs his
groups, where his arms are kept, how he gets them—in
short, he can put all the big pieces in our hands. And'—
his smile was as sharp as a nail—'mopping-up can begin.'

The Governor was silent. A sour bitter anger against
Boyd was rising in him—less to do with the murders than
with his own nagging sense of frustration: it humiliated him
that he had not been able to handle Boyd—and that Frent
knew it. The antipathy he felt for Frent at this moment
astonished him. Everything the police chief had said was
sensible and just, and he had never disliked him so sharply.
There was a tinge of fear in his dislike—not fear of Frent.
He had an obscure feeling of danger, almost physical, and
swerved from it instinctively, like a man who has begun to
suspect that he is ill.

Irritably, he thought that his face must reflect the look—
cold, efficient, calculating—on Frent's. He stood up.

'And you believe you can persuade him to tell us?'

Frent cocked his head on one side. Like a dog taking the
measure of a bone, the Governor thought. 'You know him
better than I do, sir. Is he—I imagine he is—excitable?
Unbalanced?'

'Excitable, yes. Perhaps unbalanced.'

He watched an air of reserve spread across Frent's face, dulling it.

'We'll see what keeping him awake to answer questions does,' Frent said.

The grotesque idea crossed the Governor's mind that he was handing his friend over to a surgeon who might turn out to be a lunatic. Nonsense, he thought wearily: he has only to admit he has behaved abominably and tell us the facts.

'I said last night that we'd keep quiet for the time being about the arrest. No announcement. If necessary—if there are rumours——'

'There will be, sir,' Frent interrupted.

'They must be denied, or ignored.' He hesitated. Why did he feel this acute anxiety to keep the thing dark? For Anthony's sake? Only for Anthony's sake? In the end he would have to be exposed. Another reason, formless, slid from his grasp like smoke. 'We don't'—he paused again— 'want emotional complications. No sensation—not yet.'

'Certainly not, sir,' Frent said. An expression half ironical, half inquisitive, came into his face. 'The last thing I want.'

His car was half way across Government Square when he caught sight of Andrew. The young man was walking rapidly in the violent sunlight towards the Urraca Street corner of the square. In the instant of leaning forward to tell his driver to stop the car, he saw him join Sarah Leng and turn her, his hand on her arm, towards the hotel.

A cold anger shook him. He made an effort, and forced the incident out of his mind. He could not afford the energy to let it disturb him yet.

Robin was waiting for him, with his calm air of readiness. As he stood up he allowed himself a brief and discreet glance of curiosity. He knew—the Governor had told him the night before when he returned from police headquarters—

that security had made an important capture, but he had not been told the man's name. The Governor shook his head.

'Nothing. Nothing yet. They're still questioning him . . . Come, let's get on.'

He sat down and began reading a letter from the pile Robin had arranged for him. With the slightest touch of embarrassment Robin said,

'Sir, Mrs. Boyd has been ringing up. She wants to see you. She insisted that it's urgent.'

The Governor looked up quickly, raising his eyebrows. She had never behaved indiscreetly before. Vexed, he thought: It can only be Anthony—but why the devil ring me up at this time? He said quietly,

'Urgent? What did you say to her?'

'I told her that it was extremely unlikely you could see her this morning, sir. She rang up twice. The second time I said that I would tell you as soon as I could.' A little colour rose in his clear delicate skin. 'I hope I did the right thing, sir.'

'Yes, yes, of course.' He tapped the table with one finger of the hand laid there, as he did when he was in doubt what to say. 'I'd better speak to her. Get her for me.'

In the moment of taking the receiver from his secretary's hand he had the conviction that she knew—everything. He prepared to deal with her patiently, but her voice, with its disquieting flawed note, was controlled, as if she were talking in a room full of people.

'Richard, I'm sorry, I know I'm behaving terribly, but I must see you. Now.'

He was conscious of the back of Robin's smooth head bent over the day's press cuttings. 'Perhaps you can tell me what the trouble is?'

Her voice hardened. 'You know very well that I wouldn't do this unheard-of thing unless I had a good reason.'

Without covering the mouthpiece he said, 'My engagements today, Robin? I think a dinner?' The young man had been scribbling on a sheet of paper, which he laid in front of the Governor—*You have no appointments before eight this evening.* Looking down at it as he spoke to her, Ormston went on, 'I could see you for a few minutes at six . . .'

'Stop play-acting,' she said, with contempt. 'I must see you this morning.'

'Very well, come at once.' He replaced the receiver, frowning. 'She never struck me as an hysterical woman. Go downstairs, Robin, and arrange for her to be brought straight here, will you?'

Half way to the door, Robin hesitated. 'Shall I wait, and bring her up myself?'

'Yes, do.'

He pushed aside the letter he had been reading and began carefully to read a memorandum from General Smith which was immediately beneath it on the pile. As he read he made notes. A part of his mind went on thinking, almost coldly, about Anne. She has no more sense, for all her intelligence, than stupider women. I really believe that women, all women, are incurably immature. I've never known one who wasn't. Except, he thought, my mother. She is the exception . . . He looked up as the door opened. The thought that came into his mind steadied it: A beautiful animal who reads Wittgenstein . . . He stood up, pulled a chair forward, and said formally, 'How d'you do, Mrs. Boyd?' Glancing past her, he said, 'See that I'm not annoyed by the telephone, Robin.'

As the door closed on the young man, she leaned forward in her chair and said,

'You arrested Tony last night.'

He had expected it, yet he felt a pang of dismay and irritation. In the same instant he noticed the feverish brightness of her eyes under their heavy lids, and a film of

moisture over her temples and above her upper lip. Entirely
without reflecting, he said,

'Where did you pick up this nonsense?'

She looked at him with something very nearly derision.
'Don't bother to tell lies, Richard. It wastes your precious
time. I know he was arrested——' She paused: her face
contracted briefly, but he could not be sure whether she
were hurt or sickened. 'I even know how.'

His irritation was turning to anger—not against her:
against the whole of this atrocious business and that she was
involved in it. He felt a momentary stir of his lust for her,
and thought, half consciously: She was sent into the world
for me to make love to her, not for squalid complications of
this kind . . . He had an impulse to say: Go away and keep
quiet: if your husband is a terrorist and a criminal what
business is it of yours? Glancing at her throat and bare
arms, he felt the pleasure it would give him to hurt this
delicate flesh in some way. He said calmly,

'You must tell me what you know, or think you know.'

She drew an audible breath, and forced herself to smile.
'A woman came to see me—early this morning—she was
in a dreadful state.' Her smile became a half-cynical grimace.
'I don't think I ever saw one of his mistresses—let's call
them that—before. Let alone one who came to tell me that
he had been in bed with her only a few hours ago . . . when
the security police came and pulled him out of her arms . . .'

'Anne——'

She interrupted him. 'Oh, don't think I was shocked.
But it is, you must admit, Richard, very unusual.' She looked
at him with an air of frankness. 'You won't waste any more
time lying, will you?'

Ormston did not answer at once. For the moment, the
fact that she knew was unimportant to him. He wanted,
savagely, to know what she felt, whether she were suffering
at all. His glance passed over her body to the fingers of her

right hand, tips pressed into her thigh with such convulsive force that the bones in the back of her hand showed under the thin skin. He felt a jealous twinge.

'Yes, it's true. He was in bed with a woman in a village not very far from here when we picked him up.'

She must have realised that he was watching her hands. She relaxed them and said in a light voice,

'I didn't know that having mistresses was a crime.'

'Your . . . informant didn't tell you why he was arrested?'

'She said she didn't know why——' she shrugged her shoulders. 'She was nearly incoherent, poor creature. And perhaps I didn't understand her—her English was far worse than Agathe's.' She laughed. 'She had an even stronger smell.' Her self-control gave way suddenly. 'How could he? With one of these *animals*. I can still see her eyes, great rolling eyes, like a nervous horse. Horrible.'

Shall I, he thought, tell her the truth? How badly will it hurt her? Probably very badly . . . The impulse to tell her was very little different from the one he would have felt if they had been alone in her room.

'Tony was not, this time, botanising,' he said. 'For the last eighteen months, probably longer, he has been helping to organise the rebels . . . Possibly he's mad, but I don't think so.'

Her eyes dilated—the only sign she made. 'Tony? Are you . . . is it true?'

'Quite true,' he said, watching her.

A pulse was beating furiously at the base of her throat. Almost without meaning to, he leaned forward and touched it with a finger. She struck his hand down. Jumping up, she said.

'You mean . . . you say he has killed people.'

'Arranged for them to be killed . . . He seems proud that he—he said it himself—that he has turned a number of lazy young men into efficient murderers.'

She was looking at him with horror, her hands pressed to her face. Letting them drop, she said under her breath,

'He is a devil. I always knew he was. This——' She broke off, her mouth working in an unpleasant way. 'A devil,' she said loudly, 'a cruel devil. Or out of his mind. But hateful—hateful——'

She over-acts her hatred, Ormston thought coldly. 'You realise that you must hold your tongue. There must be no publicity—nothing—until he has been examined.'

'Examined?'

'The police are questioning him now.'

She stood silent, her arms hanging. Ormston felt an access of jealousy. It was as though he had swallowed some drug that dried the inside of his mouth and throat and set his veins throbbing. The effort to move his tongue in this dryness was painful: he got out, 'Do you understand?' and stopped.

She did not look at him. In a lifeless voice, she said, 'Yes, I understand. I shan't say anything. Don't worry.'

The only thing he wanted was to get rid of her. Let her go away now. Leave him room to breathe, to collect the energy he had squandered in the last quarter of an hour. He moved his arm as if he were clearing a space.

'You must go.'

Looking round her, she took her gloves from the table, then came to him and touched his cheek, gently, the gentlest imaginable caress—if it were a caress and not an appeal. She was close enough for him to catch the thin scent of rose geranium: her touch and her nearness were unendurable. She interpreted the look on his face as impatience, and began to move away.

'Poor Richard—you were fond of him,' she said lightly.

'I only wish to God he had been shot,' Ormston said.

Her smile startled him. 'Why? For whose sake—yours or his?'

'You must go,' he said again.

'Yes, yes.' She walked to the door. He moved quickly past her to open it. Abruptly, gripping his arm, she said, 'You won't be too hard on him, will you?'

He held the door open, and she went out without glancing at him again.

Closing the door, he leaned against it for a moment. He noticed that his pen had rolled off the table, walked slowly— as tired as if he had been making some enormous physical effort—to pick it up, and sat down. His hands made the same gesture of clearing a space. After a moment, with a return of energy, he took up the house telephone. 'Robin? Yes, come now.'

CHAPTER FOURTEEN

THE smaller of the Astoria's two bars faced an inner courtyard, cobble-stoned, with one stunted bush of white jasmine and a dry chipped fountain. Along one wall were small iron tables, balanced precariously on the uneven stones and sheltered by a narrow roof made from two sheets of zinc with a crack between them: one of the concrete pillars supporting the roof immediately above their heads had some sort of vine growing up it out of a barrel. The sun striking through the crack sliced the table in half between them, and the girl's hand lay partly in the light, partly in the shade, thin fingers of smooth living wood. The impulse to lay his hand over hers tortured Andrew, and she perhaps expected it. After a minute she drew her hand back. The waiter fetched their drinks, and a carafe of water, and went back into the hotel.

'Why couldn't you come yesterday evening?' Sarah asked. She smiled at him.

The questions he wanted to ask her pressed against his mind, distracting him. An instinct that was neither cruelty nor grief, but had something of both in it, kept him quiet. Wait, he thought; let her wait.

'My father had something he wanted copied—a memorandum. I——' he was embarrassed by his lie: it struck him as a very poor one. 'I couldn't talk about it on the telephone.'

'Well, I'm very glad I ran into you,' she said gaily. 'I rang you up, about an hour ago.'

'I was out,' he lied.

'Yes, they told me.' She leaned forward, bringing her face so close to his that he saw only her eyes: there was no one at the other tables, and they were sitting at the end farthest from the door into the hotel, but she lowered her voice so that he could only just hear it. 'Tell me—is it true that one of the partisans has been captured—one of the leaders— *the* leader?'

'You call them partisans, do you?'

'Oh, call them what you like. Is it true?'

He scowled. Sunk in himself, in the discovery he was hiding from her, waiting to throw it down in front of her, he could not take any interest in what was going on outside. 'I haven't heard anything.'

'It's being said.'

'Who? Who is saying it?'

'Well, there's the grapevine, you know. One of our reporters heard something this morning from a—a source.' She laughed. 'It hasn't been officially denied yet—which would be a proof.'

She had been evasive. It exasperated him. She lies too easily, he thought. It gave him pleasure to bespatter her in his mind. 'If I did know anything about it, I wouldn't tell you, you know.'

She drew back, raising her eyebrows in surprise. 'Even if I promised not to make any use of it?'

He shook his head. An idea which excited him by its astuteness—by what seemed its astuteness—struck him, and he asked, 'If you were told—say, if your stepfather told you an important and dangerous secret, would you give it away to me?'

'You do know something!'

'No. I don't. I swear I don't . . . You haven't answered me.'

She said slowly, 'If I would tell you an important secret . . . But it all depends. If I'd been told in the strictest confidence—if I'd promised—you wouldn't expect me to break that sort of promise, would you?'

'Suppose I knew already, and asked point-blank, as you

did just now: Is it true? Would you feel that you had the right to lie to me about it?'

She seemed for the first time to realise that he had something in his mind that might turn out unpleasant. 'I don't understand,' she said, frowning. 'What are you getting at, my darling?'

He looked at her, forcing himself to see her as someone less simple, less familiar, than the girl he had imagined he knew. A confused surge of longing, misery, hope, swept away what little judgment and self-possession he had left: he half knew that his bitterness was infinitely greater than it need be, greater than any cause she had given him. This only exasperated him further, and he blurted,

'Why didn't you tell me about Julian Hind?'

'Tell you,' she said, 'tell you what?'

The sight of her face, dulled and hardened, its gaiety pinched out, settled his hopes, whatever they had been, for good: they turned and humiliated him. He looked at her without pity. 'That you were his mistress,' he said drily.

After a moment she asked, 'Who has been talking to you about me?'

'That doesn't matter.'

The contempt that came into her face startled him. 'So that's why you were so anxious to know if I would keep things from you? You . . . oh, how clever you think you are. It's exactly the sort of trick your father would play—is always playing. A—a filthy trick.'

'My father——' he began. He stopped—on the edge of telling her that none of it mattered, she must forgive him, he was a fool, a clumsy fool, he had never meant to speak about it. The streak of cruelty in him saved him from this lapse into the stammerings of a schoolboy who has made a booby of himself.

'You needn't tell me who has talked,' Sarah said. 'I know who it was—that beast Totty.'

He stared. 'Totty? Who the devil is Totty?'

'I mean Robin—he was always called that, it used to make him cry.'

'What nonsense are you trying to tell me?' he said furiously. 'I asked you a question. Are you going to answer it?'

Even before he finished speaking, a feeling of incredulity seized him: for a moment he doubted everything and everybody except the reality of the girl facing him, whose body he knew as he knew his own. He felt something like horror of himself. What have we been talking about, he thought, what sort of unnecessary drivel?

'You haven't even asked me if what he told you is true,' Sarah said. 'You took it for granted it was.' With a flash of her hot temper she struck the table. She had what he had always called her vixen face: eyes starting and lips pressed into a narrow line. He saw it with extreme sharpness, and beyond it the concrete pillar with the vine twisting round it, its leaves motionless, as if stupefied by the heat. 'If someone had come to me and told me you were a liar and a sneak thief, or any other detestable thing, I would at least have asked you if it was true, I wouldn't have believed it instantly—as if I'd always known that was what you were.' Tears—which he knew to be tears of anger—came into her eyes. 'I'll never forget that, never, never.'

She had moved her chair, so that the shadow of the vine chequered the side of her face in a ravelled pattern: he had an impulse to lift his hand and brush it away: the thought of touching her started an anguished tenderness in him—and at the same time he felt that she was evading him again. His jealousy clawed him. He almost hated her.

'Tell me the truth, Sarah, for God's sake.'

She stared back at him with as much hatred as he felt in himself. 'I'll tell you nothing at all—nothing.'

'Then it is true.'

'Believe what you like.' Her face seemed to shrivel as if in sudden cold. She leaned forward and spoke in a thin voice, feeling her way into him with it, to reach the quick of his pride. 'You're too like your father—you don't trust anybody, and you don't love anybody except yourself. I knew it, I suppose I knew it, but——'

'Shut up, Sarah,' he said quietly.

She smiled with contempt. 'Why? Don't you like to hear the truth?'

He gave way to the pleasure of hurting her. 'Why should I trust you? When I go back to London I shan't know who it is you're sleeping with, shall I?'

She had nothing more to say. She sat, hunched in her chair, for a moment, then got up and walked away, into the hotel, without glancing at him again.

CHAPTER FIFTEEN

HE walked back to Government House, trying to wear out his anger before he reached it. There were more guards than usual in the Square, and outside official buildings, but he paid no attention to them, thinking, so far as he could, of nothing except the scorching heat of the ground against the soles of his feet and the light forcing him to keep his eyes half closed. No more unhappiness, he thought, no regrets. Forget about her. You can—and without feeling sorry for yourself. . . . But, shut in his room, he became feverishly restless. A heavy sickening sense of loss drove him to walk up and down, unable to make up his mind to go out—go where?— or open a book, or do anything but endure this fever of misery and uncertainty. A part of him refused to accept it, refused to believe that this was an end, that any disaster, any loss, is final. Under everything else, a faint throb of hope persisted, belief and hope . . . When someone knocked on his door, he had no idea how long he had been walking between one wall and its opposite. His heart jumped: he clutched at the impossible, that she had made her way in somehow to reprieve him. He knew it was impossible.

'Come in.'

Robin Hind put his pale composed face round the door, and said, 'H.E. wants you in the library.'

'Tell him I'll come,' he said. He would have liked to jump at the other and knock into insensibility the brain that knew more about Sarah than he did. 'Don't wait, I'll come.'

His father was writing when he came into the library. Glancing up and frowning, he said, 'Ah, there you are. Give me a minute.' He wrote a few more words, dropped his pen, leaned back and looked at Andrew without a smile. 'Sit down.'

Andrew seated himself at the other side of the table. He noticed that his father looked strained and older, as if he were sleeping badly. Things are worse, he thought. He felt a little curiosity, but no uneasiness; he was all the more shocked when Ormston said,

'I saw you talking to Sarah Leng this morning. Were you giving her news for her abominable rag?'

The blood rushed to Andrew's head. Too taken aback to feel mortified, he stammered, 'You don't think that's what I do?'

His father seemed to hesitate. 'I don't know what sort of hold she has on you. And since I know that she's a young woman of no character, with no scruples . . .' He smiled sarcastically.

Andrew had a hot impulse to defend her. His father might be perfectly right; something cold and disciplined in him, a cold irony, admitted it, but some other instinct, deeper, reckless, flung him violently on the side of the girl against all safer older less vulnerable people. He hesitated, and rejected the impulse—it would do Sarah no good, and once and for all convince his father that her influence over him was evil and stronger than his reason and sense. He was not able to choke his resentment completely. What did he resent most? That he had been suspected of being indiscreet and untrustworthy? Or that, suddenly, he had felt, behind his father's tolerant affection, a demand he could not afford: it would cripple him. How old does he think I am? . . . He said coldly,

'Whatever hold, as you call it, she had, it wouldn't trick me into helping a newspaper I detest as much as you do.'

His father moved his arm in a weary gesture, pushing aside the papers littering the table in front of him. 'I'm sorry. I shouldn't have asked that. I know you better.' He smiled, with a mockery too detached to give offence.

'I dislike the young woman so much that I forget my place and my age.'

'You disliked her even before you knew ... before Robin Hind told you ...' Another word, and his voice would give him away—the resentment, the anguish. His father said gently,

'She's not a fit wife for you. Even if she were ... truthful and innocent, she wouldn't do.'

Would any girl, to your exalted way of thinking? Andrew thought. He kept his voice in order. 'What sort of young woman would you approve of?'

'None at all—until you are much farther on in your career. Any marriage now would be stupid. Later ...'

The warmth of the resentment Andrew felt startled himself: he was not sure what he resented so savagely, nor why he had this sense that he was facing a stranger, an enemy. He let his hostility enjoy itself. 'Later you'd perhaps choose for me.'

His father said drily, 'I don't really deserve sarcasm.'

He made the same weary movement of his arm. It struck Andrew by its heaviness, and for the first time he reflected that his father was carrying a burden so cruelly exacting that the least his son could do was not to add a straw to it. With a spring of remorse he thought: I'm a self-centred animal.

'I'm sorry,' he said warmly. 'I'm really sorry, dad.'

His father smiled without irony. 'It was my fault. I had no right to ask you what you were talking to her about.' He waited, hoping for some reassurance. Andrew said nothing, and he went on, 'I trust you completely, as if you were myself.'

'Thanks,' Andrew said.

His father said abruptly, 'To prove it I'm going to tell you'—he smiled sharply—'a state secret. The only person I've told is your grandmother ... You didn't hear anything this morning when you—when you were out?'

'No,' Andrew said. He hesitated and thought: No harm in passing on a rumour. 'There seems to be a story going about that we've captured someone important. I suppose it's nonsense.'

'It's true,' Ormston said calmly. 'We've had a stroke of luck. The chap we've caught is possibly the king-pin of the rebellion. If we can get enough information out of him we have every chance to break the thing open, pick up the leaders, stop money and arms coming in—end the killings' —he laid his ugly hand flat on the table, and drew it quickly back—'and disappoint the chaps in Whitehall who are trying to make me the scapegoat for their own weakness.' A look of bored arrogance crossed his face. 'I've never been able to suffer fools gladly. It has made me the sort of enemies any man makes who has the misfortune, nine times out of ten, to be right.'

A feeling of excitement and discomfort—very much the feeling roused in the spectator by an acrobat attempting a really dangerous trick—seized Andrew. To shake it off he said energetically,

'This really is something.'

'Not to be let loose,' his father said, smiling. 'Not until we've squeezed the last drop out of'—a barely noticeable pause—'this chap.'

'I suppose he *will* talk?'

A note of cruel self-assurance came into Ormston's voice. 'He has—never mind why—a peculiar reason to feel guilty. That is what will break him.' With an abrupt change of tone he went on, 'I want you to do something for me, Andrew. There's an epidemic of some sort—not quite 'flu, and very unpleasant and disabling—running about among the troops in a town on the coast—Zante. It's been going on too long, and Colonel Graham is going there by car to look into it. I want you to go with him. Will you?'

Does he think I don't know why he's sending me off?

Andrew thought drily. 'Of course I'll go—if I can be any use.'

'Don't if you'd rather not. What with mines and the odd ambush or two travelling isn't very safe now.'

An impulse to laugh seized Andrew. Stifling it, he said, 'When? Today?'

'No, no. In about three days' time,' his father said with relief. 'I'm glad you'll go—bless you.'

CHAPTER SIXTEEN

GLANCING as he passed it at the door of his mother's room, Andrew noticed that it was ajar: in the same instant, with the suddenness of a jack-in-the-box, she pulled it wide open. If it had not been so unlikely he would have thought she had been standing close to it, listening. She looked at him with her absent wavering smile.

'Why, Andrew, there you are. You didn't have any lunch.'

To avoid questions, he said, 'I ate when I was out.'

'I hope you did,' she murmured.

Without wanting to, and because she was standing holding the door, he went into the room, and sat down on the sofa. It was narrow, extremely hard, and covered in a slippery material with an ugly design, one of the bastards fathered by abstract painting. Why doesn't she make herself more comfortable? he wondered. The monkey had been asleep at the other end of the sofa; it opened its eyes, rubbed them with its tiny fists, like a young child waking up, yawned, stretched, and crept cautiously over the slippery surface to seat itself on the palm of his hand. Flattered—does one ever know why a child or an animal takes a fancy to one adult face and not to another?—he nursed it. The box of dried figs was behind him on the table, and he offered one to the monkey, who did not want it. He realised that he was famished and ate it, helping himself to another and another.

His mother was still standing, watching him with an air of concern. 'You look like a bird about to take off,' he said, amused. 'Why don't you sit down?'

She laughed. 'If I could take off this minute, I would.' She gave him an unexpectedly sharp glance from the side of her eyes. 'What has your father been saying to you?'

Taken aback, he said, 'He wants me to go to Zante with the medical chap, what's his name. They're having an epidemic.'

'When?'

'Oh, at the end of the week.' He was suddenly exasperated. 'They don't need anything I could do. He's sending me out of harm's way.'

'My dear child——'

'Of course he is,' Andrew interrupted. 'What's more it's perfectly unnecessary—I shan't see Sarah, I haven't anything I want to say to her.' He was surprised how easy it was to talk to her about Sarah: it gave him an extraordinary feeling of relief.

A smile flickered across his mother's dark face. 'Are you so angry with her?'

The agony he felt at this instant pulled his long mouth into a grimace. He had no idea that he had betrayed himself, but his mother saw his wretchedness as easily and clearly as, when he was a very young child, she had known that he was going to be ill. Her thin body was swollen with her pity for him and her longing to help him. She would have torn the world down about her own ears, without a qualm, to get him what he wanted, and she could do nothing. For a moment she detested Sarah because it was about her that he was unhappy.

'I'd have every right to be angry, wouldn't I?' he mumbled.

'Why?'

'If you'd been made a fool of—and told as many lies——' He stopped, and pressed his lips together.

'*Did* she tell you lies?' his mother asked. He did not answer, and she went on in her nearly toneless voice—its only tone the note of half-surprised amusement. 'You may be right about her, she may be quite worthless. But you can't—you mustn't—take your father's word for it.'

Her son was as astonished as if the monkey had spoken. 'What do you mean, mother?'

'He's desperate to keep you for himself,' she said simply. 'Poor man, you're the one of his possessions he prizes most. He *must* keep his hand on you.' She looked at him slyly, from the corners of her eyes. 'That's what he calls loving, you know.'

She made Andrew uncomfortable. Instinctively he dodged away from trying to understand her. 'Nothing alters the fact that other people—that smooth ass, Robin—know more about her than I do,' he said harshly.

'Perhaps she ought to have told you, but . . . Which do you dislike most, my dear—that she's had a lover, or that she didn't tell you about it? Is it your vanity that hurts you?'

'Does that make any difference?' Andrew said.

He said it with such violence that the monkey sprang away from him—more in disgust at the noise than fear— and threw itself into Sophie's arms: she set it on her knee like a baby; it stood there clutching her collar with one hand, stretching its slim body, thin hard belly pressed confidingly against her, small head held back so that spine and tail formed one long concave line.

'Quiet, monkey, I'm talking to Andrew,' she said. She looked at him over the animal's head. 'You're quite a lot like your father, you know.'

'D'you mean that when I want a thing I want it?' he said, smiling at her. 'You've just told me that I'm vain, too.'

'Never mind that,' she murmured. 'I don't say that Sarah isn't to blame—I don't know enough about her. But if you loved her—or if you loved her more than you hate her—in the way your father hates people he can't make do what he wants—you might feel she had the right to tell you or not tell you about something that happened before she even

knew you . . . Very likely she's noticed that you don't like
your belongings to be responsible for themselves. Any more
than *he* does.'

Her son felt uneasy—and suddenly curious about her.
'You're a little hard on him, aren't you?' He pulled a sar-
donic face. 'On me, too.'

The movement of her head reminded him of a small hawk
he had picked up in Scotland when he was a child, one of its
wings torn; he kept it out of harm's way in his room, where
it perched on the backs of chairs, striking uselessly with its
head.

'He isn't allowing you very much freedom over this
young woman, is he?' She looked at him. 'Didn't it ever
strike you that when you don't love people enough to leave
them free you are really killing them?'

'I'm sorry—that seems to me nonsense,' he said gently.
His voice hardened in spite of himself. 'If you can't count
on a—on your friends to behave decently and rationally,
what use are they? I detest'—he hesitated—'untidiness in
people. I don't care whether it affects their morals or their
manners, it's equally boring.' With unconscious cruelty,
he added, 'You probably don't know what I mean.'

I know you a little better than you know yourself, she
thought calmly. You inherited something from your father
—or *his* father—warmth—a fever of energy, sensuality, a
need, a devouring need to devote yourself to one person
(one at a time, she thought, with her half-innocent cynicism),
which will destroy you if you can't learn to live with it
without tyrannising over any woman you fall in love with,
Sarah or another—or others. Or over your children . . . She
said in a cool voice,

'Nothing is of the least importance except being able to
love. It's frightfully difficult—unless like Christ you have a
talent for it. Nowadays we're so clever and unloving that we
shall probably kill everyone in the world—which is not

worse than killing one child but, if there's no one left to repent, more malicious and stupid.'

All very true, Andrew thought drily, but what the devil has it to do with me? . . . She's good, and simple, he thought —and she knows nothing . . . A feeling he did not recognise as contempt brushed him: it came from too far back to be recognisable, from the time when he began to notice that she did none of the things his father did gloriously well; she could neither swim, nor climb mountains, talk, argue, stand an argument comically on its head . . . My father's rational way of looking at life must always, he told himself, have been hard on her and her moonshine . . . For less than a moment he wondered whether she had been happy. Whether her life lived on the margin of his father's splendid one was what, if she had foreseen it, she would have risked. He was struck suddenly by her look of secrecy and withdrawal—it was as though he were seeing her for the first time after years of not noticing her at all. A phantom rose to the surface of his mind, he saw a face bending over him, a little uncertain, shy and tender. Hers? He could not be sure. He dropped the memory again at once. Phantoms are not importunate and he had sharper thoughts.

'I must go,' he said, getting up. 'Don't let things worry you, my dear, and whatever else you do don't worry about me, I'm leathery.'

He rested his hand on her shoulder for an instant, and the monkey stretched up and closed its teeth on a finger, nipping it sharply but without breaking the skin. Startled, he said, 'Why, you little beast.'

His mother laughed. 'You weren't paying either of us any attention—and he's much vainer than I am, you know.'

CHAPTER SEVENTEEN

His mother so seldom came to his room that Ormston was surprised when, after a single gentle knock on the door, she came in. When she knocked, he had been lying on his bed, more than half asleep. It was the twenty minutes he allowed himself before dressing for an official dinner, and he did not expect to be broken in upon by anything less than a crisis: his annoyance vanished as soon as he saw her. He jumped up.

'I'm disturbing you,' she said.

It was purely a conventional gesture, but he answered seriously. 'No, you never disturb me.' As he made her comfortable in a chair, with a footstool and cushions, he noticed that she was flushed: her hands were shaking. 'Is something wrong?' he asked.

She looked at him as though he must know what was obsessing her. 'Rose has told me about the Durhams. It's horrible. Why didn't you tell me yesterday, Richard?'

'I'm sorry I didn't. I hate your hearing these things.'

'You didn't imagine I wouldn't t!' she said drily. 'It's true I never read the papers, but . . .' She shuddered slightly. 'I can still see that child who spat at me. Her eyes . . . Nothing is too bad for these wretched brutes, you must handle them as if they were animals. They are.' Her face changed curiously, as though something were at work below the delicate features to coarsen them. In a harsh voice, she asked, 'Has the scoundrel spoken yet?'

'No, not yet,' Ormston said, frowning. 'He's as stubborn as a pig.'

'You don't admire him for it, do you? Tell me—what are they doing to him?'

'Security has been questioning him, since nine o'clock

last night. They're keeping him awake.' With an inflection of distaste he added, 'In the end that works.'

'You should have him flogged,' Mrs. Ormston said, calmly.

He stifled a feeling of embarrassment, even shock. 'That won't be necessary, my dear. He's not mad.'

'He's infinitely worse.' She went on with the same arrogant calm. 'I could flog him myself.'

Her son smiled, involuntarily. 'You couldn't, you know.'

'Anything—I would do anything to end these horrors. The poor Durhams.' She closed her eyes, letting the bruised lids quiver against the dry skin below them. Suddenly, they lifted, and she gave him an anxious penetrating glance. 'There's something I ought to tell you,' she said gravely. 'I had a letter this morning from Cousin Gerald, my dear old Gerald.'

She paused. Ormston waited, unsmiling and bored, for the rest of it. He knew her dear Gerald too well to expect anything pleasant. The old man had been a house pet of every Prime Minister and Foreign Secretary during more than half a century: he was one of those perpetual filters of the political sewers through whom every secret, every scandal, flows sooner or later, is docketed, purified, and turned, as far as can be, into vapour: the filter itself remains pure. He was supposed to have written or be writing his memoirs; they might or might not be discreet, but undoubtedly they would have their poison drawn before, if ever, they were published. A wise fellow, Master Gerald, not likely, at his age, to muff his chances of an O.M., the only honour he wanted and would take.

'I don't like telling you this, my darling, but Gerald says there is a great deal of criticism of you in London—in important circles—and that it's growing . . . Perhaps I shouldn't tell you, but I felt I had to, it was a duty. You must forgive me.'

'It's hardly news to me that I have enemies'—his frigid bitterness was not meant for her, but she frowned—'or that at least one of them would be happy to see the situation here get worse and bloodier so long as it meant that *I* had failed.'

'I think Gerald could be useful to you,' she said coolly.

'I daresay.'

'Well, write to him, my dear. Ask him to help—no, to advise you—that's a better way to put it. A word from him in the right quarter . . . I could write, but I think he feels you have neglected him. He's just a little vain, dear old boy.'

At any other time he would have thanked her, and sat down to compose a letter neither too obviously a plea nor too aloof, which could be counted on to bring the filter into operation on his side. For some reason—he did not try to look at it closely, but it had something to do with Boyd, and his thoughts of Boyd, muttering on below everything else in his mind—he felt an extreme reluctance to do anything of the sort. In an obscure way he felt naked before Boyd—nothing to protect him from the other man's derisively appraising eye. It was an absurd feeling, and he could not shake it off.

'If you can write to him,' he said slowly, 'do. I don't care to.'

'A letter from me won't have the effect,' his mother said 'Why won't you——' she hesitated and went on in a lighter voice. 'One of the criticisms of you is that you're impatient, you too often cold shoulder people you think unimportant —at the time they may be, but things change—you keep them at arm's length, as if you were evading them. There's some truth in it, you know, my dear.'

'I've done my share of listening, and flattering,' Ormston said drily . . . *the right word for the right man at exactly the right moment* . . . 'If it appears to be to dear Cousin Gerald's

advantage to help me now, he will. If not . . .' He
shrugged.

The look of annoyance on his mother's face vanished as
quickly as it had come. 'Are you vexed with me for telling
you about his letter?'

'I rely on you with my whole heart,' he said warmly. Only
she and Andrew roused this warmth, this tenderness, in him,
poles distant from his love for other women. 'I can't
remember a time when I didn't.'

'I only told you because I'm anxious, I don't want anything to harm you—your career.' She smiled at him. 'I'm
so proud of you, so terribly ambitious for you. You are
my life, I haven't any other, or any ambitions except for
you.'

'I know,' he said.

Her ambition for him had brought sun and rain during
the whole of his childhood and youth. A bubble rose to the
surface of his mind: he saw himself enclosed in it, a thin tall
nervously alert sixteen-year-old, carrying the weight of her
ambitions about with him everywhere, at home where they
saw no one except each other (in those days dear Cousin
Gerald's relations with them were cooler and distant), at
school. This year, his sixteenth, he came under the only
influence that ever threatened her plans for him: a new
young master at Winchester, a classicist, succeeded in rousing in him a passion for Greek—succeeded very easily, as if
the fire had been laid and only needed a match, as if the only
thing he had ever wanted was to be a Greek scholar. He
had a feeling of release, and for two months he gave himself
up to his new dream with an intoxicated joy. He made
plans to visit Greece with half a dozen other boys the master
was going to take there in spring, to see for himself a
country he was already living in, a country of sculptured
ruins, vines, olives, lemon blossom, whitewashed walls
crossed by the shadows of swallows, thin and sharp in the

white Greek sun. At the end of that term, when he went home, his mother dealt quickly and surgically with this aberration, as if she were lancing a boil. He knew she was right—she must be right—but he suffered. He took care not to let her know that he was unhappy: he wanted her to approve of him, but more, far more, he wanted to see her smile, to feel that she was pleased with her life, happy. And soon enough he came to be grateful to her for having saved him from a grotesque childish idea before he had wasted too much time . . . She was tireless, he thought: she drove me, forcing me, my brains, my wits, to grow up ahead of time. But for her, I shouldn't have been anything—an obscure don, a schoolmaster . . .

Looking at her, he had the idea that a web of lines immediately under her skin was waiting to show itself on the surface: he felt a pang of grief, that she was old and had had so little pleasure in her life.

'I wish I had done more for you,' he said, with love.

'You were the only happiness I had,' she said in her cool voice. 'When you were a child, I mean. Now I can only watch you with pride, and feel uselessly anxious for you.'

'I always knew you were unhappy,' he said, 'always.'

He had had no intention of saying it: the words had sprung in his mind with the force of an explosion, throwing earth and stones on all sides: everything was in them, his awful feeling of being responsible for her, and the feeling of failure, even guilt, that it dragged after itself in his mind. But I didn't fail, he thought; I did everything I could . . .

His mother gave him a displeased stare and said sharply, 'What do you mean, my dear Richard?'

'As far as I can look back, I knew it. You were always self-possessed and very calm, and yet—long before I had the slightest notion what it was about—I could feel your unhappiness.' He pointed a finger at his chest, smiling. 'Here—I felt it here.'

'What nonsense!'

He was too intent on groping his way into the past to
notice that she was annoyed. 'That may be why I was so
eager to impress you with my cleverness.' He laughed.
'What a word—yet it's true, you know, my dear. You were
the *princesse lointaine*, the winter queen, the I don't know
what. I had to deserve you.'

She closed her eyes. 'Yes, you were a good boy. You
made up for other'—she hesitated—'disappointments.'

'I always meant to, you know.'

He had a brief memory of his desperate anxiety to give
her presents she would think worth having—a tiny distinct
image of her as a young woman, standing in his room and
turning over in her beautiful fingers some small object; the
expression on her face was ironical and aloof, as though she
were examining it from a distance. It must have been one
of my less successful efforts, he thought lightly.

Opening her eyes, she leaned forward and patted his arm.
'My *dear* boy.'

'It was quite a job to please you. You didn't easily please
yourself, did you?'

'What?'

'You used to look at yourself in the glass in your sitting-
room, a look of anger or disgust, as if you weren't at all
certain you liked what you saw. Once when I looked over
your shoulder, you turned and gave me a sharp slap. Do
you remember?'

'Why on earth should I? You must have done more than
look.'

He laughed. 'I don't suppose I was an attractive child.'

'You were mine,' his mother said calmly.

'What's the most satisfactory thing you remember?'

She seemed to reflect, and said, 'You never cried.'

'That's queer—I remember rushing to you, bawling,
crying like a calf, over something or other. What was it?'

'I don't remember anything of the sort,' she said, amused. She stood up. 'I must go, my dear. Rose has been waiting all this time to brush my hair.'

Crossing the room, she glanced round it, and stopped suddenly. She had caught sight of a photograph of herself on his dressing-chest. 'Where did you get that?' she asked, frowning. 'Did I give it to you?'

'You never gave me a photograph of yourself in your life.' He smiled. 'I stole it—years ago, when I was going up to Oxford. It's usually in a drawer with handkerchiefs —I took it out only the other day and put it up there.'

'Put it away again,' she said, with something very like anger. 'Please.'

'My dear, why?'

'It's not a good one—I dislike it—you must throw it away ... Or give it to me to throw away.'

She reached for it, and he stood in her way. 'No, no, leave it, I'll keep it out of sight.'

'Mind you do,' she said.

At the door he stooped to kiss her, but she moved past him quickly, with the energy she could use when she liked.

Alone, he looked at her photograph for a moment before laying it in the drawer he pulled open. Without knowing why, he felt a little resentment—on behalf of the photograph itself, he thought. It had been taken when she was a young woman, probably in her late twenties: in spite of the care he had taken of it, it had faded, but the delicate features, with their air of elegance and strength of will, were distinct enouth. There was something in the shape of the mouth that baffled him, something a little cold, something, perhaps, of the self-dislike he had seen or imagined in her reflection in the glass ... It was true, what he had told her—even as a very young child he had the feeling that her serenity was a lie and a sham. The feeling existed in him before, long before he knew anything about the griefs and disappoint-

ments of her life. As if the way she lived—and the way she
did not live, her self-deprivations, her strict refusal to ask
any soul for help—and her anger at having to live like this,
were infecting him, her child. As if there were a direct
nerve stretched between them, between his unknowing
childish mind and her cruelly stifled rage and longings. As
if he were a little sponge soaking up the waters of a dark,
a bottomless pool . . . Without warning, the moment when
he ran to her, 'bawling and crying like a calf', rose to the
surface of his mind, dragging up with it all the bewilderment and loneliness of his first months, as a day-boy, in the
preparatory school his mother had chosen for him (her
father paying the fees), a school meant less for the rich—
though these were not discouraged from sending their
children—as for the sons of the powerful and well-born:
it was a group of these who had been moved to tell him in
public that he was a vulgar mannerless little beast. He did
not remember now what he had said or done to bring this
searing humiliation on himself, but he could touch the scar
and he remembered running home afterwards and standing
in his mother's room, beside her chair, in an agony of shame
and tears . . . And that was all he remembered. What she
had said to comfort him had dropped out of his memory.
His imagination supplied it, easily: he felt her hand stroking
his hair, and heard her warm gentle voice (as he remembered
it) of those days, saying, 'Don't cry so, it's all right, we're
both here, both safe, little idiot, little love.'

CHAPTER EIGHTEEN

At this moment he recalled that during the afternoon his wife had sent a message asking him to see her before dinner. He was tempted—how he was tempted—to ignore her altogether, or at least to put her off. But she counted for so little—nothing—in his life, he knew so little about her and was indifferent to what he knew . . . reasons for taking no less trouble with her than he would take with any stranger who had the right to ask him for attention. I can spare her ten minutes, he thought coldly, not more.

To his relief, when he went into her room the monkey was nowhere in sight. Glancing round, he said,

'Sophie, I wish to heaven you'd do something about this room—or let my mother do something, if you can't bother with it yourself. It's hideously uncomfortable.'

'I like it,' his wife said.

'That's exactly what I complain of.'

'It doesn't matter,' she said, with an equivocal smile, half mocking, half friendly, 'you never come here unless I ask you.'

'I come as soon as you do . . . What did you want, my dear?'

She glanced away from him. 'You're sending Andrew into the country, aren't you?'

Now what is she after? he wondered. 'Yes. To Zante.'

'Don't,' she murmured, 'don't do it, Richard.'

He frowned in an effort to hide his impatience. 'My dear girl, why not? It will do him a world of good—give him a little change.'

In a hesitant voice she said, 'He has only two or three more weeks here. I don't see him often.'

He felt a little sorry for her, and irritated. 'My poor

Sophie, you don't, surely, expect a young man to want to hang round his parents. Andrew is twenty-two.'

A muted stubborn look came into her face. 'He likes being with you.'

A somewhat different matter, he thought lightly. 'All this is rather foolish, my dear. I don't want the boy to waste the whole of his time here; he can be useful to Colonel Graham, if only to fill out dockets—two of Graham's officers are on sick leave.' She did not speak, and he went on in a sharper voice, 'Has he complained to you?'

'No, of course not.'

'Very well, then.'

She was silent a moment, then lifted her head abruptly and looked at him with surprising coolness. 'Why did you marry me, Richard?'

Twenty-three years is a long time, in an exacting life, to remember what decent reasons you gave yourself at the time for doing a shabby thing. Glancing at her, to get his bearings in her erratic thoughts, he noticed that she was paler than usual: for a galling moment, he saw her in the dress she had worn for her wedding in the fashionable London church; it had been made by one of the great houses, it was chalk white, and quenched pitiably what looks she had. She ought never to have been put into such a dress. She held herself rigid, frowning: her hand, when he took hold of it to place the ring, was icily cold.

He was unable to keep his exasperation out of his voice. 'Ought you to ask me that now?' he said drily.

'I know why. For my money . . . It's not in the least important.'

His exasperation died in him . . . He had meant to behave well, give her an interesting dignified life, be kind, attentive to her within reason, and to see to it that any children they had were groomed from the cradle for successful lives. Was it his fault that the only part of this design which was ever carried out was the last? His fault that she had become a spectator, avoiding like the plague public men and occasions, whenever she could? She chose her place, he thought. Let her keep it. He said kindly,

'Even if that were true it would be a foolish thing to say, foolish and harmful—to your self-respect as much as mine. If I hadn't had a great respect for you I shouldn't have wanted to marry you—and you can't have thought too badly of me'—he made an effort to smile at her—'or not at the time. I don't ill-treat you, do I?'

She looked down at her small folded hands. 'Respect? Yes, of course. I'm talking nonsense. I'm sorry.'

He waited a moment, then said,

'The reason I'm sending Andrew away is to get him out of Miss Leng's claws.'

'Haven't you done that already?' she murmured.

'You can't be sure of the young.' He felt a prick of rage. 'They're capable—even the most self-possessed and intelligent—of abysmal silliness.'

One of her furtive smiles crossed her face. 'If that's true, you can never have been young.'

'Possibly not.' He stood up.

'Don't go for a minute,' she said rapidly. 'Tell me something—you hate this girl, don't you? Quite unreasonably. Why?'

He said impatiently, 'Unreasonable? It's reasonable enough, in all conscience. But in fact I don't hate her—why should I? All I'm doing is save the boy from making a ruinous mistake—now, when he could so easily spoil his whole life. Surely, my dear girl, you can understand that?'

'You hate her,' his wife repeated. 'I'll tell you why you do. Because she's taking Andrew from you, and you can't, can you, let yourself hate *him* for going.'

The anger he felt shocked him by its violence. He stifled it and said,

'What nonsense! Why on earth should I hate him?'

'You hate us all,' she told him in a matter-of-fact voice.

'My dear Sophie!'

'Andrew, you know, loves you——'

'I'm sure of it.'

She threw her hands up. 'Then why, why are you afraid he doesn't? Why can't you forgive him for turning from you to his girl? You might have expected that.'

His anger swept back, hardening in him so that he found it difficult to breathe. 'I didn't expect him to pick up a shoddy little whore.'

'My poor Richard,' she said after a moment, softly. 'If you believe that, it gives you all the excuse you need for getting rid of her. But is she?'

'You don't know what you're saying,' he said coldly. 'You're over-tired. Why don't you lie down for a few minutes before dinner?'

She smiled. 'I'm wasting your time.'

'Yes.' He frowned. 'That's abominably rude. Forgive me.'

'It doesn't matter,' she said lightly. 'But tell me one thing. Your mother . . . what does she think about it?'

'You must know what she thinks. That the girl couldn't be more of a disaster—no family, no money, and a trollop.'

'Your mother is extravagantly moral, isn't she? I've sometimes felt that she would be more comfortable if she weren't.'

The look of mockery on her face startled him. He had an absurd idea that he must get away before she said something irreparable. What could she say? he thought, vexed with himself. He did not want to believe that she was capable of surprising him; in the same instant he remembered that she had said something like this once before, years before. It was during the period when his mother was still trying patiently to mould her. A young servant in the house had turned out to be a thief—and pregnant as well—and Mrs. Ormston naturally sacked her. Sophie revoked the dismissal. He was in the room when his mother told her, kindly, that she couldn't be allowed to do it. Staring at her fixedly, from a shut face, Sophie did not speak. After a few minutes he felt that his mother had said enough, and he was on the point of intervening to help Sophie over the embarrassment she must be feeling, when she said calmly, 'You are altogether too moral. The girl will stay until she wants to go, she is my business, not yours.'—'You haven't understood,' Mrs. Ormston began, 'she's a slut——' Sophie cut her short, with the direct contempt of a child. 'It's you who haven't understood—or you've forgotten—that I pay the servants' wages . . .' This was the only and the last time she showed any hostility to his mother, any resentment. And, he thought, sharply, the only time she had spoken of her money . . .

He wanted to get away. 'Forgive me,' he said again, 'I haven't time now.'

She did not speak.

Closing the door, he pushed her out of his mind in such haste that her image, small and featureless, spun dizzily away to reach almost at once its normal state and place as a barely visible pencil mark on the margin of his thoughts.

Before ringing for his servant he telephoned to police headquarters. In an edged voice Frent told him that X was on the point of giving in.

'Are you sure?' he asked, with a leap of the heart.

'A matter of hours or minutes.'

'Good.' He added coolly, 'You've done well.'

'Thank you, sir.'

Putting the receiver down, he wondered for a second whether he had imagined a sarcastic inflection in Frent's voice. Relief overwhelmed him, relief, triumph, almost, quivering in him, an acute feeling of pleasure. And why not?

Who had a better right to enjoy his power than a man to whom it had not been handed (as to dear old Gerald) on a piece of the family plate? I earned my authority, he thought; it's mine by right of conquest, of discipline, and of knowing how to use it, decently . . . He felt a contemptuous pity for Boyd. I knew we should break him, he thought, smiling.

He had a moment's malicious joy at the thought of two or three imbeciles who were going to have to sing very small when he talked to them in London next week. Very small indeed, damn them. As always he had been justified. As always. I've never yet had a bad failure, he thought.

The excitement he was trying to suppress turned in him and became an access of purely physical energy. If I could go to Anne, he thought briefly, and thought in the same breath of the man sitting dirty and humiliated in Frent's room: he shuddered with a happiness he did not care to look at closely.

CHAPTER NINETEEN

Two days later, on Thursday evening, Boyd was still holding out, still, after four days and nights, being questioned hour after hour, his questioners succeeding each other in relays, and still mute or outrageously, often obscenely mocking. Frent reported twice a day to the Governor, who had begun to dislike the sound of his voice so intensely that he caught himself wondering why Boyd did not give in if only to be rid of it boring through his ears into his brain like a dentist's tool. He had rejected the impulse to see Boyd again, and he was obsessed by him: images of Boyd, thoughts, fragments of dialogue, ground into the back of his skull all day, behind everything else he was thinking or saying, lay down with him at night, corroding his dreams, and pressed against his eyelids as he woke. The pity, little generous as it was, that he had felt for his friend when he believed he had given in, sank in a swell of rage and exasperation. At moments he felt that if he could flog Boyd's secrets out of him he would do it.

The conference arranged for that morning filled him with an extraordinary and very disagreeable sense of futility. There they sat, the general, two of his staff, and Frent, going methodically over all the details of the plan he was taking to London next week, and it was like nothing so much as chewing sawdust. He felt it irritating his nostrils and throat. The day, too, was the most unpleasant for a long time, heat pouring from an open furnace on to the stones and dust of the city, piling up in the narrow streets like a dam that must burst, but did not, only swelled, heavy, suffocating. Inside, the shutters cut off the violence of the light, but the room was airless, and the absent Boyd more stubbornly turbulently present than any of the five persons round the table.

Even Frent, always at these conferences as alert as a cocked pistol, was lethargic. Brooding, the Governor thought maliciously, on his failure. He roused himself once. An incautious question about 'your prisoner' from one of the staff officers drew a spat of rage so unlike his normal dry temper that the startled officer apologised.

When the conference broke up, he did not leave with the others. Standing stiffly—even his eyeballs seemed to have stiffened and yellowed—he asked,

'Can you give me five minutes?'

'Certainly,' the Governor said. 'Sit down . . . You want to talk about Boyd.'

'Yes.' A curious dullness came over his face; it seemed to thicken the flesh. 'It's quite obvious, sir, that we're not going to break him by normal methods. The fellow——' he broke off, with savage impatience. 'Any sense of shame is completely lacking, and shame, y'know, is what usually breaks a man of his class, an educated man.'

Instinctively the Governor avoided trying to understand what this meant, what sort of pressure had been put on Boyd in the effort to humiliate him. 'What do you propose to do?'

Frent paused very briefly. 'To try what can be done by rather less orthodox methods.'

'Aren't there drugs?' the Governor said. As he said it he had the sensation of being tapped on the shoulder by a hand he knew to be hostile.

Frent's eyes were fixed on him. 'There are.'

The beating of the Governor's heart slowly quietened. He stood up, and walked over to the bookshelves: standing there, in a pretence of searching, with his back to Frent, he said,

'I'd better see him again.'

'If you think it will be any use,' Frent began. Realising his gaffe, he said quickly, 'I should be immensely grateful, sir, if you would. When——'

'Today,' the Governor interrupted. 'This evening. Possibly very late.' He turned round. 'I'll let you know.' Frent did not move at once and he said, 'I'm sorry to have to hurry you out. I have an appointment.'

The appointment was one he would have been delighted to avoid. It was with the father of the murdered young nurse. He had been flown out from England, from the market garden he owned and worked, to look at her before she was buried: his wife was dead and she his only child: for this reason among others the Governor had decided to condole with him himself. He came into the room, hesitantly, his shoulders bent as if under the weight of an infant, his lower lip hanging open a little. The Governor waited for him to seat himself awkwardly, sat down facing him, and said his phrases of grief and regret with all the sincerity he could bring into his voice. The father listened, with an expression of severity which did not seem at ease in his patient weathered face of a market-gardener; his hands with their blackened wrinkles and short nails gripped the sides of his chair. Suddenly, he drew a long rattling breath, and started to cry: he made no attempt to wipe the tears pouring down his cheeks: lolling in his chair, his body trembling, he breathed like a wounded animal. He had as little dignity. 'How could they hurt her?' he stuttered. 'She was only little . . . there were bruises on her . . .'

Rigid with discomfort, the Governor waited until the agony was beginning to wear itself out, then said gently,

'She was very brave.'

'Yes, but why did they do it?' her father said.

Already calmer, he pulled himself together, rubbing his grey badly-shaved cheeks with both hands. 'I'm sorry I've troubled you,' he muttered, 'you must excuse me, I'm not used to this sort of thing.' He got up stiffly. 'Can I go now?'

Does he look on this as part of his ordeal? the Governor

thought. As soon as he had seen the man out, he felt his own weariness. He sat for a minute, eyes closed. He had told Robin to come in, after a quarter of an hour, if the market-gardener were still there, and when he heard the door opening he looked up, with a feeling of affection. There was something better than pleasant in the sight of his secretary's young clear face, its smoothness untroubled by any objectionable or inexpedient passions. It was like a cool bath.

'What's my dinner-party this evening, Robin? Something quite unimportant, isn't it?'

Robin allowed himself the faintest of smiles. 'You are giving Mr. Letterby dinner, sir. Alone. He's flying home tomorrow.'

'Ah, the Labour fellow, yes. Boisterous, smokes a cigar, and has the answers at the end of his tongue. There's something wrong with a system which throws these fellows up as leaders. They don't think, they feel . . . Colonel Frent has had time to get back, I think. Ring him up and tell him I'll be with him this evening before eleven. That gives Letterby as much time to unburden himself as he deserves.' Catching a gleam of excitement in his secretary's eyes, before the smooth lids dropped prudently, he smiled. 'No, our prisoner hasn't uttered yet.'

'Isn't that unusual, sir?'

The Governor gave way to the temptation to startle him. 'No, it's not so surprising, he—I didn't tell you this, did I? —he's an Englishman.'

'Good God, is he really?' Robin stammered. He became for a moment the adolescent he may have been before he taught himself to control his eyelids and even his appetite for sweets (he was afraid of spoiling his skin) and said excitedly, 'Shooting is too good for him, we ought to hang him.'

Ormston looked at him with an amused friendly irony.

'There are moments when you make me feel very old, dear boy.'

His secretary blushed.

Well-fed, well-wined, and with the conviction that he had made an excellent impression on a courteously attentive and intelligent Governor, the guest was eased out of Government House soon after ten o'clock. Two minutes after he had left, Ormston was on his way to police headquarters.

It was still warm, with a hot south wind shuffling through dry shrubs and bringing a smell of resin and charred leaves from the fire started somewhere in the hills. The streets were a confusion of dark mouths opening into a silence broken only by his car, and once by the stifled crying of a very young child behind the black rectangle of a window. Ormston had the ludicrous idea that he was following a scent through the darkness of his and Boyd's past, a scent laid underground and crossed by others he ignored. He forced himself to lean back in the car and empty his mind of all thought of the man he was going to see. When he saw him would be time to decide what attitude to take with him: it is a mistake to prepare a scene too carefully beforehand, all the more when one member of it is as erratic, as unaccountable, as tiresomely emotional as Boyd. The effort he made to calm himself succeeded—or at least filled the time it took him to reach headquarters. In a corner of his mind a half-inaudible voice went on repeating fatuously that the game was going to be played out tonight, win or lose . . .

This time Boyd was brought to him in a small room, Frent's sitting-room, a very bare place, furnished with two armchairs, a table, a standard lamp and a narrow bookcase. He looked with a little curiosity at the titles of the books— military histories, with a sprinkling of books about birds and bird-watching. The sound of some heavy thing being dragged across the landing gave him a prick of alarm, and he swung round to watch the door open. He felt instant relief when he saw Boyd standing in the doorway. He had not been handcuffed, and he was grasping the frame of the door with one hand: with the other he made a vague gesture of greeting, then passed it across his face. In a slurred voice he drawled,

'They might have shaved me for you, I think . . . May I sit down?'

He rocked a little on his feet and blinked grotesquely puffed eyelids at the light. The two guards behind were not looking at him, but at the Governor. Ormston waved them away: they went out, closing the door.

Shambling across the room, Boyd dropped into an arm-chair. His head lolled forward, as though the neck had snapped, he breathed without a sound. He was asleep.

'Anthony!' the Governor said sharply.

He felt dismay, and then a weak horror. He had not tried to imagine the effect on the other man of four sleepless days and nights. Now that he saw it, it shocked him. Boyd's face seemed to have shrunk; it was the colour of a dirty yellowish-grey rag, and was in truth dirty, with a line of thick dark bristle up the cheeks and covering the lower part of his face. He had slumped sideways in the chair, his arms hanging as though he had died of sleep.

Ormston had been watching him for a full minute before the thought jumped into his mind: I ought not to let him sleep, it will help him . . . He made a guilty movement towards repairing the damage he might have done, and hesitated, torn between pity and exasperation. Why the devil, he thought irritably, need he have got himself into this mess?

Already Boyd's face had changed, softened. His full lips, bloodless, pouted like a sleeping child's; in spite of being swollen and inflamed, the closed eyelids with their fringe of black lashes were those of a young man, and the pursed mouth had a disturbing look of warmth, almost tenderness. Ormston felt grief and love. My poor Anthony, he thought. Guilt pricked him again: bending down, he shook Boyd gently—without the slightest effect: he was too far gone. Disgusted by himself, by his weakness, Ormston began to shake him violently from side to side. At last Boyd opened one eye and groaned, his chin trembling: the eye closed at once. Lifting him bodily by the shoulders, Ormston dragged him from the chair and held him up, a life-sized puppet, limbs dangling. Boyd opened both eyes and said thickly,

'Oh, it's you, is it? What do you want?'

'Wake up, for God's sake,' Ormston said.

'Leave me alone, Ricky, there's a good chap.'

'I must talk to you,' Ormston said loudly.

Boyd made an effort to rouse himself, muttering something under his breath.

'What d'you say?'

'If you *must* talk,' Boyd said, 'I shall have to stand up.' He stiffened, swayed, lurched as far as the bookcase, and leaned his back against it. 'What the hell is the use of this?' he grumbled. 'Didn't your policemen tell you that I'm not on speaking terms with them?' He smiled briefly. 'Nor with you, old boy, if your conversation runs on the same cretinous lines as theirs.'

Between grief and anger, Ormston lost his head and shouted at him. 'How in God's name, you fool, did you get into this?'

Boyd smiled again. 'Into what, Ricky, into what?'

'Into ruining this poor helpless country'—he had a brief vision of the face of the dead young nurse as her father may have seen it—'killing, defiling, destroying—robbing ordinary men and women of their simple decent lives and chance of happiness . . .'

'Why,' Boyd drawled, 'I believe you care. Extraordinary.

Funny Ricky—no end to the surprises you give me.' His voice changed, sharpening. 'But *you* are robbing them. Why don't you give them their freedom? It's as simple as that.'

'Don't talk your bloody nonsense to me,' Ormston said thinly. 'What does a little clerk, or a market-gardener, or a young woman, or a child care about freedom? They care about peace, bread and a handful of olives. They had all that before your friends began murdering.'

Boyd looked at him with a gleam of mockery in eyes that seemed part of the raw flesh of their sockets. 'Bread and a handful of olives—idyllic, eh? I didn't know you were a poet, Ricky.'

'I'm a sane man,' Ormston said, stung into a resentment he felt as contempt, 'not a terrorist with the heartless certainty that he can behave as foully as he likes because he has noble motives. I know better than you that there's a political problem here. We'll solve it when we've stopped the murders—not before.'

'Why didn't you solve it before they started?' Boyd said in a mild voice, yawning.

Irritated by his indifference, Ormston said, 'And why have you, you, taken a hand in it? They're not your people.'

'Yes, I know, it's absurd of me. I ought to be thinking of my career and licking the right boots. If I'd done that I might be an Excellency now instead of——'

Ormston cut him short. 'You have a filthy tongue.'

'Yes. Yes, I'm sorry,' Boyd said gently.

Ormston's feeling of anguish returned. 'I don't understand you. I don't understand why any man turns traitor —least of all you. I wish to God I did.'

Boyd moved a hand, wincing, across his eyes: the hand was no filthier than the rest of him, but it left a mark like a bruise on one temple. With the same gentleness he said,

'My dear Ricky, you wouldn't even know what I was

talking about if I said that, in the society we live in—without graces, without God—yapped at by a pack of officials to keep in line, suffocated by easy lies, without a touch, not one touch, of exaltation, if you know what I mean—you don't of course—the single hope a human being has left is to find a purpose greater than himself and his boredom and appetites, and serve it. It's his only chance to be free! Why, even a communist, serving his stupid bloody god, is freer than our respectable money-sweating bridge-playing *salauds*, or'—his bloodless lips twitched in a grimace of delighted irony—'an Excellency.'

'I didn't know you'd become a mystic,' Ormston said drily.

Boyd laughed. 'A minute ago I was a murderer.'

'You're that, too,' Ormston said. Something like a jet of hate sprang in him at a depth he could not reach to cut it off, a cold furious wish to punish the other man—but for what? For his treachery, for the young woman's dead bruised face? Or to wipe out the sick grief he felt, and could not help feeling, for all he knew that it was no better than moral cowardice, and was bitterly ashamed of it. 'You and your friends are not the first brutes to invent a religion as an excuse for killing, but you . . . when I think of some of your victims, your heroics look peculiarly indecent. Even for an idealist.'

'We do filthy things—yes,' Boyd said under his breath. He hesitated and said roughly, 'You're so much stronger than we are. You—you force us to fight as we do.'

'Then don't, damn you, complain that we treat you as terrorists ought to be treated—like mad dogs.'

Boyd lurched forward and clutched the edge of the table to save himself. 'Temper, Master Richard, temper!'

'Do you think I'm losing my temper?'

'No. I don't. You haven't enough warmth in you to do it, you cold fish.'

Ormston smiled. 'Don't you even know you're absurd —a conceited play-boy'—he groped for the phrase that might touch off his friend's peevish arrogance—'playing at soldiers and bringing off wonderful victories, the old woman your boys executed a few days ago, the schoolmaster they trussed up and——'

'Shut up,' Boyd said. Between rage and exhaustion his voice was out of control: it rose, cracking farcically. 'You'll find out sooner or later what sort of playing at soldiers I——' he checked himself sharply, stretching his lips to show his white teeth, startlingly white in his grey shrunken face. 'No, no, Ricky, you're very clever, cleverer than Frent—or you know me better—but I'm not so easily caught. Not these days . . . You resent me, don't you?'

'Why should I resent you, you poor fool?'

Boyd went off into a loud crowing laugh, his laugh as a schoolboy, absurdly unchanged. 'Why? Because I've done more than anyone to get you a black mark. We hear things, you know, in our play-boy hide-outs. There was a lot of money on you, my boy, when you came out here. There's less now, your stock's down quite a few points.'

The temptation to speak in his own voice for a moment seized Ormston: he gave way to it with relief. 'Your one real achievement,' he said bitterly.

Boyd looked at him with love. 'I wish it hadn't been you.'

Turning, Ormston walked away from him to the window. 'This room is suffocating,' he muttered. He opened the window, dragging at the shutters, and leaned out. In the last hour a half-moon had come up: below it a mesh of white spumy cloud moved slowly, thinning as it spread, like foam lifting and sliding on smooth grape-black waves. He heard a slithering noise and turned to see Boyd collapse at the foot of the bookcase. He reached him at a run, but Boyd was only asleep, his breath bubbling between parted lips. Ormston put his arms under the soiled body and pulled it up, shaking it; the breath from it nauseated him and he pushed it roughly against the bookcase, watching the eyes open again, empty.

'Anthony, for God's sake,' he said desperately, 'come to your senses. I beg you, I beg you. Drop this filthy thing, help us, help me to stop the cruelty—useless—the horrible slime of fear everywhere . . . I beg you.'

The look that came slowly into the emptiness of Boyd's eyes was purely and youthfully malicious. 'Beg away,' he said in a gay hoarse voice, 'I enjoy it.'

A sour anger filled Ormston, rising in him until he could taste it. 'We can force you to speak.'

Boyd raised his eyebrows. 'Just what do you mean?'

If he said: I have no idea what I mean, he would be telling as much of the truth as he knew. He made an effort and pushed past the confusion in his mind. 'So far you've been handled with kid gloves . . .' The stupidity of what he was saying sickened him and he stopped.

'You're thinking of taking them off?' Boyd asked, grinning.

'You . . . I don't believe you even know why you like to pose as a saviour of the oppressed. It flatters your shocking vanity . . . I called you a mad dog—you're not one, though you've been busy turning other men, younger than you are and malleable, into obscene animals—you're a man who, God knows why, has chosen to turn against his friends and to——'

Boyd interrupted him. 'You're the only friend I have,' he said.

His simplicity caught Ormston across the throat: a hard knot of shame and pity rose in it, choking him. He forced himself to ignore it. 'You've chosen'—he paused, and went on with a dry irony—'chosen to serve evil.'

'I see. I begin to see,' Boyd murmured. He lifted his

hands and passed them over his face, grimacing when they touched the rough bristles. A muscle in his face twitched and kept on twitching. 'Yes, I see. If I'm evil, you can do anything'—he pressed on the word—'anything to destroy me, because I'm a louse.' With a flickering mischief he said, 'Ricky the brave louse-killer.'

'You have only to tell us the truth,' Ormston shouted. He heard himself shouting, and thought: What's the matter with me? I'm making a fool of myself, I'm ill. 'I'll do my best for you—only tell me the truth, so that I can put an end to this squalid business before any more innocent people have been killed, any more bestial scenes like the one your friends staged three days ago in a decent little village. I give you my word I'll help you. I mean it, Anthony. I'll see you're not punished too harshly . . . I'll try . . .'

'It wouldn't be the first time, would it?'

Ormston was silent.

'All I have to do is speak.'

'Yes.'

'And give away men who are relying on me . . . Don't try to drive me, Ricky.'

'You're driving me,' Ormston said, with despair.

A pause, then Boyd said, 'Have it your own way.' He was smiling.

'Anthony, I beg you.'

This time the silence stretched out. At last Boyd yawned, and asked, 'Have you forgotten the game we used to play when we were brats, the summer you stayed with me?'

Taken aback, Ormston frowned. 'What game are you talking about? We played every sort.'

'One we invented,' Boyd said. Incredibly, a note of eager gaiety came into his voice. 'We called it Last Score—Ricky, you can't have forgotten! It went on all day, we arranged the night before to start it the instant we woke, and we went

on, scoring off each other in every conceivable way—and
some barely conceivable—under the noses of my innocent
parents until we were actually in bed again at night——'

'The last to score before we were both in bed had won.'

Boyd gave his crowing laugh. 'That's it, you've got it.'

Furious with himself, Ormston said drily, 'This isn't a
game, damn you.'

'I know, I know,' Boyd said. He grinned. 'But I can't
live up to you, you're too pompous, too much the Excellency,
too high-minded and successful . . .' He yawned as though
his jaws were loose, staggered, and fell into the armchair.

'Listen to me—this is your last chance,' Ormston said.
Why am I talking? he asked himself. It's no good, he's
corrupted beyond hope, finished, not worth the trouble of
saving, not worth . . . A pain like the severing of a nerve
distracted him.

'Persistent devil you are,' Boyd muttered.

His voice trailed off. He was asleep.

For a minute, Ormston stood looking down at him. His
body had collapsed inwards; a lock of hair, matted with
sweat, lay over one cheek, his hands had fallen lifelessly
one on top of the other, his face was that of a sick ageing
man—yet with the shadow across it of a younger face with
smooth full mouth and long eyelashes. It would be no use
trying to rouse him again.

Ormston noted all this with some other faculty than
thought: he did not touch the other man, but the darkness
and vacancy of his mind somehow received the impression
of his face and body, as if passing a blind hand over them.
After a minute he moved, and opened the door. The two
guards were squatting, backs against the wall, at the other
side of the landing. They jumped up.

'Take him away,' the Governor said.

They came in quickly and looked at Boyd. A glance passed
between them. Without a word, with a sort of clumsy

gentleness, instead of rousing him they picked him up and carried him away asleep.

The Governor watched them go with their burden. Suddenly, in the half-darkness at the head of the stairs, he noticed a man who was also watching. The lieutenant—what was his name? Hadham. The quick dark eyes in his oddly triangular face were fixed on the prisoner's body, not as though seeing it, but as though searching it, feeling in it for some place he knew was there and had not found. He was so absorbed that he did not see the Governor.

Ormston had the same—come and gone in an instant—sense of recognition that he had had the first time he saw this man. This time it could be simply the memory of a face already seen once. But it was not a recognition of that sort, it was knowledge, riddling, reluctant, obscurely felt. He had a strong impulse of distaste or fear, and went back into the room, leaving the door open.

CHAPTER TWENTY

HE was alone for a moment. His mind was still disordered, with a thread of anguish floating in the darkness behind his eyes. Frent's voice from the doorway fell across it like a clap of light. It blinded him. He turned slowly.

'What did you say?'

Frent came into the room, closing the door. 'Did you have any luck, sir?'

'No.' He had a momentary feeling of annoyance, knowing that the police chief had expected him to fail. 'Who is that young officer—Hadham?'

'Who is he, sir? I brought him out with me—an ex-commando, a very good soldier, and a good officer. Left the army at the end of the war, and I think had a shot at business. He applied to me to get him back, and I was glad to do it.'

'Have I seen him before?'

'I think you saw him the night they got Boyd——'

'No, before that.'

Faintly and politely surprised, Frent said, 'I don't know, sir.'

'It's of no importance.'

There was a silence. He realised that he was stupefyingly tired. I made a fool of myself, it was a mistake to come here, he thought. He forced himself to attend to Frent, who was talking in a low voice which suddenly reminded the Governor of the rats scraping about under the heaps of dry straw in one of the disused stables belonging to Boyd's father.

'Do you feel, sir, that there is any justification for letting the fellow hold us up in this way? He knows things that might—certainly would—allow us'—he made a curious gesture, thumb and index finger curved towards each other

—'to pick out the eyes and nerve centres of the rebellion. Like that . . . From being an active growing body it would become a heap of *disjecta membra* we could deal with easily —oh, easily.' He waited for the Governor's comment: getting none, he said, 'This being so, sir, I wonder whether we haven't—already—gone beyond reasonable limits of patience.'

The Governor was silent. Not because he was trying to find a way out of the other's reasoning—there was no way out. He had a momentary sense that he was standing much too close to Frent, suffocatingly close. Stepping back a little, he said,

'He's in the last stages of exhaustion. You don't feel that further questioning . . . ?'

With more than his usual deference, Frent said, 'Do you yourself feel that another appeal to him would have any effect?'

A silence.

'No.'

'Neither will exhaustion,' Frent said.

An intolerable impatience seized the Governor: he would have liked to push Frent bodily away. 'You knew, didn't you, that I shouldn't do any good.'

Something not quite a smile crossed Frent's thin mouth. 'I'm afraid I did, sir.' His voice rose and hardened. 'A man wicked enough to join—not only to join, but to train men to fight his own people—fight bestially—is not likely to be moved by an appeal to his decent instincts. In fact, I doubt if he has such instincts.' He paused. 'If I may say so, we're up against something purely evil.'

Pure evil, the Governor thought ironically: what a phrase! Yet it's the right one, it's the truth . . . He felt a spasm of rage against Boyd—only because of his stubbornness. 'We've been wasting time.'

Frent did not speak.

'Well,' the Governor said, 'what's your suggestion?'

Cocking his head back, Frent said briskly, 'Sir, will you approve the use of other means to get the facts out of him?'

The question: What other means? rose in the Governor's mind with extreme distinctness, in one piece, like an inscription on stone. He glanced at it, as it were in passing, without paying too much attention to it, so that a moment later it had faded. Instead, he thought of Boyd's talk about Last Score, and his half boast. The conviction that it was frantically urgent to get the information took possession of him suddenly—and gave him a feeling of relief and detachment, very pleasant. He said easily,

'Yes.'

'Any means?' Frent repeated, with the barest perceptible stress.

'Yes.' His fatigue rushed over him again, and he felt giddy. 'My God, I'm tired.'

'You carry terrible burdens, sir,' Frent said in a discreetly warm tone.

The Governor glanced at him with indifference. Was there ever a worse bore? . . . That was all he felt: boredom. He turned to go.

CHAPTER TWENTY-ONE

THE windows of the dining-room in the Astoria overlooked a strip of garden, dry, nearly unkempt, not more than a dozen feet of parched earth and shrubs between the windows and the low hedge which was all that separated the hotel from the street. Since the evening two years ago when a hand grenade lobbed into the room killed one customer and wounded three others, every window was protected by a steel screen. In spite of the screen, diners had a tendency to sit farther back, and what had been a coveted table, set in the recess formed by an angle of the wall, a window and two absurd and useless pillars, was rarely asked for. Partly because he had not lived here long—not long enough to have become cautious—Andrew had been in the habit of asking for it when he brought Sarah here: partly, too, because it gave them the illusion of sitting in a narrow room cut off from the rest. Fewer inquisitive eyes could watch the Governor's son dining or lunching with Charles Cumberland's step-daughter.

When, earlier that evening, he rang her up and asked her to see him, and after a moment during which sweat broke out on him she answered, 'I could come to the Astoria about eight,' without thinking at all he said,

'Right. Our table, then.'

There was another silence. In an uncertain voice—was she laughing?—she stammered, '*Our* table? Very well.'

The dining-room was three-quarters empty—a measure of the tension and growing uneasiness in the colony. Waiting for her at their table, his back to the window, Andrew had nothing in front of him but a line of immaculate table-cloths and clusters of wine glasses, but no guests. He might have been alone in the place.

Sarah was late. Suspense—not the reasonable suspense that had emptied the room—twisted the nerves at the centre of his body into a tight knot. If she had changed her mind . . . He leaned forward, pressing himself against the edge of the table, to endure the knot and the thought that, if she had indeed decided not to come, he had no idea, not the slightest, what to do about it.

She was there suddenly—walking across the room towards him with the quick slouching step of a schoolgirl. Like the schoolgirl, too, she had, he noticed as she sat down, a streak of ink across the back of her hand. It gave him an absurd piercing joy.

'Ink on your hand,' he said.

She glanced at it carelessly. 'It wouldn't come off, it's indelible.'

Since no one else in the room was better worth his attention, the head waiter had come to the table and was standing, with the impersonal friendliness of a minor royalty, between the pillars. Andrew took the card from him and pretended to examine it.

'What would you like, Sarah?'

'I don't mind. Choose for me.'

He chose almost at random. Pointing to it, he said, 'I ordered a martini for you. Was that right?'

'Thank you.'

For the first time since she came in, she looked him in the face. He thought she was going to speak, and waited, but she said nothing: neither did he, and they looked at each other across the table in a silence Andrew felt no impulse to break. Something, he said to himself, has been decided, already . . . as if his life until this moment in the amiably meaningless room, with its fake baroque panels and chandeliers, had been an irrelevance, or a time of waiting, which had ended when she came in. Excitement and gaiety swelled in him, pressing against his ribs. They were making him lightheaded. Whatever happens, he thought, whatever has happened, I am going to marry her. He made an effort to think coolly: Why? There was only one answer to this grotesquely silly question: Because she is who she is and what she is, and the one person I can live with for the rest of my life, for ever Amen, even at the times when I detest her and she bores me. That's a marriage, he thought, lightly.

'Shall we eat first—before we decide what to quarrel about?'

Colour rose in her face. 'Yes, all right.'

'Tell me what you've been doing since Tuesday.'

'What's today?'

'Thursday.'

'The usual things. Chores for the paper. That's all.'

She had not touched her martini. Now she drank it in two gulps. The waiter filled her glass and Andrew's with the cheap blackish red wine he had chosen; she drank hers before beginning to talk quickly, her eyes widely open and gleaming, her cheeks flushed: she repeated gossip about the crisis, and about his father, as though she were trying to provoke him, and made clumsily exaggerated gestures. Andrew listened without attending. Now and then, when a phrase caught his ear, he put in a word, but during the greater part of the meal he said nothing; his whole body was listening to something else, to words flowering from her hands, her brown arms, the turn of her head on its thin neck. He avoided touching her accidentally—with the half-conscious idea that if he did he would lose his wits altogether. Surprised, he found that he was ravenously hungry. He ate everything put in front of him, and it had no more taste than her chatter had meaning. The cheese came and was taken away again, and the waiter went, leaving them with their cups of sweet thick Turkish coffee. *Now*, Andrew thought. He looked at Sarah. She was saying,

'I'm certain it's true that Security has got hold of someone and is keeping him at headquarters, and I——'

'I'm going away tomorrow,' he said.

Her fingers tightened round the cup. 'Home? You're
going home?'

'No. My father is sending me to Zante with the chief
medical officer—to run errands for him.'

'Oh—the epidemic—yes.'

Andrew leaned towards her across the table. 'We quarrelled,' he said quietly. 'What about?'

It was obviously hard for her to speak. 'You know what
about,' she muttered.

He had an atrocious moment. It came and went. 'You'd
better tell me everything. You needn't—but it would be
simpler if you did.'

She looked down at the table, keeping her head so low
that he could not see her face. When she lifted it, he found
himself looking at the face of a humiliated child: its softness
and its humiliation stung him, and he opened his mouth to
say: No, never mind, don't tell me . . . After all, why should
she tell him anything? There was no reason. But he did
not speak. A hard, almost cruel impulse to let her humiliate
herself further seized him, and he waited.

'It's true,' she said steadily, 'Totty told you the truth.'

He forced himself to keep an expressionless face, and
nodded.

'He can't have told you anything worse than the truth,'
she went on, 'but he doesn't know all of it.' Her voice rose
a little. 'How could he? He doesn't know . . . he was a
schoolboy when I went to live with them, but his brother
—Julian—was a young man. He was as old as we are now
—twenty-two. I—I admired him more than anyone in the
world. He didn't notice me then—not for years. Four
years. Not until I was sixteen. Then one day he did see
me . . . and began telling me how pretty I was . . . and kissed

me.' She frowned and gave him a fierce glance. 'You don't know how charming he was . . . He went on treating Totty as if he were still a child, but me—he treated me as if I had grown up, and that's why I fell in love with him . . .'

'The bastard,' Andrew said.

Sarah looked at him with a startling directness and candour. 'Oh, don't think I wasn't to blame. I knew what I was doing. I was sixteen.'

'He was ten years older.'

'Yes.' She stopped, and went on in a humble voice, 'I'm trying to be honest.'

He felt an agony of pity for her. He hardly knew what it was, he had never felt anything of the sort; it clawed him. 'Why didn't you trust me about it?'

'I don't know.' She blushed so deeply that she looked ugly. 'Yes—I was ashamed.'

'You needn't have been, my darling, it wasn't your fault, and it isn't important.'

In her roughest voice she said, 'After three years he dropped me—flat. I—I suffered. That's why I came out here, I'd been going to Oxford, but I said I'd changed my mind.' A half-cynical smile came on her face. 'I'd only been here a few weeks when I knew that the one thing that had been hurt was my conceit. I have to tell you that, too, because it shows that I'm not—that I'm a rather shallow character.'

'My little love——'

She interrupted him angrily. 'You see? Your father was right about me.'

He could not help smiling. 'You don't believe that, Sarah.'

'Don't you?' she asked, glaring at him.

'No. My father's too old to know what it's all about.' He had a confused memory of his mother telling him that to love and to leave free are the same thing, but it was simpler than that. Something much simpler possessed him: an instinct to take the girl's side for no better reason than that his father was too old to understand it. A brutal joy filled him; it excluded everything and every human being except himself and the girl. No one else was alive with this energy—even their quarrels were more satisfying than other people's happiness. He knew—with an extraordinary feeling of triumph he knew that they would quarrel; there would be nothing placid or soft or forbearing about their love. It was what he wanted.

'You could, you know, have told me,' he said.

'I know now,' she said under her breath.

He wanted to protect her and he wanted to make violent love to her. The two needs tore at him together. 'I love you as no girl will ever be loved,' he said quietly.

She was shaking, and he thought: She too. 'You're all —all—I want,' she said.

'We can't stay here any longer. Where can we go?'

Sarah looked at her watch, and said with dismay, 'My goodness, I promised I'd be back in the office in an hour. It's after ten. I must go back there at once.'

'No. You can't,' he said.

'Oh, my darling, it's no use, there's nowhere we can go at this time. You can't come to the office, and I can't go home with you, can I?'

An unreasonable anger with his father seized him. Stifling it, he said, 'No . . . Very well, I'll take you back to the office.'

The *Compatriot* building was not much more than two hundred yards from the hotel: he hurried her the short distance without speaking, in a fever of impatience. The door opened on to a small ill-lit lobby, with a porter's box, empty now, and a packing-case full of old copies of the paper. Shutting the door, Andrew took her in his arms. They held each other with an equal fury and passion, like drowning swimmers, and he thought: If there could only be something closer . . . And in the same breath: Making love is less than half of it . . . He released her gently and said,

'All right, my darling, go.'

'When are you coming back?'

'Until I get to Zante, I don't know. It depends what there is to do. Wait, I'll tell you where you can telephone to me. You might need me for something.'

He caught her young triumphant smile in the half-darkness. 'But I shall always need you,' she cried. 'Always, always.'

CHAPTER TWENTY-TWO

DURING Friday and Saturday, the Governor drove to all four of the larger towns in the colony, turning off his road to visit villages, a civilian hospital, and an outpost in the low hills. He got home from the last of these after midnight on Saturday and slept late. His servant had orders to call him at nine o'clock: some time before then, half awake, he heard Robin Hind's voice in the corridor; he was talking to the servant, and a minute later knocked and came in.

The Governor knew what it was about before the door opened: lifting himself on an elbow, he said,

'You've had Colonel Frent on the telephone.'

'Just this minute, sir. I thought I should tell you.'

'Yes, of course. Well?'

'He said: Tell His Excellency that we've got through . . . That was all.'

He waited, his face in the darkened bedroom a pale oval with only a trace of excitement and interest in the discreetly attentive eyes. Sitting up, the Governor became conscious of his own breath, and the disagreeable stickiness of his eyelids.

'Run away,' he said, 'I'll get up.'

When he was dressing, he felt, suddenly, the effect of the tension he had been living with: his knees gave way, and he sat down, resting his face in his hands. Since the moment when he had watched Boyd being taken away by his guards, he had ceased to think about him—except as an obstacle, a dark shapeless mass which had to be moved or dodged round. He realised now what it had cost in energy to keep the other man more or less out of sight for as long as sixty hours, sleeping and waking. The image of a heavy body being carried across the landing towards the semi-darkness of the stairs reversed itself, like a film played backwards; the two guards, the helplessly sagging body, slowly returned, coming, this time, towards him.

Before they could reach him he stood up. Well, that's over, he thought calmly. Thank God.

The half-formed idea that he might need, not a witness but a separate record, occurred to him when he was drinking his coffee, and he decided to take Robin with him to police headquarters. The young man was pleased and showed it in the ingenuous smiling look with which he said,

'When exactly was it they caught him? Monday night, wasn't it, sir? That's nearly a week.'

'A damned obstinate fellow,' the Governor said. 'Always was.'

He caught the flicker of curiosity on Robin's face, and reflected that he had given it away that the prisoner was a man he had known. It doesn't matter, he thought. And having gone so far, he felt inclined to go the rest of the way and take the young man into his confidence. This was one of the moments when he had the sense, not serious but very pleasant, that in Robin Hind he had a substitute son, a son who gave devotion and help without giving any trouble and without expecting to be loved. In any event he would not be ignorant very long, since the facts—and Boyd's name—would have to be published shortly: as soon as he came back from London.

'Of course, when we release the story,' he said easily, 'we shall give his name. I'll tell it you now—you may even have seen him. He is Anthony Boyd.' With a foolish reluctance he added, 'The husband of the Mrs. Boyd you do know.'

His secretary's air of surprise and stupefaction made him for a moment look so unfledged that the Governor smiled. Pulling himself together, Robin said,

'What will happen to him, sir?'

'Happen to him? What do you mean?'

'What does happen to traitors?' the young man asked quietly. 'After all, we're practically at war here.'

'Ah, we'll leave that to the lawyers,' the Governor said pleasantly.

He had no intention of doing it. A feeling of warmth and magnanimity spread through him. Whatever he could do in London to help Anthony—even at the cost of offending some man he would rather not have offended—he would do. Not because of his half-promise—which Anthony after all had jeered at—but out of kindness, out of memory. Out, yes, of an old affection.

The streets were full of Sunday-morning idlers, men and boys sitting round small iron tables outside the wine-shops, and loitering in groups in front of the shops open in Urraca Street—it was hard to believe that one among them might be, or have been, a killer. Any women about, most of them older women, in black dresses, covering their ankles, were on their way to church. It had rained during the night, and the air was cooler, with points of freshness and gaiety in the swallows darting from tree to dusty tree in the Square: they were the same shape and seemed as frail as the paper aeroplane a child launched in front of the car; then, noticing what car it was, fled, leaving his toy to be run over.

Frent was waiting for them in his office. He looked sprucer even than usual; his uniform itself seemed to be new, fresh from the tailor, and his cheeks were faintly rosy. The smile with which he rose to greet the Governor had a little, a very little warmth behind the formal politeness. An elderly clerk was standing in the room at the side of the desk, with a number of typed sheets of paper in his hand. Frent took them from him and sent him off.

As the door shut, he laid the papers on the table, between himself and the Governor, with an air of contentment and

gentle pride, very like an old maid showing off her gera-
niums.

'It's nearly all here, sir—not a great deal to come. The
whole set-up. Names, stores of arms, routes, agents, organi-
sations and'—he hesitated briefly, glancing at Robin Hind
—'immediate plans.'

Robin looked at the Governor, who nodded and said,
'Go downstairs and wait for me.' An idea sprang in him
with startling suddenness, as though forced up from a depth.
One of us, he thought, should see Anthony. I needn't, if I
send him to do it, go myself—or not yet. 'Is there any objection to his seeing the prisoner? Simply to take a look at
him. Not to talk to him of course.'

This time Frent's hesitation was noticeable. He said
coolly,

'If you think it advisable.' He looked at the young man.
An expression of modest prurience—no other term would
do: it was composed, calm, and gently lewdly inquisitive—
had come over Robin's clear face. With something between
amusement and contempt, Frent said, 'If Mr. Hind would
like to look at him, why not?'

He scribbled quickly on a memorandum slip. 'Give this
to Captain Berg.'

'Come back here in a quarter of an hour,' the Governor
said.

'Yes, sir.'

As soon as he had gone, the Governor asked Frent,

'And the immediate plans?'

'Very much what I expected,' Frent said, smiling. 'But
more thorough, better thought-out—and better equipment.
Roughly, two stages: in the first, more murders of settlers,
people like the Durhams, taking care to include children,
by their own servants where possible, with their servants if
these didn't co-operate willingly. The country is divided
into districts, and in each district one man is responsible

for the killings—there is a list of proposed victims. The second stage was to be more—shall we say?—conventional: simultaneous raids on airfields, bridges, power stations—and more murders—district officials, police, more important settlers . . . Very neatly planned—with, if I may say so, imagination. What he called "B" Day—his own initial, do you suppose?—would naturally not have been the success he expected, but it would have been unpleasant enough.' Leaning forward, he tapped the papers gently with one finger. 'You'll find it very interesting reading.'

The Governor glanced at him without moving his head. 'He began to talk—when?'

'Early this morning, sir. About four o'clock.' With a simple pleasure he went on, 'It's very satisfactory. To tell you the truth, I didn't expect him to hold out for so long— fifty-three hours ten minutes is the figure, I think, the exact figure. He broke suddenly. We got everything in less than an hour.'

The conviction that what had happened was atrocious came to the Governor at this moment. He knew it in the way that a man admits to himself suddenly that the pain he has been ignoring is a cancer. Moving backwards in the darkness of his skull, the two guards with their burden crossed the landing towards him, and this time he saw behind them the short neat figure of the lietuenant, eyes and slender aggressive nose pointed, a rat or Anubis. Again, with a great effort, he forced the image out of sight. Stretching his hand out, he said coldly,

'Let me look at the report.'

Frent pushed the papers towards him. 'A copy of this draft is on its way to General Smith now.' For the first time he allowed a thread of excitement to come into his voice, raising it a tone. 'The whole situation is changed. If I were a religious man I would say that we had had God on our side.'

The Governor glanced at him. 'Aren't you religious?'

Frent laughed, a dry very brief laugh. 'I'm not easily duped. I was brought up a strict Presbyterian, and the moral rubbed into me most often was that God prefers to help those who help themselves.'

'Ah, yes,' the Governor said. 'I rather envy you.'

He envied Frent his single-mindedness, his conviction—complete, unshakeable—that he was justified in doing anything he considered necessary. It was a moral and an emotional conviction, and it must have been the greatest help to him in his career of a soldier, a good soldier, turned policeman.

He sunk himself in the report. For the first minute or so he was disturbed by an echo of Boyd's voice, rising through the lines like the ghost of a breeze in dry reeds. The obsession vanished as his mind took in the implications of the document under his eyes. He hasn't held anything back, not a single item of importance, he thought. A feeling of relief rose through him, drowning his uneasiness in a flood of cold lucid thankfulness. He thought drily: If God hasn't been on our side, at least He didn't act against us.

He read for something like five minutes, then said, 'I'll take this away with me. Rather luckily as it happens, General Smith is lunching with me. I needn't get hold of him before then. If you will——'

As the door opened he looked up, frowning, and saw his secretary standing there, his face the colour of a man who may be sick at any moment, grey and covered with a film of sweat. He closed the door noisily—his hands were shaking—and came in. He began speaking in a dull frightened voice.

'Do you know what they've done to him? They . . . I can't tell you . . . things no one would believe. Sir, I——'

He sat down, and stood up again with ludicrous suddenness, roused by Frent's voice as sharply as if a cup of icy water had been thrown over him.

'What the devil do you mean by coming in here in this state?' Frent said. He stopped as if he had remembered that Hind was not his subordinate, and said, 'I beg your pardon, sir.'

The Governor's only sensation was one of faint disgust, as though a stuffed animal he was holding had begun to bleed over his fingers.

'I'll talk to you later. You'd better go back now.'

The young man opened his mouth, closed it without speaking, and went out quickly.

'Ought he to be turned loose in this hysterical state?' Frent said.

The Governor moved his hand, brushing this aside. In the same moment, using an energy that seemed to be stretching and tearing the nerves round his heart, he brushed Boyd himself out of the way. Pressing his hand down on the papers, he thought: I can't attend to anything now except this . . . A single point gave way in his mind, a light trickle of earth on the slope threatened by an avalanche.

'I should like to be assured that Boyd . . .' A movement of his fingers completed the sentence.

Frent said quietly, 'You can feel sure that the prison doctor—a most competent fellow—is looking after him properly and skilfully.'

After a moment the Governor said, 'I'll see him myself later.'

It was not a question, but Frent answered as if it had been. 'Certainly.'

CHAPTER TWENTY-THREE

SARAH stopped abruptly at the corner of Urraca Street and the Square. It was not a place where she cared to hesitate— even on Sunday morning when, for a reason to do with her childhood in an English village, she did not believe in the likelihood of death or violence (she had, too, just been caught up in a modest little miracle, and was ready, at least for a time, to believe that goodness is nearer the bone than cruelty, and joy than loss). What had pulled her up short was the spectacle of Robin Hind. His thin blond figure, in the middle of the crowded street, was a provocation. He must have gone mad, she thought. In the hope of avoiding him, she stepped into the doorway of the nearest small shop, but he saw her and broke into a run—running towards her. Does the little beast imagine I don't know what he did? she thought, with a flash of rage.

He took hold of her arm. 'Sarah. I want to talk to you.'

As she shook his hand off, she noticed that he was ill or in trouble. She felt a twinge of curiosity, but no kindness.

'What's the matter?' she said. 'You look rotten.'

He shook his head. 'I'm all right—that's to say I'—he lowered his voice and made an effort to seem self-possessed —'I must speak to you. Where can we go to talk quietly?'

She was torn between her impulse to send him off with a very large flea in his ear and a nagging sense of responsibility left over from their childhood with its family chorus: *Totty, poor boy, isn't at all strong.* Totty, in fact, was perfectly healthy; his languor was due partly to overgrowth and more to a shrewd calculation of the benefits it brought him. She said curtly,

'All right, you can come to the office with me, I was going.'

He flinched. 'I can't go there.'

'Then go to hell . . . No, all right, I know you can't. Yes, you can. There's almost no one there at this time, and I have my own room. Come on, Totty.'

As if her use of his childish nickname had reassured him, he gave in, but kept his head well down when they were passing the soldiers outside the post-office. Sarah took him at a run up a steep flight of rickety wooden steps, into a small room as bare and dusty as the staircase: a small desk, a wash-basin, a waste-paper basket and one cane-bottomed chair.

'No one will come in,' she told him. 'Sit down.'

He looked round him unhappily. 'Where?'

She settled this by sitting on the edge of the desk; he dropped on to the chair and covered his face with both hands. On their way here she had been choosing among the most insulting phrases she could think of: now, abruptly, they were meaningless—not because he was behaving in this peculiar way but because, after all, he had only told the truth about her, as he saw it. Why blame him? she thought, with a wry candour. She asked him brusquely,

'Is something wrong?'

He sat up, taking his hands from his face. 'After all, I can't tell you.'

'Just as you like,' she said with indifference.

His carefully composed face seemed to fall to pieces. 'No, no, I must tell you—it must be stopped . . . Wait a minute.'

She felt a shock of fear. 'Has something happened to Andrew?' she asked him fiercely.

'No. Why should anything happen to him?' He bit his lip. 'I'm sorry, my dear girl, I'm making a fool of myself, but if you knew what I've been through . . .'

Her patience gave out. 'Either tell me or don't tell me, but don't sit there yammering like an old woman.'

Robin smiled unwillingly: her roughness was familiar and comforting. 'I'm sorry,' he said again. He pulled down the corners of his charming mouth, as he did when he was a schoolboy trying to impress her with his powers of sarcasm. 'You—your wretched newspaper had it in on Thursday as a rumour—you knew we'd caught a chap, one of the rebels——'

She interrupted him. 'There were stories going round. We haven't been able to pin any of them down . . . It's true, is it?'

'Yes.' He hesitated and said in a rush, 'He's an Englishman—called Boyd. He has a wife living here. Security picked him up a week ago, he wouldn't talk, so they . . . they tortured him'—he closed his eyes for a second—'Sarah, I've seen him. It made me ill . . . If I'd known it would be like that, I wouldn't have gone near him. I was a fool to go. I didn't imagine, I didn't know what it would be like, I . . .'

The horror she felt came less from what he was saying— it made no image in her mind, or one as indistinct as if he had been describing a barbarous crucifix—than because he infected her with his fear of being sick.

'Is it true?'

'Of course it's true.' A peevish note came into his voice. 'I tell you, I saw him.'

'Totty, I—I can't handle this,' she said, stammering. 'I must tell Charles about it—my stepfather.'

'Tell him. Tell anyone you like,' he cried. 'It's got to be stopped.'

She forced herself to think calmly. 'You do realise what you're doing, don't you? I mean—you're the witness . . . the only witness . . . Are you going to stand to this—publicly —when you're asked about it? Think.'

She watched him. Something like consternation came into his face; she could almost see another, older person pushing

aside the young man who had been speaking without any
thought of himself. He lifted a hand slowly and passed it
over his smooth fair head. He scowled, and said harshly,
 'No, I can't do that.'
 'Then what's the use of your telling me?'
 'You can use the information,' he said. 'You must. Only,
don't say who told you.'
 Poor Totty, she thought involuntarily, with contempt and
pity. 'If we don't support the story—and you're the only
person who can support it—we shall be shut up—broken.
They've been waiting for a chance. Surely you can see
that?' He did not answer, and she went on, speaking carefully, watching his face, 'It would finish you, you know.
Some people would say you were lying. Most of them would
know you were telling the truth—even most people at home.
But you wouldn't be thanked. I expect—I don't know, of
course, but I suppose you'd have to resign or something.'
 'Or something,' he repeated ironically. 'You're talking
like a child.'
 'I may be,' she said drily. 'I don't know very much, but
I know that when you tell scandalous truths about authority
—any authorities, not just ours here—even if you're believed
it puts you on the other, the wrong side of a line drawn
between people who are—what's the word?—sound, and
people who are unsound, not reliable, likely to be a nuisance.'
 For the second time since he came into the room Robin
seemed about to break down and burst into tears. He looked
at Sarah with a despairing appeal. 'But what am I to do?'
 Now he's going to be sorry for himself, she thought.
'Don't ask me to tell you that. I'm not competent. Anyhow,
it's your choice, your funeral.'
 'But why need you drag me in?' he said petulantly. 'Why
can't you just publish the story, without involving me?'
 'You know why not.'
 He tried to pull his face into its normal look of composed

amiable good sense. 'Sarah, I thought I could count on you not to damage me,' he said, in a reproachful voice.

She smiled unkindly. 'The question is: Can we count on *you*?'

Instead of answering, he jumped up and began to walk up and down the narrow room. 'Do you think he knew?' he said abruptly.

'Who? What are you talking about?'

'About H.E., of course. D'you think they told him they were going to use torture? I can't believe it.'

'I can't see that it matters.'

'It doesn't, except'—he turned on her a face in which anxiety and mortification had drawn under his eyes a line that certainly had not been there when he got up that morning—'I've ruined myself with him. Whatever happens he won't forgive me, or trust me again. And I have no one else backing me now. No one. I'm done for——'

She was silent, then said, 'Poor Totty.'

'You're laughing at me,' he said coldly, 'but it's serious for me.'

'I know it is. I wasn't laughing.' For the first time she saw him as fully grown-up, a stranger, with his reserves, his vanity, his power to do harm, his impulses to malice or grace or kindness. 'You're very ambitious, aren't you?'

He gave her a cool glance. 'What's wrong with that?'

'Nothing. But it makes it harder for you than it would be for me.' She was balancing on a knife-edge between contempt and a rough kindness, the one as close to her hand as the other. 'Here's where you choose,' she said simply. 'If you tell, it will be a frightful scandal. You *may* be ruined with him—with your precious Excellency—already. If you tell, you'll certainly be ruined, no *may*, with everyone except the kind of people you loathe, like my stepfather. That's the score. So—what are you going to do?' An impulse to be better than honest with him made her say, 'You can, you know, choose—I shan't give you away unless you tell me I can.'

She almost added: And don't bite your nails . . . It was a childish habit, for which he was always scolded. He was doing it again now.

'Can't you—are you sure?—leave me out of it?' he muttered.

She tried to speak patiently. 'If I repeat to Charles what you've told me and don't tell him where I heard it, he'll either laugh in that ghastly young-at-heart way of his, or go on probing until he gets it out of me. Totty, it's no use. Either you come out with it yourself, or . . .' She spread her hands.

The young man did not answer. He was sitting stiffly, a faint frown pulling his thin eyebrows together, blue limpid eyes fixed in a worried stare. Sarah thought: What's going on behind them? I bet I know. His ambition is on top again: he means well, he always did, but he has to get on.

'You'll think badly of me, won't you? If I refuse.'

'No,' she said.

With a little horror she realised that she had scarcely given a moment's thought to the poor man they had tortured. In a queer way, she felt a profound cynicism—as though she had always, young as she was, known that human beings did these things to each other.

'I—I can't, Sarah.'

'Very well.'

His voice sharpened. 'You won't give me away, will you? Promise.'

'I promise,' she said coldly. She added, 'But the story will get out. These things always do.'

'How? Why should it?' he said, scowling.

'I don't know how. All I know is that somehow, in some way or other, when a thing like this has happened—has been done—it gets to be known. Perhaps someone's conscience gets to work. Or—or as if——' she broke off, with a confused gesture. She had been going to say: As if the cries you can't hear through the thick walls are picked up outside by people's nerves . . . Instead, she muttered, 'Don't, if there *are* rumours, think I've said anything. That's all.'

Robin got up. Stretching himself, he walked over to the wash-basin and turned the tap. No water came.

'It doesn't work,' she told him.

'Oh, damn. And I'm filthy.'

There was a small looking-glass hanging from a nail above the basin. Bringing his pretty face close to it, he smoothed his hair, using both hands, then took his handkerchief to the sides of his mouth and eyes. Sarah watched him with curiosity. Suddenly she said,

'You've been talking about me—about Julian.'

His shoulders jerked. He did not turn his head. 'I'm sorry, Sarah.'

'It was a foul thing to do.'

He turned round. He looked much younger again, and ashamed. 'I didn't mean to tell anyone. It—it happened.'

'It doesn't matter.' With a start of joy, she thought: And that's true.

He hesitated and said, 'You know, Sarah, Andrew might have found out.'

'That's no excuse for you,' she said sharply.

'I know.'

'But it's really true it doesn't matter. I'm even glad he knows.' A regret—and something less avowable than regret —pinched her. 'But I wish *I'd* told him. I hate myself for that.'

'Don't,' Robin said in a low voice. 'It only means you think you're better than the part of you you hate. That doesn't get you anywhere.'

She looked at him with astonishment. How does he know

anything like that? she asked herself. She felt a spring of
sympathy for him—not simply the familiarity and off-hand
affection of their childhood, but the sense that, after all, he
was as uncertain, as vulnerable to the world and nakedly
young as herself. And as Andrew. But Andrew and I are
together, she thought, with a choking happiness.

She said warmly, 'I hope you'll be able to make it all
right with him.'

He lifted his eyebrows. 'With . . . ?'

'With the Governor.'

His face twitched. 'My God, I hope so—I can't think
what came over me to make such an ass of myself.' He took
another quick look at himself in the glass. 'I must go.'

In the doorway he hesitated. He said, 'Thanks, Sarah,'
and ducked out of the room.

Alone, she stood looking out of the one cracked dirty
window. The sun was at its height, pouring a hot yellow oil
over all she could see from this angle, the end of a roll of
barbed wire outside the post-office, a sliver of scorched
dusty ground, and a bored-looking soldier, eyes narrowed
against the glare. Abruptly, as if a whip had been laid
across her young baffled shoulders, she saw all these as a
meagre scrap of earth jutting from a darkness where nothing
was pleasant, decent, or even human: only fear, violence,
squalid deaths and the threat of death. For the first time
the thought of Boyd started a shudder in her, at such a depth
that it was painful and frightening. She sat down, folding
her arms across her thin body, and tried to think it out
clearly. Not a great way from this room, a man had been
tortured, by his countrymen, by men using the same words
as he for bread, pity, pain. No, no, it's too frightful, she
thought. She felt ashamed of herself and horribly inade-
quate. I let Totty off too easily, she thought with a spurt
of anger. Far too easily. But what can I do? If only I could
ask Andrew . . .

Without giving herself time to have doubts, she decided to ring him up. I can't tell him about it on the telephone, she thought, but I can tell him he must come back, I need him, he must come at once.

She got up and hurried across the landing to her step-father's room, where there was a telephone. If Charles is already there, I can't do it, she thought. But if he isn't, it's a sign—it means I'm right to tell Andrew.

The room was empty.

CHAPTER TWENTY-FOUR

IT was after five when the Governor called his secretary to his room. During the hours of waiting for the summons, the young man lived through all the circles of his hell of uncertainty and self-accusation, at one moment up to his neck in the ice of disgrace and failure, at others clinging against hope to a belief that he could still save himself by finding the right words of repentance and promises of amendment. He had never felt more mortified, more ashamed of himself. Only let me get safely through this, he prayed, and never, never, will I make such a fool of myself again . . . What, after all, did Boyd matter to him? Why had he let a nervous shock drag him into such a mistake? What did anything or anyone matter to him except himself and his needs and sane decent hopes?

Long before he was summoned, the thought of Boyd had dropped below the troubled surface of his mind, out of sight.

When the young man came into the library, the Governor allowed him to stand at the other side of the table for a full minute before glancing at him. He was coldly angry. Robin's behaviour at police headquarters had not only irritated, it had deeply disappointed him. It touched him personally. He had taken the young man—recommended to him, it was true, by a man (now dead) whom he was willing to oblige—on an impulse of liking, very rare indeed with him; and liking had become something close to affection. He felt now as though he had spent a large sum of money on a painting or a piece of china which had turned out to be a fake. His judgment had been badly at fault. And—the real point of his bitterness—Frent had been looking on at the exhibition.

'Well?' he asked ironically. 'Are you recovered?'

The young man's eyelids quivered. 'Sir, I can only apologise—very humbly.'

'Your behaviour was . . . inexcusable.'

'Yes, sir.'

The young man's effort at self-control was slightly pathetic —or would be if the whole tiresome business were not unnecessary, irritatingly unnecessary. 'What the devil possessed you?' the Governor asked, frowning.

Robin hesitated. For less than a moment Boyd's mutilated face and body floated to the surface. He choked down the sickness and said quietly,

'I thought that the prisoner was in pain.'

'Was that a sufficient reason?'

'No, sir.'

Since he left police headquarters, and during his luncheon with the G.O.C., Ormston had been able to shut away almost entirely any thought of Boyd. The shadow of an irrational anxiety—completely irrational, he told himself —remained: it concerned himself. All through the meal— as during the last minutes with Frent—he had been plagued by a sense of dislocation, very disconcerting, as though one side of his mind had detached itself from the other and become a spectator cynically watching his gestures, listening to all he said and waiting for him *to give himself away*. Had he given himself away?—to Frent? to the general? And given away what weakness?

'I haven't had time to decide what to do with you,' he said coldly. 'You can go.'

Robin's face expressed nothing but his sober acceptance of a punishment he had deserved. He went out without a word.

For a moment Ormston sat still under the weight of his uncertainty. Never in his adult life had he doubted himself and his power to handle any situation, any person, and turn them where he wanted—never until now. He thought suddenly: I shall have to see him.

Oh, nonsense, he told himself sharply, sheer nonsense. Pointless . . . But—he knew it—now that he had allowed Boyd in, he would have to see him. Unless he had seen him he would not be able to sleep—and he needed sleep. I must go at once, he thought. An unfamiliar impatience, an impatience and irritability of his whole body, seized him. It gave him energy. His mind cleared, and he felt confident.

As the car passed through the inner town he looked at it with more attention than usual: the narrow streets were decomposed by the strong light into piles of white crumbling stone; a house-front here, a column there, stood out, intact, but the whole effect was of confusion and disintegration, and the only face he noticed clearly among those turned to the car, the face of a woman, had its nose eaten away, like an old statue. He had an impulse to turn back. Exasperated by his levity, he thought: What the devil is wrong with me that I don't know my own mind for as long as ten minutes? . . . It had been stupid to come. He shrugged his shoulders. Since he had come this far he would go on, go through with it, and see for himself what effect the . . . drugs . . . or other treatment . . . had had on Boyd. It was possibly the sensible thing to do—better at any rate than not knowing.

Frent, he learned at police headquarters, was out. An officer called Senior was on duty in his room, a big stout comfortable fellow with burnished cheeks and twinkling blue eyes, the spit of a country grocer, very reassuring. The prisoner, he said cheerfully, had been put to bed in one of the cells, he was not sure which, but the prison doctor had seen him, and if His Excellency would like to talk to that officer . . .

Ormston cut him short. 'I want to see the prisoner. At once. I haven't much time.'

Did he catch or imagine a trace of embarrassment on the fellow's good-humoured face? If it had been there, it vanished instantly and its place was filled by the blank pseudo-face Captain Senior kept in readiness, behind his features of a decent only slightly rascally village tradesman, for use when some important person, so important that Hector Senior should never have been left to deal with him, was behaving out of character. Deplorably out of character. What call had His Excellency the Governor to appear here, without warning, without an aide, and demand to see a man who was no longer of any interest since he had been squeezed dry? It was all very difficult. Not the least of his difficulties was marching sideways, so that he led the way without leading.

A little to Ormston's surprise—he had not known it existed—they went down, by a flight of stone stairs cut off from the ground-floor corridor behind a door and a grating, to a basement.

'Has the prisoner been down here all the time?' he asked.

'No, sir.'

'How long have you had him here?'

The captain could not say.

When did they move him down? Ormston wondered. For the final interrogation? Why?

The staircase and the narrow passage in which it ended were lighted by electric bulbs set in the walls—well-lighted. But he had an impression of airlessness and gloom, stifling, as though the light were being beaten back by darkness pouring from the walls. Yes, dark, he thought vaguely.

A young soldier was on guard outside a cell. Wagging a hand at him, Captain Senior opened the door. He seemed about to edge his large body inside.

'You can go,' Ormston said.

He shut the door against Senior's face. A single electric

bulb, hanging from the ceiling, lit the cell. It was not a strong light, but strong enough to light up so narrow a place —and the man on the bed.

Standing with his back to the door, Ormston looked at him, in the first sickened instant taking in only the face, or what he could see of it: there were bandages over one eye and across the jaw, and the flesh between them was black and tumefied. Also there was something not right with the unbandaged eye. As he took a step forward, Ormston thought that the lid had been singed.

He stepped back again. The door he thought he had shut had only been ajar; it closed sharply when he leaned against it. Boyd's single eye opened. It seemed to focus with difficulty. Very slowly, in silence, his hand moved, and pushed at the bandage over the other eye.

'Don't,' Ormston said instinctively.

Boyd's lacerated mouth twitched, in the parody of a smile. The fingers of the hand he could still use tried to push the covering from the lower part of his body, gave it up, and lay still. A trickle of blood came from a corner of the contorted mouth. He had not said anything.

Ormston forced himself to move nearer the bed. He began, 'I didn't know . . . I didn't intend . . .' The same mockery of a smile cut him short. He controlled himself to say, coldly and distinctly, 'There has been a mistake, a horrible mistake. The men responsible will be punished— I'll see to it.'

The rasping thread of sound coming from Boyd was almost inaudible. 'No, you can't. You have no right.'

Ormston had been struggling against nausea: it rose again at the back of his throat.

'Anthony——'

'I talked—yes,' Boyd muttered. 'I vomited answers. But don't think that finishes us. You'll have to kill or torture thousands of us to do that.'

'Don't blame yourself,' Ormston said, with pity.

The flicker of Boyd's single eyelid was a point of irony. 'D'you know what you've done?' A little energy came into his voice. 'I believed there was something in me—in any man—that could survive anything, torture, anything. I believed that. If you like, it was my religion. Now I don't know whether it's true, I don't know whether what is human in us is stronger than what is inhuman and obscenely cruel. I no longer know . . . That's what you've done to me.'

'Forgive me.'

Had Boyd tried to laugh? 'My dear boy, I don't flatter myself. The role of victim is less disturbing, far less interesting, even less elegant than that of his torturer.'

Ormston said again, 'Forgive me.'

'It's not'—Boyd paused: from somewhere he gathered strength—'*not* true that . . . at a certain point . . . anyone will give in. I was unlucky to be so hard to kill.' The brutal contempt in his voice was not, Ormston thought, for himself, though he went on, 'Another man might not have given in. *I* did. You made a rat of me. You, Ricky.'

A phrase forced its way up in Ormston from so far back that he did not recognise it. When in his life, his childhood, had he cried it before?

'It wasn't my fault!'

Silence. Then Boyd whispered,

'Come a bit nearer, can't you?'

Ormston came to the side of the bed. Looking down, he saw only the disfigured eyelid, and the lips, split open and blackened, pushed against each other by the bandage below them. Beads of sweat lay along the upper lip. An unpleasant smell came from the bed.

'Something to say,' Boyd muttered. 'Closer, can't you?'

Ormston bent over the grotesque face. A second later he stepped back, lifting his hand blindly to his cheek.

The effort of spitting had exhausted Boyd. His eyelid dropped.

There was nothing his friend could do but go.

CHAPTER TWENTY-FIVE

HE came out into the sharp honey-yellow light of early evening. Turning his head he saw, floating in this light, the pure hull of a mountain. Behind it the sky was a dead calm, clear through depth below depth.

He was infinitely astonished that none of these had changed.

The sense that he was a spectator of himself returned. Sitting in the car, he noticed his hands move, crossed his legs, as though watching another man go through these habitual gestures. The feeling of separation, of being not-there, not in himself, persisted: it was his other self who acknowledged the salutes of the sentries at Government House, crossed the hall, walked with him up the great staircase to the library.

He sat for some minutes, in the same more than half oblivious state. The sound made by his hand tapping the polished wood of the table startled him into consciousness. He realised that during these minutes he had been thinking about Robin Hind, and had come to a decision. He had decided to get rid of him. For two reasons, both as clear to him as if they had been reached by a rational process. That they had not, he well knew. One was the certainty that if he kept Robin he would always, at the back of those pale seemingly candid eyes of his, see the tiny obscene image of Boyd. And for the rest, I dislike him, he thought . . . It was, he knew, a wholly unjust dislike, born of his own error of judgment.

A sudden access of energy sent him to the telephone: he had himself put through to police headquarters. Colonel Frent was still absent.

'As soon as he comes in, tell him I want to see him,' he said. 'Here.'

Putting the receiver back, he touched the bell that rang in his secretary's room, and when Robin came in said drily,

'Sit down. I'm going to talk to you for a minute.' As if speculating what use the young man could be to him, he watched Robin seat himself stiffly in the chair facing him across the table. 'You realise that you've shown yourself capable of something very like hysteria—at best a shocking lack of control.'

'Yes, sir,' Robin said quietly.

'I hope you realise, too, that another such . . . indiscretion —whether it happened here or in London—would be the end of you. No one cares to have a subordinate about whose nerves are not under control.'

'I realise it entirely, sir,' Robin said, in the same low steady voice. 'I ought to have held my tongue. I know.' He went on with a light touch of urgency. 'It would never happen again.'

'I hope not,' Ormston said, 'for your sake.' He felt a cold pleasure in what he was going to say. 'I can't keep you. You must go elsewhere to hold your tongue.'

Except for a heaviness that came over it, like a fluid gathering under the clear skin, Robin's face showed no emotion. He sat rigidly still. Ormston felt a twinge of admiration for his composure. For a minute longer he allowed him to believe that he was going to be broken, then said,

'You'll have a pressing family reason for returning to England. I'm commending you to a safe friend of mine in the Department. You'll be all right—so long as you behave yourself properly.'

The young man's lips trembled—the first sign he had given of distress. In a voice you could believe very deeply moved, he said,

'Thank you, sir. You . . . I'm immensely grateful.'

'You ought to be,' Ormston said coldly. He moved his hand. 'That's all. Go away.'

Frent came ten minutes later. He brought news which his dry precise voice offered as though he were seated behind his desk, dictating it to one of his clerks. A just perceptible gleam at the back of his eyes—gaiety? elation? —made him seem affable. During the morning a security force had surrounded one of the hide-outs given away by Boyd and picked up not only two so-called area commanders but the plans for a raid on three villages, with the names of the men to be shot or hanged, and details of a scheme for poisoning wells used by English troops on patrol in the hills.

'Perhaps,' he said, with his aseptic smile, 'this scheme would not have been carried out. But the other, the attack on the villages and the massacre that was to follow, would certainly have come off in the next week or so. So, at some time, would "B" Day and its murders and destruction. We have been very lucky.'

'Yes, yes,' Ormston said, almost absently.

As though he were slightly, very slightly, taken aback, Frent insisted a little. 'The importance of this, I may call it, first fruits of Boyd's capture is something we can congratulate ourselves on without'—he smiled again—'without being too cock-a-hoop.'

'Tell me,' Ormston said drily. 'Was it necessary to be so . . . brutal?'

Frent's eyebrows rose. As it always did when he was driven to explain himself at any length, his language became not so much colder as clinically disinfected. 'You understand —there was no time to proceed slowly, or by careful stages. And it was impossible to allow any but the very briefest intervals for recovery. Time, in fact, was of the essence.'

Ormston was unnecessarily irritated by the cliché. After a moment, he said,

'I have seen Boyd.'

The glance Frent gave him was rather more calculating than inquisitive . . . How deeply shocked were you? . . . It was inquisitive, too: it had something of the neutral curiosity with which a child watches a fly trying to struggle out of a jar of treacle.

'Sir, I regret sincerely that we had to use strong, even cruel methods. But—as you yourself agree—we were up against an evil thing, and you can't fight evil with blunt weapons.' He paused a moment. 'By sacrificing one man— and after giving him every chance to save himself, don't forget—we have saved I hesitate to say how many lives, avoided God knows what atrocities.' He hesitated again, and went on in a livelier voice, 'The fact that the man in question is a traitor—of the least excusable sort—if any treachery is excusable—is surely also of the essence.'

He stopped, moving his shoulders in a hint, without disrespect, of a shrug.

'Yes,' Ormston said. 'No doubt. A great many lives have been saved.'

'Impossible to guess how many.'

'You believe it justified the use of torture to break Boyd.'

Coldly, with polite surprise, Frent said, 'Sir, I don't follow you.'

Ormston looked at him. 'You've seen him?'

'Yes.'

'Well?'

The wings of Frent's nose quivered a little. 'They all break at some point,' he said quietly. 'Some need longer —more pressure—than others.'

'You gave the orders,' Ormston said.

'Yes, of course.'

'Did you watch them being carried out?'

'Certainly not.'

Ormston thought: He gave the orders, he knew what

would be done, he saw the result. He didn't like it, but he feels no remorse, no excessive discomfort. Why not? Why is he immune? How? . . . Noticing that he was tapping the table, he stopped and put his hand in his pocket. Perhaps, he thought, it happens in the same way as a scientist who is helping to perfect a bomb which will kill human beings in the greatest agony is immunised against images of the effect. Insulated from them. But by what? By a sort of cold insanity which splits a part of his mind from the rest: in one part he is a normal decent intelligent human being; in another he is capable of an obscene act.

I, too, he thought. But I'm viler than Frent. He knew what he was doing, but he knew it without feeling. He was only the instrument—in *my* hands . . . With a drop into darker colder waters, he reflected that he had taken care not to know too much beforehand: he was a coward as well as vile.

'It sickened me,' he said calmly. 'It shouldn't have been done.'

The oblique glance Frent gave him between half-closed eyelids conveyed—under the indifference of the bureaucrat —all a soldier's contempt for the civilian.

'With the utmost respect, sir—you authorised me to use any means.'

Ormston stood up. 'Yes, I did.'

Frent held himself stiffly. 'If you consider the value of the information—incalculable . . .'

'I have considered it,' Ormston interrupted.

'He—Boyd—is not a pleasant sight. True. But men— and women—with their throats cut across are not pleasant.'

'I have,' Ormston repeated, 'considered that.'

CHAPTER TWENTY-SIX

HIS night was short and untroubled; a heavy sleep fell on him almost as he lay down; he woke at six, with a light shock, like a swimmer coming to the surface after a plunge —the sensation of breaking through a brittle skin to find himself in a suddenly luminous world, full of sounds and wings. He got up and pushed open the shutters. Without warning he was invaded, again, by the overwhelming feeling of surprise that the world outside him had not changed in some drastic way. Leaning against the window, he tried to decipher, in the curves of the hills, in the early sun moving across them like a flight of migrating swallows, a sentence that would answer the disturbance in himself, as obscure and menacing as a disordered heart-beat.

No, nothing has changed, he thought.

The change was taking place in himself. There, the whole landscape had been torn up, as by an earthquake, houses reduced to rubble, trees torn down, all the known contours effaced. He turned to go back to the bed-table, to ring for coffee: to reach it, he had to step over Boyd's torn body lying between window and bed.

Vexed, he thought drily: This won't do—it mustn't happen again.

During the afternoon, about five, when he was working in the library, his secretary came in and asked,

'Sir, will you see Mrs. Boyd?'

He detected a changed note in the young man's voice. Composed and sober as always, it seemed to come from the farther side of a gap—as though Robin had been trying to put a distance between himself and a tiresome and unpleasant past. As though I were his past, Ormston thought. He felt indifference and a derisive amusement.

'Is she here now?' he asked without turning his head.

'Yes, sir.'

Must I see her? he thought, with a reluctance which had little to do with Anthony: she must have come about him, but, he told himself, I can deal with that. What he detested was this sense that one side of him had been flayed and was a raw naked surface, the ends of the nerves exposed, and that she might catch sight of it.

'Very well. Bring her in.'

He stood up as she came in. She had wrapped herself in a long thin coat, and was wearing a hat with a veil that covered her face; drawn closely under her chin, it was knotted on the crown of the little hat. From the way she walked, he saw that she was nervously tense: she had a faint colour in her cheeks, which only happened when he had been making love to her: there was even something insolent in her good looks, and Ormston thought: No one has the right to affront life with such a face, and she has no right to affront me with her body, not now . . . He had a hostile impulse, grotesque in this moment, this place, to tell her to undress; she felt it, and closed her eyes for a second in instinctive rejection and fear. Her gesture threw him back on himself, and he said quietly,

'Why did you come?'

She sat down, and began to pull at the knot of her veil with impatiently blundering fingers. It did not give way; she stopped trying and folded her hands. Without any haste she said,

'I've heard—I heard it from Agathe, who has so many cousins and uncles that they are a grape-vine in themselves —that Anthony—not that Agathe knows his name—is . . . ill. In pain.'

'So naturally you came here to ask.'

'Naturally.'

'It's not true.' Why am I taking the trouble to lie to her?

he thought ironically. 'He's exhausted—they've been questioning him for a long time.'

She looked at him with an almost sullen attentiveness, and said brusquely, 'I want to see him.'

Ormston smiled. 'You can't do that, my darling, it's not possible.'

'Why not?'

'It's not possible,' he repeated.

'You mean you won't give me permission.'

He hesitated. 'No. I won't.'

Anne stood up and leaned against the table. The fingers of the hand she rested on it were shaking. 'Then it's true. The police have ill-treated him.'

Ormston did not answer. It was not that he had any dislike of lying, but he was suddenly bored: it was almost too much trouble.

She came close to him, close enough for him to catch the light scent of geranium, and began speaking in the low voice its flaw made more charming, more of a caress. 'Tell me the truth, my darling. I can forgive you anything—you know that. But tell me.'

'Take your veil off,' Ormston said.

Slowly, working at it, she got the better of the knot so far as to be able to push the veil off her face, and offer him her mouth.

'There,' she murmured. 'Are you satisfied?'

He felt a strangely numbed joy. It was more than longing for the release, the comfort, she could give him—and no one else could. A confused notion of atonement came into it: there must be some restitution he could make, a simpler life—simpler and harder—that he could live, with her . . . once she had forgiven him. Absolved him . . . It was absolution he wanted from her. He believed, his body believed, that she had been sent here to give it to him.

'It's true,' he said, 'true. I'm sorry.'

The change in her face, to loathing, did not at once make any mark on him. He was holding her too closely against him, the warmth of her body under her thin coat penetrating his, to see her distinctly; it was only after a moment, when she began to struggle against him, that he understood. For another moment he went on holding her because he was afraid, if he let her go, that she would fall. She was crying, long harsh cries, that must tear her throat. He made her sit down, and dried her face gently with his handkerchief. She pushed him away. No longer crying, she looked at him with a cold, vindictive, almost evil expression. Her face was distorted by it.

'You had him tortured,' she said, 'you. You're quite loathsome. D'you know that?'

'If you say so,' he said, staring at her. A great deal of his energy was going on the effort to hide his anguish from her.

'You were jealous of him—always—long before you began making love to me. That's why—why you did it.'

'Why I made love to you?' No, that isn't what she means, he thought: she's not—not so ill-bred.

'Why you wanted to hurt Anthony, to kill him.' Her eyes dilated. '*Have* you killed him?'

'No.'

She's not, he thought, ill-bred, but she is stupid—with the peculiar stupidity, an affair of the soul or the senses, of clever women. He had a strong impulse to tell her the truth: that it was not jealousy of her husband that had goaded him. He was jealous, yes. But there were other infinitely more solid reasons—there was his ambition, and there were reasons below that, deeper, older, more twisted. For the moment he could not see what these were . . . It would be unkind to tell her the truth. Let her believe that it was jealousy, only jealousy; let her comfort herself by believing it. Any comfort is better than none, he thought coldly—and to a woman any flattery.

Anne stood up. She was making an effort to be calm. The look of rancour had settled on her face again, ageing it. 'I'm going to see that you're punished.'

'As you like,' Ormston said.

She stared fixedly for a moment, as though seeing his offence laid out in front of her. Suddenly, without any warning, she broke down again. There were no more tears, but she trembled violently, pressing her fingers into her cheeks with such force that they left long reddened marks in the white flesh.

'It's no use,' she said dully, 'of course it's no use. I can't do anything. You'll hush it up. No one will believe it, no one will *want* to believe it.'

'My poor girl,' he said very gently.

She shrank from him. 'I should like you to suffer.'

He watched her for a moment. 'Did you ever love me?'

She did not answer. She smoothed her dress, pulling the veil over her face, where it hung clumsily loose, and went out of the room.

It was six o'clock. He had agreed to see Gouraud at that time, before the old Frenchman left on the evening plane for Paris, where he had business. On the telephone he had said that he would be away a month or six weeks, and wanted to say goodbye. 'After all, at my age, one never knows. Not that I have any intention of being buried in France, but there is the risk . . .'

He came in, with his amiable lipless smile, and held out a limp hand to be shaken. Dressed in dark clothes for the journey, in place of the shabby linen or silk he wore here, he looked more than ever the small provincial shopkeeper —a French province. All the greed and cunning of his peasant grandparents had taken refuge in his sunken eyes, together with their energy, patience, and deeply ironical disbelief in any virtue except the virtue of survival. The arched forehead above them protected his own virtues of curiosity and kindness.

It was exactly eight days since Ormston had talked to him for two minutes, on his way to see Anne, but their talk had taken place in a former life, between two other men. The man in front of him, friendly, smiling, was a stranger, as much a stranger as if he had come from another world.

Gouraud ran over him a glance used to uncovering, in a formless mass of earth, the outline he expected.

'You're tired,' he said.

'Not more than usual.'

'Forgive me,' Gouraud said, 'you are not usually tired.' He did not insist, but went on to explain why he was going to Paris—a question of an inheritance, and the French law, which was going to put every obstacle in the way of his doing as he wanted: to sell out at once and spend the money on his obsession. 'But I shall defeat them,' he said, rubbing one delicate bony hand over the other, 'they are only lawyers, and I, I am the grandson of the man who drove all his children out of their home except one, the heir he wanted. They haven't a chance with me.'

'I hope you'll win,' Ormston said, with affection.

'Of course I shall win! . . . Tell me, you'll be here when I come back?'

'Yes. Oh, I believe so. I might be'—his mind refused him the English word—'*dégommé*. One never knows.'

'That would really break my heart,' Gouraud said. 'You have become the salt of my life here.'

'You're very kind,' Ormston said smiling.

Gouraud folded one skin-and-bone knee over the other; his hand smoothed the dark cloth, appraisingly, as though he were going to make an offer for it. He turned the same gaze on his friend. 'I didn't come only to say goodbye. You know how inquisitive I am—I had a question, but don't answer it if it annoys you . . . My foreman—I call him that to flatter him—tells me that an English officer has been captured working with the rebels. He believed it. Have you heard the rumour?'

'It's true,' Ormston said.

The old Frenchman's eyes brightened, but he kept a serious face. 'Ah. Embarrassing.'

It would so delight him to be told the story that Ormston could not refuse it to him. 'I'm going to tell you the name,' he said, 'then you'll know more than all but a very few people—it's not being published until I come back from London next week . . . The man is Anthony Boyd.'

No trace appeared on Gouraud's face of all he must be turning over in his mind—that storehouse of secrets, experiences squeezed to the last drop of pleasure and bitterness, ironies, subtle egoism—about the relation between his friend and Anthony Boyd's wife. He spoke with unaffected kindness. 'I am sorry that you are having to deal with treachery in one of your own people. It is very mortifying. We French know a good deal about it, we know it's not a simple affair of good and bad, wickedness and piety, and we know that it corrodes. I am really sorry.'

Ormston had a sense, very consoling, that he had been taken back into a civilised society. I can talk to him, he thought. If anyone could help him to clear his mind, it was this man. But could he tell him? No question of prudence: Gouraud was far more secret than the grave. But had he the right to burden with his squalid secret an old over-used mind? Tough as a strong root, Gouraud was also acutely sensitive, from the ends of his archaeologist's fingers to his nerves and stomach.

His desperate need of companionship drove him. 'I knew Boyd at school,' he said slowly. 'We were close friends. He was—is—very stubborn, very hostile to the more respectable virtues and persons.'

'It's even worse for you than I supposed,' Gouraud said.

He moved his hands in a gesture of extreme delicacy. 'A friend as well as a fellow-countryman.'

'Yes. Yes. It doubles my—my guilt in allowing him to be questioned brutally——'

Gouraud's hands swept this away. 'My dear fellow! What some over-zealous or clumsy subordinate does is not your business. But it's repugnant—of course it is—to have to hand a friend over to justice. One of the burdens of your position. You're not, I think, a believer?'

Unhorsed, Ormston said, 'In God? No.'

'Neither am I. Let's say that I believe like Pascal—but without his anguish—that the few years of our life are all that is given, our whole destiny. Because I believe it, I also believe that men like you, intelligent, informed, sane, upright, have the right—I say: the right—if you wish, to impose your feeling for order on the anarchic mob. Order, discipline, are not in our nature, they have to be imposed, human beings have to be persuaded, or coerced, if necessary with the greatest severity, away from the miseries of their inborn slackness and disorder and puerile malevolence. Men of your sort have the right to do anything necessary to achieve this. Anything. You are the depositories of our civilization and its values—its reasonable scepticism, curiosity, tolerance . . . but you know the rest . . .'

'How far would you go to preserve them?' Ormston drawled. He hesitated and said calmly, 'As far as torture?'

'No. Not so far. It would be a contradiction, and I am very logical. Passionately. Also'—he smiled—'I have a weak stomach.'

Ormston was silent. An idea came into his head for the first time—was it the first time, or had he only just noticed its shadow falling between him and the light?

'I could resign.'

Dismay and disapproval tightened Gouraud's mouth to the point where it became a sunken line, a wrinkle in the

worn sallow skin. He sat up. 'No, no, you have no right.
You are our Creon, you carry that burden. Some of your
duties are repugnant, like signing the order for an execution
—or handing over a friend. But you mustn't resign.' He
checked himself and said gently, 'I'm tiring you further.'

'You never do that.'

'Yes.' He stood up. 'I'll go. Goodbye, my dear fellow,
until I return.'

'Take care of yourself.'

'Nonsense. I'm not important—except to myself. To
myself, very . . . But you must be careful. Remember—
it is in you, in men like you, that the future lies.'

'The future?' Ormston felt himself beginning to smile;
he checked his smile before it could spread and disconcert
the old Frenchman. 'Thank you.'

CHAPTER TWENTY-SEVEN

HE had no engagement for this evening, but the thought of dining between his mother and Sophie, the one exacting and intelligent, the other silent, bored him. If he could have his mother alone . . . Not possible . . . On the excuse of work he had sandwiches and a bottle of claret brought to him in the library: afterwards he set himself to write what, as a younger man, he called a clearance: a curt summing-up of his position at the moment, its chances, risks, benefits. It was a trick he had taught himself early. It gave him confidence, before a dinner-party where he was going to meet the man on whom his future might depend, or when he had to decide between two risks, or simply when he had run into debt, to know exactly what he was worth, and what, if he could create the opening for it, he ought to say: sometimes he rehearsed before a glass, watching himself.

This evening the trick did not work. His mind refused to draw any confidence from the summing-up. There were too many unknown quantities. It was no longer a question of saving Anthony from the harshest penalty—what was it? —for his treachery. He might be given a long prison sentence, but at the end of it he would be released—and then what? Would he or would he not make a scandal?

There were two things that might shut his mouth. His vanity. And his hostility to society, his habit (it was that) of contempt for the very men—politicians, journalists, publicists of any breed, even the most high-minded—who would make use of his sufferings for their own purposes. At the worst—if he told his story—could he be discredited? Probably. Possibly. He had a great many enemies—and, after all, a confessed traitor . . .

The strong possibility remained that he—he, not Boyd,

he ('our Creon', he mocked himself)—was the one who would be discredited. He, too, had enemies, those he had chosen and those he had earned by succeeding too well.

He turned over on his tongue the irony of his position if what he had done turned out to have saved the country and ruined himself. The taste was sharp and, curiously, subtly, familiar.

I am very much alone, he thought. Abruptly he decided that he would bring Andrew back, at once, tomorrow.

He felt tired. It was early, not yet half-past nine, but he could read himself to sleep: he tore up his clearance, hesitated a moment whether to ring up Frent, to ask after Boyd, and decided that it was useless and unwise. Outside the door of his bedroom, he stood still. An impulse as unreasoning and instinctive as any of his childish fears for her and need of her, sent him to cross the corridor to the door of his mother's room.

When he went in she was lying back on the sofa, her head propped on a mound of pillows, and Rose Bain was busy massaging her throat and face. Rose's tongue was well out between her teeth and quivering slightly, and her face twitching in a pious ecstasy. At the sight of him she threw up hands glistening with cold cream and exclaimed, 'Heavens. But nearly finished, nearly finished. If you come back in ten minutes operation beauty will be over.'

She burst out laughing at her joke. She was flushed and in pain: sciatica was wracking her, but she believed it would go away if she ignored it, and Mrs. Ormston encouraged her in this stoicism.

'Shall I leave you?' he asked.

His mother looked at him with a trace of annoyance. 'My dear boy, give me at least a quarter of an hour.'

He turned to go. The impatience that seized him was as anguished and irrational as the child's to whom a minute is eternity. He said roughly,

'Go away, my dear Rose. You can come back later.'

Flustered, she looked at his mother for orders.

'If my son is in such a hurry . . .' Mrs. Ormston said, closing her eyes. 'But take the cream off first—you can begin again when you come back.'

He watched the other woman gently wiping and dabbing, and his mother's aquiline features emerging from the linen towel with a dull faintly nacreous gleam over them. Quite suddenly he saw her hand; it was lying on the striped damask of the sofa, the hand of an old woman, wrinkled diagonally from its outer edge almost as far up as the exquisitely shaped nails. Below the middle finger a whirlpool of deeper lines mimicked a swollen knuckle. For all the time spent on them, and for all the delicacy of their abnormally long fingers, her hands were old, the only unmitigatedly old part of her body: her carefully-tended face and throat were creased, but they had not, as had her fingers, this obscene look of naked separately-living things, ageing at a different pace from their body. A freakish image sprang in his mind: the hard ribbed sand of a tidal estuary, pinkish-brown in the setting sun. He tried, frowning, to pin it down. There had been an estuary, but where? when?

'There, my dear one,' Rose cried, 'will you be all right?'

Carrying towels and the jars of face cream, she shuffled out, leaving the smell of camphor behind her: as she reached the door Ormston had been holding open, she dropped a towel: her foot in its black ludicrously pointed slipper shot forward like the snout of an animal and kicked it into the corridor. 'Brute,' she said under her breath.

An instant later she opened the door, put her head into the room, said, 'I meant the towel, of course,' and disappeared again, closing the door with a foot thrust out, groping, behind her.

Mrs. Ormston was sitting bolt upright on the sofa. She

waited until he had crossed the room to her, then said calmly,

'Well?'

He did not answer at once. With savage self-mockery he realised that he had come here meaning to throw himself in her arms. The delay while Rose wiped the cold cream off had chilled him strangely. How ridiculous, he thought. A man over fifty, kneeling before a handsome old woman, bawling for comfort.

'Well?' she repeated, a little irritated. 'Why are you staring at me? Do I look odd?'

'How old are you, mother?'

'You know exactly how old I am—seventy-two.'

'When I was born you were nineteen,' he said, smiling. 'It must seem a long time.'

Mrs. Ormston raised her eyebrows. 'Your interest in our ages is—what shall I say?—eccentric.'

'A man of fifty-three and a woman over seventy . . . they're not the same two people as a child and his mother.'

'Do you want to be admired for making the discovery?' she mocked him gently.

His mind made an abrupt jump. 'You may have made a mistake in pushing me into an ambitious life. Why did you do it? Can you remember?'

'I haven't the least idea what you want me to say, my darling. You're in a strange mood, aren't you?'

Pulling a chair close to the sofa, he sat down and lifted one of her hands. She frowned and drew it away, without haste.

'You won't remember something that happened years ago —when my father was alive: it was during the war and he must have been home on leave. We were in Essex, at the cottage. I'd been out playing—the estuary—wet ribbed sand—I can see it.' To have trapped the image gave him an acute pleasure. 'I came in, and you and my father were quarrelling: the door of your room was closed, I stood outside it, listening. It was a frightful quarrel, my father shouting, roaring, and you—as always—controlled and very calm——'

She interrupted him. 'I hardly know which to applaud, my dear, the memory itself or your tact in reminding me.'

In his groping absorption he did not hear her. 'What happened next is the real, the surprising thing—that I oughtn't to have forgotten. Suddenly the door opened and my father came out. He nearly fell over me. I was crying and he picked me up, kissed me, then put me roughly down and went off. I remember that I ran into your room, still crying, and you made light of it all, it was a game you had been playing, not a quarrel at all, a joke.'

He stopped abruptly.

'Well?' his mother said in an ironically indulgent voice.

'I'm not sure now that you were right to keep all your anger and resentment from me.'

'You were a child.'

He searched her face for traces of the young woman whose arms and cool authoritative voice had stood between him and the angers, the unpredictable violence, of his barely known father. Nothing, not a trace—unless it were the clouded eyes, behind which, then as now, lay a country largely forbidden to him. He had an extraordinary sense that he had crossed a frontier and must go on, driven by he had no precise idea what furies.

'They seeped, you know, through the walls of closed rooms. But not honestly, not in a safe form. As a poison, an infection—of fears, suspicion—I suspected every kind of horror—lies. You didn't need courage to hide your difficulties from me—it was easier than telling me. It would have been better for me—for both of us—if you had raved, wept, told me my father was a devil—anything would have been better than that festering calm . . . My father must have found it intolerable.'

His mother spoke in the tone, plangent, very distinct, she used with inferiors—when she was forced to speak to them. 'Your pity for him is sadly out of place. He was an ill-tempered brute. Ill-bred.'

'Oh, I didn't pity him then,' Ormston said. 'I can now, a little, because only now I realise how implacably you resented him, and were ashamed of yourself for having fallen in love with one of your father's servants.' He looked at her. He had no idea that he was smiling. 'Do forgive me, my dear, but how soon after you had married him did you begin to think that you had—as Rose would not say, but you might—become a *déclassé*? Very soon? Before I was born?'

'You will oblige me by ringing for Rose before you go.'

In an unknown country every step is an excitement. 'He and I were up against the same thing—you had no warmth.'

His mother closed her eyes: her hands shut, then opened convulsively as if she were letting everything fall. 'Perhaps even then,' she said calmly, 'I was afraid that you were the son of your father.'

A moment of silence.

'Did you always dislike me?' he asked.

'Are you out of your mind?' she cried. 'How can you sit there and talk this rubbish?'

Ormston had the sense that the room was full of light, a desert of light in which he was alone. 'You were very intelligent, mother. You wanted to behave well, and you did everything you could to hide from me—perhaps from yourself, too—that if I hadn't been born there would have been nothing to remind you of your . . . mistake. Your frightful mistake. You could have crossed it out and forgotten it.'

His mother looked at him with cold anger. 'Rubbish,'

she said, 'rubbish, rubbish'—as if only the repetition satisfied her contempt—'rubbish. What's your grievance? That
I tried to keep you from knowing that your father was a
savage animal?'

'I don't——' he began.

'Or that I was ambitious for you? I didn't know that was
a sin.'

'If I became a success,' he said slowly, 'it would wipe out
part of your disgrace. I was——'

She cut him short. 'Yes, I see,' she said drily. 'My
crime—as well as protecting you—was to want to make an
eminent man of you. I'm sorry.'

'No, no, it's laughable—I can't remember a time when
I wasn't desperately anxious for your approval.' He smiled
sharply. 'I must have decided that if you didn't love me
you should at any rate admire me.'

She had recovered her self-control. With something like
kindness, she said, 'My dear boy, I do admire you. You
have done extremely well. Always.'

'Yes.' He had an insane longing to tell her about Boyd.
It swept through him like the crisis of a fever, and left him
giddy and trembling. 'Forgive me the nonsense I've been
talking—I made myself what I am. I wanted to be successful, I wanted power. I still do. Nothing else has any
real value. And surely I had the right to it? Do you
agree?'

'You don't need to justify yourself,' she said gently. 'Not
to me.'

I don't believe a word I'm saying, he thought. He had a
terrifying sensation of collapse, as though his body were
caving inwards, its veins emptying, the sockets of its bones
cracked open. He got up and dropped on his knees, feeling
blindly for her hands.

'Help me. You can. You'll understand, you're so calm,
so wise. The one person I can trust.'

Her voice reached him from a great distance. 'What is the matter, Richard? Are you ill?'

'Tell me—if everything I've got for myself—for you, too—yes, for you—were going to be destroyed, if I were disgraced, my career broken——'

'What in heaven's name are you trying to tell me?' she cried.

'—would you—as you always did—go on believing in me and—what was it you said?—admiring me?'

His mother made a noticeable effort to stifle the distaste she felt for this frenzied emotion, but her voice gave it away. 'Really, my dear boy, must you behave like your father? This extraordinary scene . . .'

With a physical shock, he saw himself kneeling ludicrously at the side of the sofa, clinging to one of her hands: he saw the hand, too, brownish ribbed skin and long narrow pointed nails, with stupefying distinctness; he dropped it and got up. In the same instant, as though the shock had broken a way into some walled-up recess of his mind, he felt a murderous rage, a wish to hurt, even strike her. She was wiping her fingers on a ridiculously small handkerchief. His own hands were shaking and he folded them behind his back, out of harm's way.

'Our prisoner decided to talk,' he said. 'I had him tortured.'

She rolled the tiny handkerchief into a ball and let it drop. 'You——?'

He hesitated. A question that had plagued him, and was unanswered—perhaps unanswerable—chose this moment to return. *Had* he, after all—when he told Frent that he could use any means—had he known clearly what these would be? I don't know, he thought wearily, I—do—not know. It's not important . . . He said calmly,

'It was the only sensible thing to do—since he refused to help us.'

'Is he . . . badly hurt?'

'Yes.'

His mother was silent: no change in her face, but the fingers of one hand scraped across the sofa with the unpleasant sound of nails on silk. 'Is there going to be trouble —a scandal? Is that what you meant?' She lost her composure suddenly. 'Richard, you must stop it, you must protect yourself.'

Ormston smiled. 'You mustn't be disgraced.'

Both words and smile stung her. 'You had no right to tell me,' she said icily. 'Why should I have to know about such horrors? You should have kept it to yourself.'

'Yes, yes, you're quite right.' His anger, like his weak longing to be comforted, had gone: something, at the back of his mind, was trying to draw his attention to itself; it wavered and came closer, then slipped aside: he felt curiosity and a prick of fear.

'Aren't you making too much of it?' his mother said. 'The man was surely worthless?'

'Perhaps,' he said with indifference.

'*Why* did you tell me?'

'Why?' He frowned. 'I have no idea now why,' he said simply.

Her glance moved over his face, slowly, with a controlled disgust. 'You must have been mad to do such an unpleasant thing. Even your father—brute as he was——' She checked herself.

A feeling of boredom seized him: it bored him to go on talking. 'Yes, I daresay,' he said. He yawned. 'He wasn't a self-righteous hypocrite. His—his lusts didn't need an unnatural outlet.' Unnatural? he thought. Nonsense. Entirely natural and human.

'I don't know what you mean.'

'You ought to know,' Ormston said. 'You and I are much more alike than I am like my father.'

'I tried to make a gentleman of you,' his mother said softly, with extreme bitterness, 'a man able, as he wasn't, to behave decently.'

He looked at her with amusement. 'My poor dear. What a disappointing life you've had.'

'We won't discuss my life, my dear boy.'

The memory that had been evading him stepped forward, slyly, like a clown with a stick held behind his back. 'Oh, but we will,' he said lightly. 'D'you remember the time I'd been laughed at and told I was a common little beast, and I came howling to you to be comforted? It's of no importance, but I've just remembered how it ended. You were as cold with me when I told you as if I'd said or done something offensive. You pushed me out of the room: I was disgracing you, you said.'

His mother smiled slightly. 'By crying?'

'Oh, no, not at all. By existing.'

She said nothing. He reflected that the best thing he could do was to leave her at once: there was still time to retreat, back over the frontier, to draw a few respectable rags over his nakedness and over the nakedness of their two lives; still possible to pretend that nothing irrevocable had happened. An impulse too strong and obscure to be suppressed pushed him to go on.

'You didn't even care to see your photograph in my hands, did you, my dear?'

Silence.

'Yes,' she said at last, 'it's true. I never liked you. I never wanted you.'

He looked at her with a mocking smile. 'Now we know.'

He turned and walked quickly to the door. It was ajar. Rose's clumsily groping foot had not quite closed it. Pulling it open, he was astonished to see his wife standing in the corridor, against the opposite wall. He stared at her. She was very pale. How long has she been there? he wondered absently. How much did she hear? . . . He felt indifferent. Did it matter what she had heard? Drawing the door to behind him, he walked past her and went to his bedroom.

Sophie stood looking after him for a moment, then tip-toed across the corridor, and, stealthily, without sound, pushed the door of her mother-in-law's room open a few inches, and peered inside.

Mrs. Ormston had her back to the door; she was looking at herself, leaning into the glass with an air of bewilderment and stupefaction. If she lifted her eyes very slightly, she would see Sophie reflected behind her, watching. She did not lift them.

Stepping back, Sophie closed the door carefully and went unhurriedly along the corridor to her own room.

CHAPTER TWENTY-EIGHT

As his father opened the door of the room, Andrew turned
sharply. He had been standing staring at the titles of the
books in his father's bedside shelf—all of them, except a new
life of Napoleon, were books of memoirs—without paying
them any attention. He frowned and began,

'I came back——'

'I see you did,' Ormston interrupted drily. 'May I know
why?'

He knew why—had known the instant he set eyes on the
boy's face. Unexpectedly, he felt a lift of the heart, excitement, almost pleasure. The agony of disillusion he had
barely had time to taste dropped out of sight. My last
chance, he thought swiftly. He brushed aside the half-
formed question: Chance to do what? Andrew was his—
even more than his son, his creation. He knew, knew certainly, that he could convince him of the rightness of what
had happened. With him I can't fail, he thought. His
mind had cleared suddenly; he felt quietly confident and in
control, like a surgeon picking up an instrument he knows
precisely how to use. It was a familiar sensation, as old in
him as the moment when, a young man, he was waiting
with two others to be interviewed for his first job: then as
now he had had this calm certainty of being able to please
and impress men not easily impressed or charmed. Glancing
at his two rivals, he had felt a touch of contempt: compared
with him they were ignorant amateurs at the game of handling people. It brushed him again now, this contempt:
never, he thought, never at any age had he been so young,
so defenceless, so capable of giving himself away as Andrew,
without knowing it, did in every line of his young hard
face.

With an effort, Andrew said, 'Is it true that you have had Boyd tortured?'

His father took this clumsy thrust easily. 'Let's sit down.' He settled himself in a low chair. 'No, no, sit down, boy, I can't do with you standing up like a sentry . . . That's better. Who gave you the fellow's name?'

'You did.'

'No. I didn't. Tell me who did.'

Andrew moved his long fingers. 'Everyone knows it.'

'Everyone? That's nonsense. They will next week—when they open their newspapers. But who told you this story that he had been—what was it you said?—tortured?'

'It's being said——'

'Bazaar gossip,' Ormston interrupted, smiling. 'And you swallowed it?' He watched Andrew as the young man jumped up. 'Can't you sit still, my dear Andrew? All right —but it's time you went back to England.'

'Then it's not true?' Andrew said in an uncertain voice. He paused, scowled, and said, 'But it is. I know it. I know what was done to him . . . Don't try to make a fool of me.'

'I'm not,' Ormston said gently.

He hesitated. But this is my last chance, he thought again, coldly and lucidly; my last and only card . . . If he continued to lie it ceased to be, in any sense of the word, a chance. By cheating he would be throwing his card away. There would be no victory, no triumph, no reconciliation. Nothing. Nothing except his flat pointless refusal to play his card, trust his luck, or skill. He said slowly,

'Suppose it's true—and suppose there were no other way, beyond all argument *no other way* to save this country from more bestial killings, misery, useless deaths—wouldn't you say it was justified?'

'No,' Andrew said.

'Tell me why,' Ormston said patiently.

Andrew's grimace of contempt made him look older and less vulnerable. 'If you want to know—I mean, if you really don't know why a torturer is the filthiest creature on earth, worse than any murderer, too filthy to touch—I can't tell you.'

His son's insolence stung Ormston because it was involuntary: the boy did not mean to be insolent, was not conscious of the loathing in his voice. He felt a momentary doubt, an almost physical queasiness. Mastering it, he said coolly,

'Don't let yourself become emotional, Andrew. I want you to use your head—not react like an hysterical woman. Think. If you were responsible—as in effect I am—for the lives of all the people in this country, from helpless old ladies like Mrs. Durham to children, even unborn children —they killed one of these the other day, when they shot a young woman who was pregnant—what would you do if you were faced by the refusal of a man, one man, to give you the information you needed to break a rebellion which is both a civil war—they kill their own people—and a vicious circle of fear and hate? What would you do? Would you sit down and say piously: It's too bad he won't speak, but I've kept my hands clean? Or would you use violence—if you like, cruelty—to force him to speak?' He lifted his hand quickly. 'No, wait a minute. Remember that we spent four days, four long days—while the killings went on—unarmed men, a young English girl, a boy— trying without any physical pressure—except keeping him awake—to get Boyd to speak. We tried every argument. Every sort of appeal. *I* tried. I'—he paused briefly—'I implored him. I almost went on my knees'—he smiled, a half-ironical smile—'I would have crawled on them if it had been any use. We—I—failed . . . Well? Would you, at that point, have given in and let him get away with it—with our chance of stopping this cruel bloody mess? Think, my dear, think.'

Andrew was pale and scowling. 'I don't know,' he said under his breath.

His father's heart leaped; he looked down, to hide his triumph. 'It's not easy to govern,' he said quietly. 'If you have to decide between one man, one criminal—that's what Boyd is, you know, a peculiarly evil criminal, unreliable, vain, arrogant—if you have to decide between him and all the helpless men, women, children, he is condemning to misery, it becomes an agony of mind that is——' He broke off. He had been going to say: that is worse than the agony of a man twisting and screaming between the hands of his torturers. *No*, he thought . . . He closed his eyes for a moment. And it would be a mistake to say it.

His son did not speak. He waited. As so often, he had the sense of using his energy and charm as a violinist uses his bow. He had a brief memory of Andrew as a very young child: between his third and fourth years he had gone through a phase when he fell into fits of rage for no reason, or none he had words for, and the one person who could manage him then was his father: he had only to speak to the furious child to calm him into tears or smiles. This power he had over his child was his sharpest most exquisite joy. It returned again for a moment.

'Could you have tortured him?' Andrew said abruptly.

'No.'

He had spoken without thought, the word jerked out of him. Andrew's face, distorted by disgust and an almost childish grief, told him what he had done.

'You see?' Andrew cried. 'You order other people to act like—like animals, and you, you keep your gloves on. It . . . it's the most contemptible thing I've ever heard.'

The blood rising in Ormston's temples was followed by a sensation of cold, moving behind his eyes, across his skull. He looked at the furious young man facing him—his son. For a moment he wanted to say: You're not better than I

am. You don't know what you would have done in my
place. Until you're actually in a situation, you don't know
what it will force you to do; you'll do what it tells you. And
it will tell you *what you are*. You don't know that yet—you
don't know who you are . . . An image of Boyd's scorched
twisted hand pushing weakly at the bedclothes clapped
itself across his mouth. He steadied himself and said,

'My dear child——'

Andrew interrupted him rudely. 'If it had been anyone
but you . . . I suppose you'll deny it if it gets out, but people
won't believe you. You'll be discredited—a leper——'

The puerile insult, the wish to hurt, stiffened his father.

He said drily, 'You're wrong. Nothing is forgotten so
quickly as unpleasant facts. Nothing.'

Andrew's mouth twitched. '*I* shan't forget it.'

He's going to break down, Ormston thought. With deliberate sarcasm, he said, 'Your self-righteousness does you
credit.'

Andrew bent down, bringing his face close to his father's,
and seized his arm. Instinctively, Ormston drew back.

'*No!*'

Taken aback, Andrew stammered, 'What? I'm sorry,
I'm sorry.'

'Nothing,' his father said, 'it's nothing . . . For a moment
I thought you . . . it was a mistake.' He made an immense
effort, and said, 'You haven't been tested yet. You've been
safe . . . I shan't always be able to protect you.'

'You?' Andrew said. He smiled. 'Do you think I want
protection from you? I loathe your idea of safety.'

Ormston did not speak.

'I'm sorry,' Andrew said again. 'It's no use, is it? I'd
better go.'

His father felt an anguished need to keep him. 'Boyd
isn't dead, you know. He's being well looked after . . .
Nothing irreparable has happened.'

Andrew smiled with the same young cruel mockery. 'Is that what you think?'

'You . . . you don't believe me?'

Andrew seemed to hesitate. 'That you did it is irreparable,' he said, almost gently. 'You can't put that right. You're'—he spread his hand in a confused gesture—'No, it's despicable and disgusting.'

His father did not go on. I can't get near him, he thought. Yet if he put a hand out, he could touch him, touch the hard warm flesh, feel its warmth, its energy of a young animal.

'You mean that I am?' he murmured.

Since Andrew said nothing, he went on,

'I've always tried not to fail you.'

'What I can't bear is that *you* did it,' Andrew said.

It was a child crying out. Ormston smiled without irony. 'You don't trust me—not any longer—to know what ought to be done?'

'I don't trust you at all,' Andrew said.

He walked towards the door.

Ormston stood up. He had the sense that something in his body had given way under the pressure—he felt it—of his son's rejection of him. He can't wait to be rid of me, he thought: he wants me out of his sight, out of his life.

'Don't go,' he said involuntarily. 'Stay with me.'

Andrew stood still, his reluctance so plain it was like a blemish on his face. 'I can't. I'm sorry.'

'Help me.'

His son looked at him with an embarrassed smile, as though watching him do something clumsy or humiliating.

'How can I help? There's nothing I can—is there?'

A single thought steadied Ormston on the edge of he scarcely knew what—despair, laughter. My last card was no good.

He said very gently, 'You'll see Sarah, won't you?'

'Yes. Tomorrow.' No point in saying that he had seen her already this evening. Besides, his father must guess.

'Well, go,' Ormston said.

Alone, he stood for a long time, several minutes, without moving, afraid to move, afraid of the vacancy round him, the absence of all voices and absence of himself.

CHAPTER TWENTY-NINE

It was late, but he could not go to bed. Not yet. He had first of all to clear his mind of the—he hesitated—the fog of unreason clouding it. The memory of something Gouraud had said returned, and he thought coldly: What, after all, did I do? A responsible act. I have been responsible for *a saving crime*. Both words are just. It was a crime and it saved—many many people. Anthony was a dangerous man, a criminal; for their sake he had to be made harmless; he himself made brutes of us. Then what did I offend against? Not any Christian law . . . Forgive your enemies . . . Is it my place to forgive the murderers of innocents? And not against any creed of tolerance—the flabby indifference of intellectuals. Tolerate a mad dog? . . . All that is irrelevant, sentimental, neurotic . . .

'I was right,' he cried suddenly. 'I had every right.'

He did not believe what he said. He believed it with his reason, and his reason was foundering in cold and darkness. At some moment he had crossed a threshold, a door had shut on him: he was in a locked windowless cell: other lives went on, his mother's, Andrew's, but his ended, here. His offence—'Yes,' he said softly, 'I offended'—was against something so deep, so old, that with better luck he might never have stumbled over it, never torn his hand on it in the darkness. And very likely I shan't be accused, he thought, or not openly. My trial, my damnation, is taking place in darkness and silence, before no human tribunal—and no God, since I don't believe in Him . . . What shall I do?

'What shall I do?' he repeated.

Resign. I shall resign . . .

The decision made itself; it had sprung in a recess of his

mind, fully-grown, even before his son left him. Of all the
decisions he had made during his life this, he thought
lightly, was the one with which he had had least to do—he
had had almost no part in it, no choice.

He felt an overwhelming relief. Now I can sleep, he
thought: he stretched his arms, smiling. It was two o'clock.
Usually he slept with closed shutters, but he felt he wanted
air on his face; he turned off the lamp beside his bed and
pushed every shutter open. The soft warm night came
into the room. He undressed and lay down, and fell
asleep.

He dreamed. He saw himself standing in front of a glass,
looking at his face as a young man: overjoyed to see that he
was still young, he ran his finger round the firm outline of
his chin, touched the deep smooth eyelids, smiled with the
perfect mouth, and when the figure turned away from the
glass, followed it, losing sight of it almost at once, but going
down, always down, an endless descent into thicker and
thicker darkness pouring from the walls on either side of
him, the air heavy and stifling, to a recess where in complete
silence two men were working over a third whose indistinct
face he looked at, looking down, seeing it and its atrocious
pain through his own eyes which were at the same time the
narrow half-smiling eyes of one of the torturers, with whom
he identified himself while still keeping his own identity
as spectator, now able to see only the hand lying on the
floor of the cell, pressed palm down, an old curiously
wrinkled hand the colour of wet ribbed sand; he backed
away from it in horror, drawn towards a grey fog, hearing
himself, or a shadowy companion, mouth soundlessly words
I will arise I will arise, lift me, save me with a kiss, and then,
with relief, an agony of relief, seeing the dream (he knew
now that he was dreaming) waver and blow away like
smoke, as the bed, the sheet under his hand, the wide rectangle of the window, moved smoothly into its place: he

heard a bugle, so far off that the thread of sound spanned an immense distance.

Lying there, eyes widely open in the early light filling the room, he thought almost with surprise: I have no one . . . He remembered that he had embarrassed Andrew last night by asking him to stay, and for the first time saw the injustice, egotism, folly—the folly especially—of expecting a young man, with his own life clawing him, to help.

There is no one else, he thought calmly.

He began, with the greatest lucidity, to sum up in the case of Richard Ormston versus . . . versus whom?

A prudent fellow, this Ormston, fastidious, well-mannered, charming, intelligent, scrupulous on one level, only unscrupulous in the service of his lawful ambition. There were no vulgar betrayals to confess: he had always veered away at once from any possible entanglement or start of interest in pretty but dowerless young women: the married woman who was his mistress when he was a young man was kind, sensible, and approved of his marriage: there had been no unprofitable friends he needed to shed as he climbed, since instinctively he made friends in the right places. From the start, even when he was poor. (As soon as he had money he was able, not only to choose the right friends, but to indulge himself in a few enemies.) Had Anthony, as boy and young man, been what he became during the war, he would not have been intimate with him . . . For less than a second he remembered the bawling child. It wasn't the first incident of its kind, he thought sharply. There had been others, irrecoverably buried, a frozen buried lava of grief. He felt a frightful bitterness, and checked it, telling himself derisively: Before you begin to feel sorry for this unloved child, notice what he became.

He had nothing but the most unshakable contempt for the notion that a child is bound to be the victim of its foolish unhappy parents. I was born greedy, violently sensual, he thought. Is it my fault that I never learned to live with so much violence? Entirely my fault. I could have done better . . . Another thought touched his mind as lightly as one of those spider's threads stretched across a path, invisible until they cling to your face . . . Your indifference to Sophie—inexcusable . . . He brushed the thought away. He had no time now for her. He had married her, and she had borne his son: her money, at a time when he had little of his own, had been very useful to him, and he had not been unkind to her—but she meant nothing to him . . . All that's completely unimportant, he thought impatiently. Nothing is of importance except to remember that I made myself: I *wanted* to be what I am—a power in a world where the greedy, the single-mindedly ambitious, the hard, survive and flourish. I willed it. There is no excuse. No defence . . .

With something very like excitement he thought that the sleepwalker who wakes to find himself on the edge of the precipice over which he will fall bloodily must feel exactly this shock of disbelief, despair, and, yes, exultance.

He raised himself to look at his watch. Six o'clock. There were sounds outside, all the sounds—voices, footsteps, a distant aeroplane, cock-crows—of this early-waking country, a rumour as deep and continuous as the beating of his own heart. He had a fleeting sense of being part of it, part of the life of common men, with their courage, fears, cruelty, kindness, hate, love, their desires and deaths—the last the only thing they succeed in without having to learn the trick.

Something else, infinitely weak, stirred in him. He had no clear idea what it was, and he watched it with as much uncertainty, as mild a pleasure as, when he was a child, he watched the first blade of the crocus break through in the garden behind his mother's house.

CHAPTER THIRTY

IT was late in the afternoon, nearly five o'clock, before he found time to sit down in the library to draft the letter of resignation he meant to take to London with him. Unexpectedly, he found it very difficult to get the right tone, cool, aloof, final. He made several drafts before one satisfied him, and he could put it aside.

He felt tired and empty. The thought, only half-formed, of some kind of expiation—but what? What could he possibly do?—came into his mind. First of all—and at whatever cost to himself—he had to try to get leniency for Boyd. After that . . .

Robin Hind's entrance annoyed him. He looked up, frowning.

'I told you not to disturb me.'

The young man's engaging air of embarrassment was followed, momentarily, by a gleam of excitement and curiosity. He said quickly,

'I'm sorry, sir, but there is news.'

'What news?'

'The prisoner . . . Boyd . . . has killed himself.' He paused, but when the Governor, staring at him with a heavy attention, did not speak, he went on in his cool pleasant voice, 'A nurse and an orderly were taking him to the operating theatre in the hospital. It's on the third floor, and he broke away when they were passing an open window and threw himself from it—on to the concrete.'

Relief—was it relief he felt? 'You say he's dead?'

'He was alive when they picked him up,' Robin said. 'He died in a few minutes.'

'Is that all?'

'No, sir.'

'Well?'

His secretary held out a memorandum sheet on which he had written a sentence. *Tell His Excellency that I forgive him* ... Glancing at it and laying it on the table, the Governor said drily,

'What *did* he say?'

Robin lowered his eyelids. 'That is the message I was given, sir.'

'Be good enough to give me the exact wording,' the Governor said, coldly, brutally.

Robin stammered, 'He said: *Tell . . . tell your poor old bastard of a Governor that I've let him off.*'

A slight smile crossed the Governor's face, a smile which lifted the ends of his mouth in a spasm of contempt, and ironical pleasure. He said calmly,

'Yes, I see. Last score to him ... You can go.'

Robin was shocked to the heart by this smile—or what he took to be his heart, an organ which so far had given him more satisfaction than trouble. He hurried out.

As soon as he had gone, the Governor picked up the draft of his letter of resignation, read it carefully through, altered a phrase, read it again and tore it into the smallest possible shreds before dropping it, together with his secretary's memorandum, into the waste-paper basket.

CHAPTER THIRTY-ONE

HE finished destroying the few personal letters and documents kept in a leather case in his bedroom. His watch, which he had only half wound the night before, had stopped and he had to cross the room and look at the travelling clock on his dressing-chest to see that the time was going on for midnight. He had one more thing to do, a letter that ought to be written. Since it mattered very little to whom it was written, he chose a friend whose name caught his eye on the political page of *The Times* lying open in front of him.

Composing the letter gave him a mild amusement, it came so easily and quickly. I should have been a novelist, he thought.

My dear Alan,

I hope to see you next week in London, and congratulate you then on the new job. But since you may, if I am unlucky, have left before I arrive, let me tell you now how delighted I am that for once the right man and the right job have coincided—I don't wish you luck, you scarcely need it. When—if—we meet, there are one or two personal matters, not very important, on which I'd like your advice. I could ask for it now but—to tell you the truth—I'm too tired to write personal letters. Really I'm abominably tired, and sleeping abominably badly. The sensible thing to do, and in five minutes or less I'm going to do it, is to take a couple or more of old Dent's knock-out pills—do you still go to the old boy, by the way?—and turn in.

Remember me to Mary—and try to be still in England when I come.

Yours ever
Richard Ormston.

He addressed an envelope, but left the letter lying on the table, open, as though he had been too tired or too lazy to fold and seal it.

For a moment the image of the sleepwalker returned to him, and he thought, with a little irony, that nothing protects from the final gulf, nothing hides it from our sight, placing a hand over our eyes, except the body of another human being. Without feeling sorry for himself, he thought again: I have no one. My mother never was with me; that was an illusion of my own making, entirely of my making . . . With pity, the first pure pity of his life, he thought: My poor mother. I wish to God I hadn't told her about Anthony; I did it out of malice and spoiled what little pleasure she had in me. Oh, fool, fool . . . Anne? . . . Something half grief, half self-contempt brushed him as he watched the current sweep her away. She was no use to me, he thought . . . Even on the edge of the precipice, he had not changed . . . A mortal cold and solitude, complete, final, inescapable, enveloped him. He felt it, suffered from it, and thought: A pity if I can't take a few steps alone, without a hand over my eyes . . . He smiled.

Suddenly energetic, he got up and went over to the dressing-chest, pulled open a drawer and began searching it for what he wanted. Just as his hand knocked against it, he heard the door open behind him, and turned.

His wife had never looked plainer or less impressive than she did in the dressing-gown she was wearing, dark grey wool, shapeless, held together by a cord; probably she had bought it in the boys' department of a London store. A plait of her grey hair hung over one shoulder: she might have been a prematurely aged schoolgirl if her lean dark face, flat cheekbones, and hooded eyes, had not given her the mask of a peasant, a Spanish peasant. Exasperated, Ormston thought: The last person I shall see—no, no, it's too much . . . He forced himself to speak gently.

'What do you want, Sophie?'

Except by one of her absent good-humoured smiles, she did not answer. She took her time about crossing the room. When she reached him, she quite coolly whipped the little bottle of sleeping tablets from his hand, glanced at it, set it down, and said in a light voice,

'What next, I'd like to know.'

He could not keep his irritation out of his voice. 'Really, my dear girl, what is it? What do you want? I'm just going to bed.'

She glanced at him with a frank malice. 'Don't bother, Richard. I know what you're going to do.'

'My dear Sophie, what kind of nonsense have you got into your head now?'

'Since I tell you I know, why are you taking the trouble to lie?'

He felt terribly bored. There was no reason why he should take her into his confidence—even if he had wanted to.

'My dear, do go to bed,' he said, sleepily polite. 'It's after midnight.'

'And leave you to kill yourself?' she murmured.

'You have more imagination than is good for you,' he said drily. He went on in a mocking voice, 'Even if I meant to make such a fool of myself, why should you bother?'

She frowned. 'Perhaps I shouldn't—you don't care what I think. But you care about Andrew. Do you want to give him that burden to carry for the rest of his life?'

'The rest of his life? Nonsense! My dear girl, the young recover a great deal more easily than that. They don't let us burden them with our troubles—rightly and very naturally.'

'I daresay,' Sophie said. 'But you have no right to do it.'

He struggled against his annoyance. It was very much

the annoyance he would have felt if he had been asked an impudent question by a man who had no conceivable right to ask him anything at all. He suppressed it and said coldly,

'I value your opinion.'

She sat down. In a light, almost childish voice, she said,

'Before Anthony Boyd died, he had been tortured, hadn't he?'

Angered more than taken aback, he said, 'Did Andrew tell you that?'

'Oh, I don't need to hear things from Andrew.' Her eyes flickered. 'I'm not quite without friends here, you know. The man I get bananas for the monkey from is one of them, and the girl who washes my hair when I don't do it myself is another . . . It's true, isn't it?'

She had not answered his question about Andrew. He did not persist. 'Boyd was in the hands of the police.'

'You gave them the order, didn't you?'

Ormston shrugged his shoulders. She had exasperated him to the point of wanting to punish her for inflicting herself on him now. Meaning to hurt her, he said,

'Yes, I did.'

Her face did not change. 'Why?'

To his immense astonishment, he felt a wish to justify himself. No, not to justify, but only—for the last time, at the last moment, and before this nonentity, this puppet of worn dark wood—to know himself, to know what, what cruelty, what cowardice, he was capable of.

'I didn't torture him. And if I'd been told—I say: told— what they were going to do, I should have been forced to forbid it. I wasn't told.'

'But you knew.'

He hesitated. After all it is not so easy to look at yourself without first arranging the image. 'Yes, I knew what they were going to do—and I didn't stop it.'

She gave him a shrewd, almost merry glance, and he caught himself thinking that there was a kind of earthy mischief in her that he had never noticed: it must always have been there. 'He was a terrible nuisance to you, wasn't he? Your career . . .'

'Yes. Yes, that's true, too,' he said. He felt lighter suddenly, relieved, as though something that had been eluding him all his life had rolled gently into his hand, as though he were not, not absolutely, destitute.

A curious smile crossed her narrow face. 'You don't know yourself very well, do you?'

A ray of light—or this smile—fell through some crack in the bones of his skull across his mind. He thought: There is something more.

'I—yes—I got a satisfaction out of it.' A shudder started in him and wormed its way upwards. 'What am I? What am I, Sophie? I used to love him—I thought I did—I thought I loved Andrew—and my mother.' He looked at her with a hard stare. 'The truth is, the only person I've loved is myself. That's what you mean, isn't it?'

'No. Oh, no, you didn't love yourself. It would have been much better for you if you had. Why, my poor Richard, you hated yourself.'

Stupefied, he thought: And that's true. There was a store of hatred in him, more of it, far more than he could have used up on any other human being; it overflowed on to Anthony when his stubbornness became a stumbling-block, a threat: on Sarah Leng when she took his son from him: on his mother. And on myself, he thought. An unexpected laugh shook him.

'When I look back, I see myself as a thoroughly dislikeable brat, all self-satisfaction and careful charm.'

In a light voice, she said,

'That's not how I see you. I see you keeping a sharp eye on people you were afraid of—yes, afraid—but with a secret

hope that they'd suddenly become good and kind.' She
gave her quick clear laugh. 'Poor child!'

If she had thrown a cup of water in his face, the shock
would have been less rude. In the same instant he had a
feeling of release, almost gaiety. She had not changed, not
suddenly become moving or attractive: it was as if she had
stretched a finger out and touched in him a nerve that had
been lying inert, dead, for years, for almost the whole of his
life; the pain for a moment was excruciating, and then the
gaiety, the warmth, took over, he wanted to laugh aloud,
to talk, to drag everything from his mind and lay it in front
of her, a child bringing his mother the pebbles and rubbish
he has picked up. He said gently,

'Why, Sophie, I never knew you.'

'You never cared to.'

'Can I talk to you?' he asked. 'You're not tired?'

'Don't be absurd, my darling.'

So much to say, so little time, and so few words that did
not belong to the *literature* (and parody) of his life: there
must, he thought, be people in the world who were not
their own models, whose lives were left to write themselves,
in goodness, in simplicity. He was not one of them; he had
so twisted and glorified and falsified himself that to find a
few nakedly true words was almost impossible now.

'In the last day or two I've realised, you know, that there
is a point of—of selfishness and unkindness—cruelty—that
I can't step beyond and endure myself. I thought I could
do anything—for a good motive. Or even a merely sensible
motive, such as getting on in the world. That's simply not
true. I know that now. There's a line I can't cross and forgive myself for crossing it . . . And this has nothing to do
with my evil nature—I mean, with the evil which is part of
me. I had all kinds of good motives'—he smiled in an embarrassed way—'I wanted—I sincerely wanted—to save this
poor country from any more horrors. But my good motives

don't excuse my bitter offence against'—he hesitated—
'against all men.'

All the wrong words, he thought wearily. It was against
myself. Letting them torture Anthony was a final arrogance,
a final violation—of myself, a final act of hate, the arrogance
of a devil . . . For the first time he noticed that his wife's
eyes were not, as he had always seen them, flat and shallow;
they were clear, so clear that he had the illusion of looking
through them, through depth after depth, one olive-black
darkness merging into another, as in the sky at night when
there are clouds and no stars.

'You believed you had the right to save it by hurting
atrociously one man, only one man.'

'Yes.' He stopped, and went on with a sick bitterness, 'I
made myself believe it, Sophie. There is no excuse for me.
I did something that was absolutely evil.'

Sophie's smile was half sad, half quizzically amused.
'Goodness me, how d'you know there is any such thing?
Aren't you being rather vain?'

He had begun to walk about the room, suddenly very
restless, and the word brought him up like a whip cracked
in front of his eyes. He blinked, and turned on her.

'It's incredible that I'm talking to you like this.'

'It's easy to talk to a stranger,' Sophie said, smiling, 'a
woman you don't know.'

He made a confused gesture. Her calmness and simplicity
did not surprise him—not any longer. What was surprising
was in himself: the extraordinary ease he felt, the surrender,
the solace of leaving himself in her hands, no need to guard
himself, to think a move ahead, to finesse. It had never happened to him in his life—or so long ago that he had forgotten
the taste of it. Almost humbly he said,

'No, my wickedness is a fact, not . . . I didn't just make
an error of judgment, a mistake.'

'Your mother——'

He cut her short, harshly. 'My mother is sickened by this.' He paused, and went on in a meditative voice, 'She never liked me, you know.'

Sophie was looking at him with a serene gentle irony. 'Surely she knows that you wanted success—beginning with your school prizes—more than anything else to please and impress her?'

'How did you know that?'

'I love you.'

He moved his hands. The words meant nothing to him —as little as his mother's caresses mean to a child. They passed over him in the same way, a touch too simple, too usual to distract him from . . . from himself, and from the discoveries he was making.

'I'm the only person who is to blame—no one else. You must see and believe that, Sophie. No one did me any harm. I harmed myself. I'm what I made—I could have made something quite different. I needn't have served this evil in myself.' He thought she was going to interrupt him, and he said savagely, 'No, no, don't say anything, and don't tell me it doesn't exist. If I didn't—now—believe that, I couldn't believe that goodness is possible. I couldn't believe in your goodness . . .'

He stopped. To his dismay, he was shaking; he felt dazed for a moment, as though he had been struck on the head. Too late, he thought, it's too late to discover these things.

He forced himself to attend to Sophie. Poor Sophie, he thought. What am I doing to her? I ought to send her away . . . He made no effort.

'No one has any right to judge you,' she said tranquilly. 'Neither your mother, nor Andrew, nor'—she paused very briefly—'your present mistress.'

'I'm my own judge,' he said sharply. 'Even if they forgave me, I should hate myself . . . How can I forgive a man I don't know?' Unconsciously, with an unconscious timidity, he bent down and touched her cheek lightly. 'Do *you* know who I am?'

Startling him by the loudness of her voice, she cried, 'Yes!'

'I don't believe you. I can't.'

'You're very obstinate, Richard,' she said simply.

Could anyone, he thought, go on living with the truth about himself—without dying of disgust, or being frozen to death by its cold, its final hard deadly clarity?

He said almost inaudibly, 'Nothing can save me now—and no one. *I can't live with myself.*'

A silence.

'Richard—one thing. In the end, when all's said and done, you weren't indifferent.'

'Well?'

'Indifference is the worst face of cruelty—not to see, not to know, not to admit the pain you've made another person feel.'

He had no words—hers had entered him with a humiliating bitterness. Indifference was the face he had shown her, always, throughout their marriage. Although that is not what she was saying, he thought.

'Forgive me.'

'I don't forgive you, my darling,' she said sorrowfully, 'I don't want to—there's no need—I love you.'

He was standing now in a light so cold and blinding that it must, he thought, sear his eyelids; just able to see himself in it, and reject himself. In this moment of final, only half bearable lucidity, the thing in her he had called sentimental pity, and disliked as a very sickly form of egoism, was the most nearly pure face of human gentleness and goodness, and an ironical comment on his certainty, his life-long certainty, that anything he was clever enough and powerful enough to do he had the right to do, and that he would never —being what he was: civilised, intelligent, far-seeing,

rational, and the rest of it—stumble into doing a clumsy or
ill-judged or disastrous act.

'I sicken myself.'

'You needn't, you know, forgive yourself,' Sophie said
lightly, 'it's not your job. But you can be patient, and live.'

'No,' he said, 'I can't.'

'Why? Tell me why.'

He did not answer. To talk, even to her, had become
useless—an effort he needn't make. He had seen himself
now, it was finished; all he wanted was to shut his eyes and
mouth, and keep them shut . . . It struck him that perhaps
the last and the least thing he could do for her was to push
away this lethargy closing on him, pressing him down like
stone hands laid on his shoulders, and tell her—tell her
what? Tell her the truth, he thought—as much of it as I
know.

'The truth is I've reached breaking-point. My breaking-
point. The fact that I had a man tortured is something that
. . I've broken some sort of law between men . . . that
makes my life strictly insupportable. I'm—what is the
word?—yes, irreparable. Past mending. Even if I were to
do some kind of public penance . . . I did, you know, have
a childish idea of expiation, but I've given that up.' No
expiation is possible, he thought calmly. Not for me: what
I really want is to destroy myself, not try—he could not help
smiling at the word—to redeem myself. 'I've been able to
realise what it was I did and that's as far as I can get—the
very limit of my strength. Even'—he smiled at her—'even
with yours added to it. I *can't* live with what I did.'

Sophie's voice carried a sadness to which there were no
limits. 'My love doesn't help you.'

He imagined that this was the first time she had used the
word. Love? he thought . . . He felt a queer bitter amuse-
emnt ready to twitch his lips, and pressed them closely together. I should tell her I love her. It might mean some-

thing to her. It might console her ... He couldn't do it. One doesn't change, he thought drily. She is the only person I want near me, the only one. The only person I trust and know—and who knows me. But I don't love her. If she can believe I do—so much the better ... He roused himself to say,

'Yes, of course it helps—with everything except going on living.'

His exhaustion struck him suddenly, like a fist—exhaustion and something else. Light, a different light, warmth breaking through it, as clear as a beckoning hand. He went on his knees beside her. A confidence far beyond ordinary trust filled him.

'But it can help me to die ... I'm strong, Sophie, I should have to go on living for years and years—heaven knows how many——' he laid his forehead on her hands folded on her knee. 'Must I face that, or can I run away?'

He waited for her answer. He could feel no tremor, no movement at all, in her hands or her body. She was holding herself perfectly still. At last she said,

'Oh, my poor love. Yes—yes, you can run away.'

'Then help me.'

He had to wait another long minute.

'Get up, Richard.'

He got to his feet, and watched her go to the table and bring back the little bottle of tablets. She asked calmly,

'How many of these ought you to take?'

'I don't know.' He felt lightheaded with relief and gratitude, and laughed. 'I asked old Dent how many of them would kill me. He told me and I've forgotten.'

'There are about eight left,' Sophie said.

'That may have been what he said. I rather think so ... Well—give them to me, Sophie.'

Filling a glass with water from the carafe on his night-table, she brought it to him, then shook the pills—exactly

eight—out on to the palm of her hand. When she held it
out to him, he noticed its smallness and fineness.

'You have very pretty hands,' he said.

The least gleam of mockery came into her eyes; she
blushed, hotly, wave on wave of colour rising in her sallow
cheeks. She laughed a little. 'It's not the time to notice
that.'

'I suppose not.'

Turning his head, he caught sight of the letter he had
written, lying on the table. 'That will make it seem an
accident.'

She gave him an absent little smile. Had she even heard
him? The hand she was holding out to him remained
steady, until he had swallowed the last pill. Then, only then,
its fingers stiffened and curled inwards, as if shrivelling. She
said quietly,

'Lie down now, my dear.'

He had undressed before he began clearing up: he lay
down on the bed, pushing the single blanket out of the way
—and suddenly knew that what he had done was irrevocable:
everything was lost. Cold entered him like a nail driven in.
The agony did not last; it drifted away raggedly, like the
vestiges of a dream. Sophie had seated herself on the edge
of the bed, so that she could take his head on her shoulder;
his body in its thin pyjamas settled itself against her with
complete familiarity, although he had never done it in his
life—with her or any woman. But his body was now no
longer his business. It was hers: he left it to her. He asked
idly,

'Am I heavy?'

'No.'

Immediately over his head the ceiling was lightly cracked,
a single line, meandering out of sight: he saw the Itchen near
Winchester, and a boy stooping to dip his finger in the
water. 'What I did to Anthony was abominable, wasn't it?'

'Yes.'

'How can you bear to touch me?' he asked—for the pleasure of hearing what she would be sure to say.

She did not answer. She went on smoothing the hair above his temple with one finger. He felt peaceful and coolly happy—and indifferent. I have been accepted, he thought. As I am, for what I am. 'In spite of my sins,' he said aloud.

'My love, my only love, you haven't . . . you're not more a sinner than the rest of us.'

He turned this over for a moment. 'The man you loved didn't commit any sins, but—I wasn't that man.'

'I always loved you,' she said very gently. 'Always. Before I knew you—when you were a baby. I shall never stop loving you.'

A feeling of heaviness seized him, heaviness and speed, as though something were rushing past him, a swirling torrent of wind and darkness, rising in front of his eyes and flowing behind them, soundless, penetrating; he rose and fell with it. He had to make an effort to move his tongue.

'Why didn't I know?'

'You know now.'

'It's too late.'

'Nonsense,' she said, 'nonsense, my darling. We have plenty of time.'

The word echoed in his head, returning and dying away in that dark labyrinth, baffling him with its sense of a double flow, the one in himself and the one, rising silently from an unseen well-mouth to fill the whole boundless height from earth to night sky, outside. But what time *is* it? he thought: what year? I don't know . . . Images, and fragments of images, drifted by him, as towards the end of a dream, unseizable, all but unidentifiable . . . a young man's hurt angry face . . . hair blown across a cheek . . . a stretch of water glittering close to his fingers; he did not try to touch it . . . He became conscious again of his wife's arms holding him, of a warmth and softness against the side of his face, and thought confusedly that if he could tip all these fragments into her hands she would understand everything about him.

'Why, Sophie, why was I so cruel?'

'I don't know. So many questions we can think to ask have *no* answers. Simply no answers.'

'It's not important,' he murmured.

Again something dark rushed past him and he felt himself ebbing with it into a blackness infinitely greater than the speck of light he had become, a speck flickering in and out on the horizon, many miles away, separated from him by a cloudy landscape, dark smoke of trees, fields, rivers, an estuary, gently swelling hills. The sea must be over there, he told himself, a lighthouse or the lights of ships; then, for less than a moment, he felt his wife's arms again; the shame and silliness of his life, drawn into the little flame of her love, wavered and disappeared; the room behind her darkened and dissolved into smoke: she, too, left him, her features first, then the echo of her voice speaking to him, and last of all the light pressure on him of her hands.

What she had said was, 'I don't know why you did this evil thing. There *is* evil, there is violence, there is cruelty. And there *is* love. One has to leave it at that.'

The stiffness and acute pain in her shoulders and the joints of her arms had become paralysing: two and a half hours is a long time to sit still, holding up a man as heavy as Richard Ormston. His weight against her grew heavier. She looked down at him—and moved awkwardly from the edge of the bed, laying his body down as she did it. She drew the blanket up over him.

Two or three minutes passed before she felt able to walk easily. She was not certain where the bell near the foot of the bed rang: she pressed it and stood in the centre of the room, waiting.

A very young orderly came in. Standing between him and the bed, she asked,

'Do you know whether my son is in the house?' He ought to be, but she suspected that he had found a way to be out of it at night.

'I don't know, ma'am,' he mumbled.

She sent him off to Andrew's bedroom to find out. He came back and told her that there was no one in the room: she reflected for a moment, and said,

'You'll see anyone who comes upstairs, won't you? As soon as he comes, ask him to come here—at once.'

The boy saluted and hurried out, and she went back to the bed. Bending down, she whispered in his ear. 'You don't mind waiting a little longer, do you? You needn't be afraid, I'm here.'

CHAPTER THIRTY-TWO

As the door opened, she turned, expecting Andrew. Mrs. Ormston had come in and was walking across the room with the same step she would have used at a reception, short, dignified, neither reluctant nor hurried: she was made up as if for a reception, too; her hair had been dressed, by Rose, of course, with elaborate skill, and she was wearing a dark velvet house-coat. At the sight of Sophie, she allowed a surprised half-smile to cross her lips. Very probably, she did not know herself whether she were speaking maliciously or not, or condescendingly.

'Why, Sophie, my dear girl, what are *you* doing here?'

Sophie did not move. 'What do you want?'

Mrs. Ormston glanced past her at the bed. Lowering her voice very slightly, she asked,

'Is he asleep?'

'Yes. But what do you want?'

'I heard people walking about—you know, I sleep so badly that I never put my light out before two o'clock— and I know that Richard often doesn't. I thought . . . but, really, my dear, I needn't explain to you, need I?'

'Did you come here to scold him?' Sophie asked. 'You're too late. You won't be able to do him any more harm— ever again.'

She stepped aside, to let her mother-in-law come to the side of the bed, watching her as she looked down at her son's body, stooped, lifted one of her long marvellous hands and touched his face delicately with a finger: the light caught its polished nail. She drew back, straightening herself carefully, and looked at Sophie with an expression ludicrously out of place on her powdered cheeks and carefully painted lips—

bewilderment, horror. Suddenly these took on the look of an ill-fitting mask.

'Is he——?' She could not finish the sentence.

'He has killed himself,' Sophie said quietly, without a trace of emphasis, her face calm.

'Impossible,' Mrs. Ormston said at last. 'Quite quite impossible. You're mistaken, of course.'

'It's true,' Sophie said. I should be sorry for her, she thought. Her only child. I can't. Forgive me, I can't.

The hands Mrs. Ormston drew down her face disturbed more than her complexion: together with the powder they removed a skin of arrogance and fine effortless reserves. She was left looking dull and heavy. Speaking to herself, she muttered,

'What will people think? What will they say?'

'I can't think that matters.'

'Sophie, I came here to—to forgive him.'

'Forgive him for what?'

Mrs. Ormston made an heroic effort: her voice almost, not entirely but almost recovered its smooth amiable tone of having to keep in their place, impersonally, without any dishonest consideration for their feelings, stupid people and inferiors.

'You wouldn't understand it, my dear girl.'

This glancing, half deliberate insult, so like those she had been ignoring for years from this quarter, did not touch Sophie. In some queer way—perhaps because, although she did not know it yet, the older woman's power to hurt, to condescend, to be uncommon, and uncommonly intelligent and detached, had died with her son—it started a movement and a warmth in her that she did not yet know to be the beginning of pity.

'Anyhow, it's too late to forgive him now,' she said gently.

Mrs. Ormston swayed, and caught at the back of a chair.

Controlling herself, she asked in the same strong drawling voice.

'Did he complain to you about me?'

'Had he reason to?'

'No. But he might—he hasn't been himself lately, you know—he might have imagined he had.' She pressed a handkerchief to her mouth for a moment. 'Poor deluded boy.' Tears came into her eyes, she let them pour under her lids, those heavy bluish lids, and trickle over her cheeks. 'How could he do this? I loved him so, Sophie, and he was all I had. I don't know how he could leave me alone in the world. He knew how I have suffered. How could he do it?'

Shall I tell her? Sophie thought. 'The only person you loved was yourself. He didn't find that out until yesterday. Well, perhaps some part of him always knew it—always believed he was unlovable, and disliked himself for it.'

'What nonsense, Sophie,' her mother-in-law said loudly. 'Childish hysterical nonsense. Or lies.'

'I'm not lying.' She took a step forward and looked closely into the older woman's face with its bruised lids, thin dark nostrils like a hare's, and the scrawl of fine lines. 'He told me so himself. Four or five hours ago.'

'I don't believe you.'

Sophie shrugged her narrow shoulders. 'Just as you like.' She turned away. 'I'm sorry. Don't let's argue in front of him.'

The slow shambling noise behind her startled her into turning back quickly. Mrs. Ormston had collapsed into a chair. It was not only her body that had given way: the face she lifted to Sophie was that of a terrified old woman, grief and fear rising in her, in the breathless sounds forcing their way out between her lips; her cheeks quivered in a very disagreeable way: somewhere in her had been dammed up a timidity at least equal to her vanity and arrogance, a great weight of timidity which had broken through at last and was sweeping dignity, self-possession, sense, away in its muddy torrent. She pulled at her mouth with hard finger-tips.

'Have I . . . did I do something wrong ? . . . How, tell me how.'

Leaning forward, arms folded across her body, she rocked herself and whimpered. Sophie touched her gently.

'It doesn't matter.'

Her mother-in-law snatched at her hand. 'Don't leave me. Don't send me away to live with only that fool Rose.'

Was she always afraid? Sophie wondered. Compassion for the clutching unhappy old woman came to her from—from where? She half turned towards the bed. Some other feeling, something shrewd, ironical, not unkind, made her say steadily,

'I'll have to think about that. I might resent you, you know, and then it wouldn't work—for either of us. You must give me time to think.'

'No,' Mrs. Ormston cried, 'don't leave me.'

'I'll think about it and tell you,' Sophie repeated. With an effort she added, 'Would you like me to leave you with him for a short time ?'

Mrs. Ormston pulled herself out of the chair with surprising energy. 'No, no, no . . . Get Rose for me.'

Sophie frowned. 'She shouldn't be got out of bed at this hour. She's really ill, you know.'

'I must have her, I need her '

On the edge of an angry protest, Sophie closed her mouth. One can't save everybody.

Her mother-in-law hurried across the room. Before she reached the door it opened. She brushed past Andrew without glancing at him: her voice filled the corridor with its blind need. 'Rose, Rose, I want you. Rose!'

CHAPTER THIRTY-THREE

ANDREW closed the door and came forward, raising his eyebrows, with an air of sleepy amusement. 'What's going on? What's wrong with None?'

His mother looked at him. He has grown a great deal older since he came out here, she thought. But at this moment his face had a blurred smoothness, eyes half closed to keep the warmth and violence of his happiness from showing itself plainly; a smiling fold at their corners gave it away. The girl, his mother thought absently: he has been with her. How do they manage it? He has his pass, of course, but . . . where? Some shabby little hotel? It's not my business . . . She felt sorry that his happiness and contentment were going to be broken into, but only lightly sorry. He's young, she thought, he'll recover very easily—as *he* said . . . She spoke carefully.

'Your father is dead, he killed himself.'

He stared at her without any expression—then walked quickly past her to the bed. He looked down at the body for a minute, touched it, the face, the hands lying half-folded on the sheet, and drew back. He turned, his face working. Frowning, he began, 'Mother——' and stopped.

'It's all right,' his mother said kindly, drily.

'I don't . . . why did he do this?'

'Don't you know? Don't you know what he did? Surely——'

'Yes, but——' Tears came into his eyes, and he waited to get rid of them.

'He didn't want to go on living with himself,' his mother said. A scalding grief filled her as she said it, with the thought: I was no use.

'It's my fault,' Andrew said thickly. 'If I hadn't turned against him he wouldn't have felt . . . he . . . I'll never forgive, myself, never.'

Sophie roused herself to deal with this. 'Don't imagine that *you* could have saved him, my dear boy. That's only conceit.' She saw the blood rush to his face and said gently, 'I'm not laughing at you. I'm only reminding you that as long as a man is alive he is able to work miracles——'

'What on earth do you mean?'

'He doesn't die until the last instant. Until then, until the very last second, he can always begin again. You had nothing to do with his—his refusal. Nothing. You'll forget what you said to him—whatever it was—I don't know. But you'll forget it and be happy. You'll see.'

'No,' Andrew mumbled, 'I shan't forget.'

'Well, don't,' she said carelessly, 'don't forget it. But remember everything, not just the last. And be happy.' She felt a sudden triumphant energy, almost elation. 'Don't be ashamed of being happy again at once. It's not the whole of life, but it's worth having—when it exists. Horrible things happen, but they're not the final thing, and death isn't final, he is dead but you, you and Sarah, go on. Surely you see that?'

Her energy left her as sharply as it had come, and she had no sense that she had made him see what, with this shock of certainty, had broken through to her. He was shaking again, and trying to control himself. Going back to the bed, he leaned over it as though he meant to kiss his father, but drew back again, a hand over his mouth. Sophie watched him and did not move. I should comfort him, she thought; I can't, I'm too old, too tired. Sarah will do it much better.

Andrew turned round at last, and came to her.

'Poor mother,' he said, and kissed her.

She let herself lean against him for a moment, but there